WHITEOUT

DHONIELLE CLAYTON

TIFFANY D. JACKSON

NIC STONE

ANGIE THOMAS

ASHLEY WOODFOLK

NICOLA YOON

ELECTRIC MONKEY

First published in the USA by Quill Tree Books, part of HarperCollins Children's Books, a division of HarperCollins*Publishers*, 195 Broadway, New York, NY 10007

First published in Great Britain in 2022 by Electric Monkey, part of Farshore
An imprint of HarperCollins*Publishers*
1 London Bridge Street, London SE1 9GF

farshore.co.uk

HarperCollins*Publishers*
1st Floor, Watermarque Building, Ringsend Road
Dublin 4, Ireland

Text copyright © 2022 Dhonielle Clayton, Tiffany D. Jackson, Nic Stone, Angie Thomas, Ashley Woodfolk and Nicola Yoon

The moral rights of the authors have been asserted
A CIP catalogue record of this title is available from the British Library

ISBN 978 00084 9305 9
Printed and bound in the UK using 100% renewable electricity at CPI Group (UK) Ltd
1

Typeset by Avon DataSet Ltd, Alcester, Warwickshire

To Black kids everywhere:
your joy and love warm the hearts of the world.
We still see you.

WEATHER.COM REPORT

ATLANTA

H: 36°F L: 18°F

Special Weather Statement Until Midnight EST

Issued by National Weather Service, Atlanta, GA

AFFECTED COUNTIES

Cherokee, Clayton, Cobb, DeKalb, Douglas, Fayette,
Forsyth, Fulton, Gwinnett, Henry, and Rockdale

A historic winter storm is gaining strength along
the East Coast, dumping record-breaking snow
accumulation from Jacksonville, FL, to the nation's
capital, coupled with a threat of coastal flooding
from Savannah, GA, to Wilmington, NC, and 70 mph
offshore winds. The National Weather Service has
reported that large swaths of the southern United
States will see up to eight inches of snowfall,
prompting emergency conditions across four states.

Heavy snow and high winds have created near-whiteout conditions. Authorities ask that everyone stay indoors and avoid all unnecessary travel. Icy patches likely on roads. All flights at Hartsfield-Jackson Atlanta International Airport have been grounded, and a winter storm warning is in effect from 3:00 p.m. through 12:00 a.m.

ONE

STEVIE

Morningside—Lenox Park, 3:01 p.m.

THERE ARE INFINITE ways that terrible night could've turned out differently.

Some quantum theorists believe there's another you out there. Another me. That our universe is really, really big—infinitely large—and because of that, there are only so many ways matter can arrange and rearrange itself. Eventually, everything has to repeat, they say.

So there's another version of this reality. A parallel one. Another me. Another you. Another version of the people we might love. Another outcome to every mistake we've made . . . living in another version of this universe as if we're only a deck of cards shuffled and reshuffled, beholden to the numbers.

I should know. I understand the science. I have the highest GPA possible in my grade, shattering all the records at Marsha P. Johnson Magnet (or MPJM, as we call it). I could've tested out of high school in the ninth grade, but chose to stay for . . .

Whatever. Anyway, back to the point. There are infinite ways that terrible night could've turned out differently.

Imagine if I hadn't gotten so wrapped up in my experiment that Sunday afternoon, and hadn't left the lab late covered in calcium sulfate and stinking of acetic acid, my super-long locs needing a refresh and my hands tinged green from overflowing graduated cylinders.

Imagine if I actually had taken the time to look like a perfectly put-together girlfriend, someone worthy of being loved instead of an overly anxious mess. And if that anxiety didn't push me to make the most catastrophic decision ever as I tried to get myself to relax. I can't even face what I did.

Or even the night before *it* all happened: Imagine if I hadn't wasted our Saturday presenting ~~my girlfriend~~, ~~ex-girlfriend~~, my hopefully *still* girlfriend, Sola, with my charts, animated brain models, chemical equations, and study data for my AP Chemistry midterm project on love. The hypothesis posited that love was simply a biological response built into human brains to ensure the survival of the population . . . so is it even important?

Imagine if I hadn't pontificated on my hypothesis, drilling down on how my results proved that love holds an overblown significance in our society and is most often wielded to make people believe that having a partner is some sort of accomplishment.

Being the smartest person in the world . . . now *that's* a feat.

Curing cancer . . . ending pandemics . . . those are achievements.

Building libraries in communities that lack them . . . something to shout about.

Being in a relationship, though? There's no need for a trophy or gold sticker . . . right?

Imagine if my whole experiment hadn't invalidated our relationship.

Back to the awful Sunday night in question: Imagine if I hadn't been so on edge, worried about being impressive, trying to show off that I was, in fact, the smartest person in school and would be able to go to the college of my choice; that I could identify every Nigerian dish her mother had made with the correct pronunciation, even as an outsider; that I could be *so* perfect, Sola's parents and aunties and uncles and cousins would ~~like me~~ *accept* me. Accept *us*.

Accept our love.

If I hadn't talked so much.

If I hadn't been such a pompous ass.

If I hadn't driven home that way.

Maybe in a parallel universe, like the one the quantum theorists theorize, that other version of me is less awkward, less nervous, less needing to know everything to feel tethered to reality, and maybe that *me* didn't ruin her relationship three days ago. Maybe the cards were shuffled differently there. Maybe there's an outcome where I didn't blow up my life.

A knock rattles my bedroom door. "What—I mean, yes?"

The door creaks open. Pop crowds the doorway, forehead molasses brown and crinkled like the gingersnap cookies

Aunt Lisa brought over yesterday for the holidays.

"I'm going to pick your mom up at the aquarium so we can go Christmas shopping at Lenox Mall." Pop's gaze scans my bedroom, the purse of his lips telegraphing his unhappiness with its current state. His once perfectly neat, perfectly behaved child would never have a messy room. Future scientists are *never* messy.

"First, you can drop the 'mall,' Pop," I correct, fixing my eyes on the observation log in my lap. "While it's *technically* correct, colloquially, it's just Lenox. Second, you shouldn't say Christmas shopping because there are other winter holidays happening right now, and more to come later in the month. It's not inclusive."

Pop sighs. "Stop giving me a hard time, baby girl."

I cringe and look up. Pop *knows* how much that second word grates. How limiting it feels right now. How I'm trying to figure things out. I've told him. "Don't call me that."

He puts his hands in the air. "Sorry. Forgot all your new rules."

"They're not new, Pop."

"Well, I'm still making sense of it all too," he says.

"So am I," I mutter, feeling like everything I thought I knew about myself, Sola, my experiments, the world, is changing.

Pop sucks his teeth. "Look, I'm just here to remind you that you're still grounded."

"I haven't forgotten."

"That means no visitors."

I refocus on my log. "She doesn't want to see me, so no need to worry there," I say. "Pretty sure I ruined everything, and since you all won't let me have my phone back, I can't even do anything about it."

He sighs and starts his lecture on consequences for one's actions, blah blah, full-on rolling into Reverend Josiah Williams mode. "And no leaving this house." He clears his throat like he always does before he has to be a hard-ass. "You better answer the house phone when I call to check in."

"I know."

"Do you?" Pop strides deeper into the room. "'Cause lately it seems like all the things I *thought* you knew, things I taught you, went straight out the window . . . and you're acting like you lost all the sense you got. Where is my brilliant girl?"

I curl deeper into my window nook and gaze out at our front yard. The sky is a powdery white as precipitation drifts down. "No two snow crystals are alike. Did you know that?" But there's no avoiding his monologue about my current moral failings and his surprise that his poster child, his *only* child, could mess up. He quotes some scripture that goes in one ear and out the other, and I wish I could remind him that we're not in his megachurch and he's not at the pulpit. That the last thing I need to hear about is "respecting my parents" and "following my elders' leads." It's too bad he can't tell me what to do when you've made the worst mistake of your life and hurt someone you love.

I cut in again: "Some are flat plates with dendritic arms shaped like small columns. Pencil flakes or needles, you could call them."

"You really talking to me about *snowflakes*, Stevie? Did you hear anything I said to you?"

"Snow *crystals*. The word snowflake is more a general term. Could mean one single snow crystal or a few of them all stuck together."

"Stephanie Camilla Williams!" Pop's voice deepens in that warning way, the kind when Black dads say your name, you know you're toeing the line.

"It's Stevie," I mumble, crossing right over it.

"Stevie." (Pop hates calling me that but has acquiesced because he knows I'll just keep correcting him.)

"What? It just started snowing, and I thought you should know, so you'd be careful. All that condensed water vapor coming out of those clouds"—I point out the window—"could make the streets messy. Statistically, there will be an average of six point seven motor vehicle crashes in these weather conditions."

"Aren't you glad you aren't going?" Pop winks, then darts over to kiss my forehead before I can protest. I'm going to need a surge of endorphins to get through what I *have* to do tonight. "Be our perfect gir—I mean, child, please," he says as he exits my room.

I want to grumble that I'm not a child anymore. That I'm almost seventeen, but it wouldn't matter to him. I will be a child even at forty, because he's the "elder."

I gaze out the window again, watching as Pop's car backs out of the garage, then disappears up our street and out of view.

I sigh and thumb through my observation log, combing through all the experiments I've done. The failed ones, the adventurous ones, the complicated ones, the prize-winning ones.

I can't stop flipping to the one that blew up my relationship. It stares back at me. My once pride and joy, earning me an A+ for the semester. The one that sparked an argument that bled into what was supposed to be one of the biggest nights in my relationship history with Sola—one where I finally got to meet her parents, not just as her best friend . . . but as her girlfriend.

Date: 9/8
EXPERIMENT TITLE: LOVESICK, THE OXYTOCIN OBSESSION
SCIENTIFIC QUESTION: What is the biochemistry of modern teenage love?

I gaze at my data tables of saliva samples and oxytocin measurements. Data that supported my theory: teenagers who claim to be "in love" will have oxytocin levels that mirror those of a person addicted to recreational drugs. Maybe if I hadn't chosen this experiment or told Sola about it at all, we wouldn't be in this mess. *I* wouldn't be in this mess. But I told her everything. Because I *always* tell her everything.

I slam the log shut and walk to my desk. I pluck the tiny LEGO bouquet I always keep there, squeezing it over and over again, hoping it'll slow down my heartbeat. I click a button, and the automatic blinds I had installed across the left wall of my room lift. Instead of revealing a stretch of windows, there's a map of my life laid out across my mom's wallpaper like a complex multitiered mathematical equation.

I wish life was as easy as a chemistry experiment. Choose the right reactants and blend them the right way to yield the product you desire. Chemistry makes things simple. If you know how the elements behave, you can predict the results. Voilà: no one gets hurt or burned . . . frustrated or disappointed.

The life wall journey begins with my baby pictures, then includes every newspaper clipping about my genius-level IQ and science experiments, with headlines shouting about the youngest-ever kid to break the world record for mental math equations completed in under a minute. There are articles about my desire to be a biochemist, and there's my series of medals, and there are cheesy portraits of me with famous scientists and politicians, all fawning over me being a tiny smart person. All before sixth grade . . . all before meeting Sola.

Everything changed when I met her. Which is evident in how much space she takes up on this wall. Her kid photo is here too, right next to one of me holding a trophy from my middle school science fair. Her little-girl face stares back at me. Round and chubby cheeked, hair beads hitting her shoulders.

I can almost hear the *click clack* they used to make every time she turned her head to be nosy.

On Sola's first day of sixth grade, the front office lady, Ms. Townsend, marched her into Mr. Ringler's classroom. That *click clack* of her braids echoed in between all the introductions. Her dark brown skin glistened so much, my mama would've said she looked like candied pecans fresh from the oven. And Sola was grinning so hard, *my* cheeks throbbed in sympathy.

I remember being jealous. Her ability to step inside a room full of people she didn't know and just smile. And not just a regular, sheepish smile . . . no, the deeply happy kind, as if somehow she was excited to be the new kid or felt like she'd just started a brand-new adventure or something. She wasn't afraid that someone would call her cheesy.

I spent a lot of time making sure people didn't know how I felt. I could be angry or sad or frustrated or even happy, and no one would ever know. I could control every one of my facial muscles. But Sola let it all shine through.

She'd plopped down next to me, filling the empty chair at our two-seater desk. I'd tried to ignore her, burying myself in Mr. Ringler's math worksheets or playing with the LEGOs hidden in my side of the desk. If I didn't make eye contact, maybe she'd stop glancing over at me.

"Hey," she'd whispered. "Excuse me . . ."

I'd pretended to not hear anything, but then a little paper tent appeared in my line of sight. I couldn't resist opening it. Inside sat a gummy worm and a story about its dastardly life as a worm burglar. I giggled and looked up to find her intense (and beautiful) brown eyes aimed right at me.

She unleashed that sunshiny smile. "We're going to be best

friends. I know it," she said, her voice confident and tone prophetic.

"How do you know?" I couldn't look away from her.

She pushed another worm in my direction. "Because you laughed at my story. Which means you get me. And I knew you'd like it, which means I get you."

I tried to hide a smile, then pretended to pay attention to Mr. Ringler's fractions (even though I already knew how to do them). While she ignored the math lesson, scribbling away in her journal—writing more stories about the worm burglar, I presumed—I made a tiny bouquet of LEGO flowers and left it in her side of the desk when she went to use the bathroom. I waited the whole rest of the day for her to find it, and when she did, she beamed like I'd left her a million dollars. At that moment, I knew: I wanted to make her smile like that forever.

Now, I set my own LEGO flower bouquet back on the desk in my room. Over the years, I've made dozens of these, leaving them in her locker or on the dashboard of her car or tucked away in her purse. A tiny way to remind her that I love her and I'm always thinking of her, even when I go quiet and get lost in my work and can't get the words out.

I run my fingers over the wall and sigh, tracing how Sola intersects with almost every milestone in my journey. She probably should've been there from birth. There are pictures of her—of *us*—everywhere: hanging out after school while our classmate Kaz and I tutored people struggling in science; avoiding my dad's sermons and hiding with Porsha in the wings of his church; going to hear Jimi sing at gigs all over the city; sending old-fashioned care packages to Evan-Rose at her fancy boarding school (a school where Sola and I went to sleepaway camp, and that we almost wound up attending); the two of us hanging out at the aquarium with Ava, staring up at the largest saltwater fish tank in the United States, while my mom handled boring fish logistics stuff in her office.

I move down the life wall to my most prized section: everything laid out under the words THE FUTURE.

All of ~~my~~ *our* plans sit there like a dream poised to evaporate into thin air.

Howard University after high school.

A shared apartment in DC.

A gap year post-graduation, to travel the world together.

A job in a lab or with a big pharmaceutical corporation so I can earn enough for her to stay home, write, and become a best-selling romance author.

Marriage.

Three kids.

Lifelong love.

Forever happiness.

An anxious bubble balloons in my chest. I grab my observation log and hug it close, hoping it can make the bubble burst. "You have to fix this, Stevie," I say to myself.

I flip it open again and pore over the elements of my newest experiment. The most important theory I'll ever test.

EXPERIMENT TITLE: MY GRAND PLAN TO FIX THE
ULTIMATE SCREWUP.
SCIENTIFIC QUESTION: Can you get someone to forgive
you and love you again?
HYPOTHESIS: If Stevie combines the proper romantic
elements to create the perfect romantic gesture, then Sola's
heart can be recaptured.

I recite the step-by-step plan, all the people I've already texted, all the favors I've requested, all the parts of this experiment that have to work for me to achieve my desired outcome. The biggest and riskiest pseudo chemical equation of my life. The only way to fix all the things this version of me has done in this version of the universe.

I dart to Mom's home office at the front of the house and retrieve my phone from the safe that she doesn't think I know the code to. But Mom chooses numerical passcodes the way most people do: she uses an already-meaningful set of numbers for easy memory retrieval. For five-digit codes, the house number where she grew up—52404—is her go-to. Her ATM pin is the last four digits of her phone number: 9860. The eight digits for her cell phone? Her and Pop's wedding anniversary: 10221995. And this safe? It's my birthday: 1230.

I punch in the numbers and hear the triumphant ping of the bolt releasing.

Of course the phone is dead. I plug it in and sink into Mom's worn-out desk chair, my legs finding the leather grooves she's left behind from sitting for so many hours poring over aquarium reports.

My heart thuds as I wait to see what might be waiting for me on my phone. There are papers scattered all over Mom's desk— board meeting minutes and research on moon jellyfish. Maybe marine biologists are messier than biochemists . . . but I guess I don't have room to judge right now. It's not like my room is exactly *clean*.

The phone glows, and as it comes back to life, the lock screen fills with social media notifications, alerts, and email previews. And messages from Sola. One after another. Single lines of anger. Thick text blocks of sadness and frustration. All built up over the last few days.

S SOLA

I can't believe you did that.

I lie awake at night replaying it over and over again. From your ridiculous "experiment" that basically invalidated how we feel about each other to you ruining the dinner with my family. Our BIG dinner. Our big moment. All in one weekend.

And you won't even text me back! It's been THREE DAYS, and NOTHING!

Do you even believe in love? Do you love ME?

How could you?

OUR RELATIONSHIP IS NOT AN EXPERIMENT!

The final *long* text is from this morning:

You know what? Since you love deadlines
and dates and precise expectations and only
seem to respond to those, I'll give you one.
If I don't hear from you by midnight tonight,
it's over. You owe me an explanation, Stevie.
What the heck was going on with you? Why
did you behave that way in front of my family?
And don't give me any science bullshit. I want
to know that you aren't a robot. That you feel
something. Anything. If you can't show me,
please don't ever call me again. In fact, you can
just forget you ever knew me. I'm sure there's a
biochemical way to do that. . . .

My vision blurs and the words jumble on the screen, scattering in all directions as my heart sinks. Right down into the pit now, burning a hole in my stomach. What Sola said the last time we saw each other echoes in my head as if she's right in front of me, shouting.

"Do you even believe in love?"

"If it's all just science, how could you possibly love me?"

"Is our relationship a complete lie?"

I call her.

It goes straight to voicemail.

I try again.

And again.

Nothing.

I get up. Pace. She thinks I've ignored her for three days. She had no clue that I'm grounded and my parents took all my devices and have been watching my every move. Once she hears the explanation for my silence, everything will make sense. It'll cool her anger. Rational heads will prevail . . . isn't that the phrase? She should know that I would never ignore her.

I message her on every app I can think of. Then I click open my email app—which won't sync. (Typical.) So I retrieve my laptop from Mom's safe and power it up. All the folders load neatly on-screen, freckling a photo of Sola, her beautiful hair swaddled in a gorgeous gele made by her mother. The deep peacock blues and rich oranges of the fabric make the deep brown of her skin glow.

I send her an email. Then wait, and recheck social media.

My computer chimes.

Delivery status notification (failure)

Did she delete her email account? Or is this some sort of evil blocking software? Am I blocked? Would she do that? Can she do that?

I call Sola.

Nothing. Still straight to voicemail. Why is her phone off? *She* couldn't be in trouble because of me, could she? I remember her saying, "Yeah, my parents don't believe in the whole *grounding* thing."

I hold my breath and dial her house phone. It rings and I almost don't say a word when her mother answers.

"Hello?" the thickness of Mrs. Olayinka's Nigerian accent pours through the phone. "Hello?"

I clear my throat. Sweat skates down my back. I tug at my sweater. A long silence crackles between us.

"Who playing on my phone?" she barks.

"Hi, Mrs. Ola . . . Mrs. Olayinka." I gulp.

"Who is this?"

I hang up and put my hands over my eyes. "Pull it together, Stevie," I say to myself. "All this cortisol is going to lead to the shrinking of your prefrontal cortex. Something you *need* to become the best biochemist in the world. You have to calm down."

I drop my head between my knees and take three deep breaths. I can fix this. My plan from three days ago won't work, since there's no way all the favors I called in can be pulled together by Sola's midnight deadline. (*Midnight!* Is she trying to destroy me?) I have to come up with something new—and fast.

I check all the apps again. No response from Sola.

I rush back upstairs to my room and stare at my life wall. At our history, all laid out. I see a photo of the fireworks we saw together on the Fourth of July last year, and another one of us at the stadium where we suffered through a football game for my dad's sake (so *brutal*, that sport). The only thing that made it bearable was Who's on That Plane?—the game *we* played where we counted the planes we could see flying overhead through the gaping circle of Mercedes-Benz Stadium's open roof, guessing who might be inside.

And then it hits me like lightning, what I could do. What I *have* to do.

I scroll through my phone until I find Ernest, the older brother of my other best friend, Evan-Rose. Because he's the only one who can help me now.

S STEVIE

> Mayday, mayday! SOS, Ern!

E ERN

You're so silly, Little Stevie. What's up?

> Hey now, I'm not that little anymore. And I need your assistance with a very high-stakes situation.

High stakes, huh? You young ones are so dramatic. Name it, and you got it.

> It's, umm . . . kind of outrageous? Like, it's a BIG favor. E.R. told me you're at the stadium working on a secret engagement stunt.

Ummm . . . my sister has a big mouth, but yeah. It's for this celebrity's big wedding proposal but that's all I'm saying.

So . . . can I get in on that?

What do you mean?

I'll call you with the details,
but I'm on my way.

Okay, cool. I'm still running tests, but the snow
is causing problems so I don't know how long
I'll be here. Mr. Celebrity is blowing up my
phone for a report so . . .

I smile and request a Ryde. Hopefully Ern already being precisely where I need him is a good omen. After telling him my plan, I grab my observation log. Make a few changes to the procedure section, and jot down the new variable: *midnight deadline*.

As more logistics details fill my mind, I *know* this is a good idea. I just hope I can pull it off. On time.

Or I'll lose Sola forever.

OPERATION SOLA SURPRISE

3:42 p.m.

Stevie

Hey y'all! So, I apparently made things worse by being grounded and not having my phone. 😒 Sola gave me an ultimatum . . . with a midnight deadline. Which means the original plan for her big Christmas surprise would be too late and I have to do something different . . . NOW. You don't have to get those gifts anymore.

But thanks!

Stevie has left the group.

Jimi

Wait . . . did she just . . . ? Does that notification say Stevie LEFT the group? After dropping that bomb?

E.R.

Sure does. Typical Stevie for you. Of course. Just changes the plan AFTER I already went through hell and risked expulsion to get this damn thing she asked for.

Ava

Stevie can't do that. Can't just CHANGE the plan at the last minute. Right?

Porsha

I mean, technically I guess Stevie CAN . . . but
nah. If she's getting ultimatums, she CLEARLY
needs our help. Time for a plan of our own.
Y'all in?

Kaz changed the group name to OPERATION SOLA AND STEVIE SURPRISE.

⊙ OPERATION SOLA AND STEVIE SURPRISE

3:46 p.m.

Jimi

Like, for real. We gotta come through for Stevie. She's certainly done things to help US out in the past. . . .

Porsha

You right. Lord knows Stevie keeps me awake at church, analyzing the scientific accuracy (and inaccuracy) of Bible verses.

3:47 p.m.

E.R.

Stevie was my steadiest anchor to home my first semester at boarding school. Picked up every time I called to vent about *my* issues. AND she sends bomb-ass care packages.

Ava

Yeah. We're cousins, but also kinda sisters? I know she's got me and I always got her.

Jimi

Stevie and Sola are always at my gigs. Even the ones no one else shows up to.

And they're the happiest couple I know. Usually, I mean.

3:56 p.m.

Kaz

Right. I'll certainly never forget all the times Stevie helped me out with my tutoring service. Wouldn't have survived MPJM without her.

Porsha

So we still on? Everyone understand the assignment?

Jimi

Yup.

Kaz

On it.

Ava

You know it.

E.R.

Hell yeah.

TWO

K A Z

Lenox Square Mall, 4:35 p.m.
Seven hours and twenty-five minutes until midnight

FROM THE START, mistakes were made.

"I can't believe you're making us come here," I groan.

No one in their right mind would come to Lenox four days before Christmas. If you know anything about shopping before this hyper-capitalist holiday, you know that the week prior, every mall around the world is filled with ravenous, bloodthirsty shoppers trying to scoop up last-minute gifts and stocking stuffers.

But here I am, circling the parking lot for what seems like the twentieth time, looking for a place to land. And next to me, Porsha Washington, my best friend in the whole wide world, is harmonizing with Mariah Carey's "All I Want for Christmas" for the millionth time.

Porsha laughs, the bell on her Santa hat jingling. "I'm not 'making' us do anything. Only place to get what we need is the mall. Our Jack and Jill homie is in need!"

I laugh thinking about how me, her, and Stevie have been stuck doing leadership and cultural events (and tons of community service) because our parents have had us in that secret bougie Black kid organization since we were nine. So, when Porsha busted into my room shortly after we all agreed to help our friend and said, "I found where to get what Stevie asked me for," there wasn't any room for hesitation. "We need to go by Lenox immediately."

But then I looked up from my three-dimensional scale model of the aquarium, squinted at the screengrab, and glanced out the window at our shared snow-covered driveway.

"Bruh, it's snowing."

"Yeah," Porsha shot back. "And Rita is the only car that'll get us to the mall alive. We're going. Come on, it'll just take an hour."

So we piled into my truck, sat in traffic for twenty-four minutes, despite the mall being really close to where we live, and I've been circling this lot ever since. If I had thought it through, I would've checked the news before stepping out the door, to see what was going on. Atlanta is in a damn state of emergency over the snow. There's about two inches on the ground, enough to bring the city to a standstill.

As I said: mistakes were made.

But after everything Stevie and Sola have done for me . . . I owe them this favor. Still doesn't stop me from strangling my steering wheel.

"Aye, why do people drive like they got nowhere to be?" I snap, weaving around an old woman worming her way through the parking-lot lanes.

Porsha chuckles. "You're being Grumpy Kazeem."

"I'm Hungry Kazeem."

"So . . . Hangry Kazeem?"

Fasting ain't never easy, but the last day of any fast always hits hard, like a steel bat to the face. Dad got COVID during Ramadan, so we decided as a family to reschedule our fast until he was healed and have our own little Fake-Eid tonight to celebrate. I've mentally been trying to distract myself from thoughts of food by working on extra-credit projects for AP classes, putting together puzzles and 3D models. I saved my hardest model for today, the one that required the most thinking, to keep me straight until sundown.

But like always, Porsha comes and changes up the game plan.

"Ooh there!" She points to an empty space, one lane over. I step on the gas, swerve around the corner . . . but lose the spot to a green Jeep.

"Dang," she mumbles, then perks up. "Ooo! This is my song."

"Every song on this album is your song."

"But this one is, like, top three favs on the album. Come on, you know you wanna sing," she says, bopping in her seat.

"I wanna find a parking spot," I grumble.

She rolls her eyes. "Extra-Hangry Kazeem. Ooo! Look, that truck has Christmas lights."

"I already let you put antlers on Rita."

"And Rita is better looking for it," she says, petting the dashboard.

Rita is my truck that's probably older than the two of us combined. My dad bought it when we first moved to Georgia from Sudan, and it survived my two older brothers before it was passed down to me. Passed down, meaning earned, as I needed straight As for two years before I could ever think of touching our much-beloved rust bucket.

I glance up at the Christmas tree sitting on the roof of Macy's, the sky above a dark slate gray. The falling snow isn't the pretty kind you see in Christmas cards. It's the wet, icy kind, making the parking lot look like the black slick top of a frozen lake.

"Bruh, my to-do list is wild," Porsha says. "Imma look up and Christmas will be here, like, tomorrow. Oh, don't forget on Friday, we're building gingerbread houses. Oh, I have to put in an order for the honey-baked ham for Christmas dinner. There's probably going to be a long-ass line for pickup."

"Oooo, Christmas swine. Yummmy. Cough . . . BARF!"

She laughs. "Relax. Dad already said he's making that honey-glazed salmon you love."

"At least your father is thinking of me."

"Boy, bye. I always make sure you have the hottest of hot sauces and ginger beer."

"That you do," I concede. "But for real, though, why do you even order a ham when you don't eat it?"

"'Cause it's tradition," she replies. "Mom ordered one every year. The table will look weird without it. Oh! That reminds me, I need to pick up some sharp cheddar blocks for the mac and cheese. I hate pre-shred. And the fruitcake and lemonade. Oh, and I need some more green food coloring. And some ribbon for presents . . ."

While she's distracted, I put on the new Lil Kinsey track I was listening to earlier, before making the dumb decision to leave the house.

"Uh, you ain't serious," she snaps.

"What? This is fire!"

"No trap music during the Jesus season." She quickly switches back to Mariah's "Joy to the World," then grins at me. "There. And please miss me with your 'never touch a Black man's radio' dad joke."

Moving next door to this Christmas junkie in the third grade, you'd think I'd be used to her tyrant ways when it comes to the holiday playlist. Literally, when the clock strikes midnight after Halloween, she turns from a pumpkin to one of those Christmas bulbs and teams up with Sola to terrorize us with all things Santa.

Some people are dead serious about Christmas. My best friend is one of those people. Like, Thanksgiving straight up doesn't exist. It's just a break to refuel. The house decorating, the ice skating, the chopping down of those innocent trees, the movie schedule, the fussing over a menu that hasn't changed since cell phones were invented, the gift wrapping and subsequent paper cuts. She approaches Christmas with precision similar to that of a military drill sergeant. "Don't you dare try to veer off from the plan or schedule!"

But this year feels special. Our fast is landing right in the height of holiday season, putting us on somewhat equal footing. And tonight, my family is hosting a big dinner for Fake Eid. No way Porsha can come up with an excuse not to come like all the other times.

"Yo, they canceled all flights at the airport," Porsha says, her nose up in her phone.

"What? All of them?"

"Yeah. I just saw it on Ava's feed. Everyone's talking about the traffic. People calling 75/85 a parking lot." She flashes a ten-second clip at me.

"We better take the back roads home."

She sucks her teeth. "We took the back roads here."

"It's really not even snowing that hard. Everyone's right— Atlanta drivers are already garbage, but add some *snow*?"

Porsha chuckles, throwing me a mischievous smirk. "Hangry."

That smile. I'm talking strictly as her friend here, but let me tell you: Porsha Washington is fine. Like, straight-up beautiful. Pretty brown eyes, short hair that curls right under her adorably chubby cheeks, with a runner's body that would make any guy do a double take. But that smile, bruh . . .

"Okay, ready?" She stretches her arm out for a selfie and smiles. I gaze up at the camera, clocking her dimples.

"Kaz! Smile!" She laughs, slapping my arm. "Come on, get closer. Stop trying to mess up my picture! You look like you about to choke."

Man, pull it together.

I hold my breath, lean over closer, give my best "I'm not in love with my best friend" smile, and try not to breathe because then I'll catch a whiff of her body spray that sends me. Sometimes when she borrows my hoodie, I don't wash it for weeks. I even sleep in it, just to bury myself in her scent.

Simping big-time over this girl.

But tonight, that all changes. Tonight, I'm going to tell Porsha that I love her. I've already got it all planned out. After the dinner, I'm going to bring her to the dessert table and present her with her favorite cake, the words written in the icing. (You don't understand, the girl *loves* cake.) Depending on her reaction, I could just say it was a mistake at the bakery. 'Cause . . . well, I could never say those words out loud. That'd be nuts.

"Oooo, this one is cute!" she shrieks, showing me the photo. "Maybe I'll frame this one."

Porsha has been talking about printing, like with actual photo paper, a picture of us for years. She even has an empty frame waiting. But every year she forgets.

Just like she forgets about all the holidays my family celebrates.

Not this time. I knew the only way she couldn't get out of coming to tonight's dinner is if I stayed up in her face all day.

"Oh!" Porsha looks at her lit-up phone and turns down the car volume. "Hey, Ummi."

"Ummi? Wait . . . are you talking to my mom? You have my mom's cell?"

"Shhh! I can't hear," she snaps, returning to her call. "Oh, nothing, just looking for a parking space. . . . Yeah, I hope Stevie can win back Sola too. They're so cute together. . . . Sure, I'll remind him. . . . Yep . . . okay . . . great! Talk to you later. Love you too! Ma'aasalaama."

I hold back a prideful smirk, always impressed that she at least attempts the few Arabic words I've taught her over the years, even when she butchers them.

"So what, you two girls talk often?"

She rolls her eyes. "I can't help it if your mom loves me more than you."

I get it. She's easy to love.

"Anyways, she called me to remind you to pick up the rolls from Mrs. Ahmed for tonight's thingy."

My stomach roars at the mention of food. You ever been so hungry that if someone said, "Two plus two equals five," you'd say, "Bet," just to cop yourself a single cracker? I've reached that level of desperation, and it's all on me. I overslept and missed suhoor breakfast. Now I'm craving Ummi's fried sambuxa bad.

We stop at the roundabout as a couple crosses the street headed for the Cheesecake Factory. I shift my eyes to Porsha watching them holding hands and giggling, her face smooth, but I could almost swear there's a bit of longing in her eyes. Just the thought of reaching over and touching her hand makes my heart sprint.

BEEP!

A car honks behind us. Porsha turns, catches me staring, and gives me that smile. "What? What you lookin' at?"

I snap forward, slam on the gas, and clear my throat. "Uh. Nothing. I was thinking . . . that I can't believe Sola and Stevie are breaking up."

"Maybe not," Porsha says. "Maybe whatever this thing Stevie is cooking will squash that."

"You think it'll be that easy? Sounds like she messed up bad."

She shrugs. "Sometimes people just belong to each other, so it doesn't matter how bad they mess up. Besides, it's Christmas! Ooo! There! Over there! A space!"

I'm so caught off guard by the comment that I almost forgot where we are. I swerve, bumping into a curb, wheels shrieking as we slip into the spot. I drum the steering wheel in victory as Porsha cheers.

"YASSS!"

"Aight," I say, and turn off the car. "Game plan."

"Okay, ready!"

"We gotta make this quick. It's getting bad out here and it's probably gonna take us half an hour to make it home. So we need to roll through, grab the goods, and dip. No stops."

Porsha secures her Santa hat and gives me a thumbs-up. "Got it. Let's roll."

We jump out the car just as a lime-green SUV skirts to a halt in front of us. The window rolls down and we're eyed by two brothers in black hoodies. I take a step closer to Porsha.

"Aye, man! You took my spot." Gotta love Atlanta.

"Your spot?" Porsha snaps, glancing at the ground. "I don't see your name on it."

There she goes with that hot-ass passenger-seat road rage.

The driver raises an eyebrow. "Imma say it again. You took my spot."

"You weren't even over here!"

"Well, I saw it first."

"Bruh, you can't call dibs without anyone hearing you. And whatever, 'cause we got here first."

The driver's face darkens before he puts the car in park, as if preparing to hop out. I quickly jump in front of Porsha.

"Hold up, man, hold up!" I push Porsha aside. "Look, bruh, we finna run in here and pick up something real quick. We'll be back in, like, fifteen minutes. You can either circle around for half an hour like we did or just wait till we get back. It's on you."

The driver eyes me, then peers at Porsha.

"Aight. You better be back in fifteen."

"I hear you," I insist, dragging Porsha by the arm. "Girl, come on."

"Why you being all nice to them?"

"Besides trying not to get us killed out here . . . to use your words, 'It's Christmas!'"

That's her favorite line. Whenever people act up around this time of year, she blows it off by saying, "It's Christmas!" Like it makes it all okay. Like everyone celebrates it or something. Truth is, she's just a big softie. And I love that about her. I love everything about her. Which I plan on telling her tonight.

Passing through the metal detectors, we enter the mall, and it's worse than I could've imagined. Stores jam-packed, crying children, shoppers shoving through with arms full of heavy bags. And the entire place smells like . . . cupcakes. Completely forgot there's a cupcake store at this entrance. My stomach cramps in need.

"Damn," Porsha mumbles as we fight our way through the crowd. "Which way is GameStop?"

"It's near the food court, I think." Which is at the *far* opposite end of this madhouse.

We head deeper into the packed mall, and Porsha says, "I'm still shocked that LEGOLAND was sold out of the set Stevie asked for."

"Well, I'd rather be there than here, for sure, but now I feel like the parking situation wouldn't have been any better at Phipps." It's still a mystery to me why Atlanta's two most popular shopping malls—Lenox Square and Phipps Plaza—are across the street from each other.

"Awww, Santa Land," Porsha says, pointing. "Looks even better than last year." Santa Land was set up in front of the stairwell by the Macy's, with three giant Christmas trees, a sleigh full of presents, and giant twinkling white reindeers. The line wrapped around a candy-cane fence. Santa sat on a tall green sofa-like throne, perfect for taking photos with children.

"Oh yeah. Beard almost seems real."

"Here," she says, passing me her phone. "Take a picture of me."

"Now? Bruh, what did I say? We gotta go!"

"Just take the damn picture! Dang!" she snaps.

She stands in front of the Christmas tree, striking a pose. I step back, positioning myself, tilting the camera just right so I can fit the top of the tree in the frame. As she plays with her hair, I take a few candid shots that I'll send to myself for my own personal collection.

"Ready?" I ask.

"Yeah."

"Three, two, one . . ."

Just then, Santa turns around, right into the shot.

"Ha. He winked," she points out.

"What?"

In the picture, Santa leans over his throne and looks directly at the lens with a wink, making it the perfect picture.

"Ha, so he did. That's a dope picture," I say, thinking about how beautiful she looks.

"Ooooo, these are so cute. You always take the best photos of me," she says to me.

"I know."

"I'm posting this one. Quick, what's the caption?"

"Holly jolly I'm in the mall lobby?" I offer.

"Made it through the snow bando?"

Head down, she plays with some filters as we debate captions before settling on "Hottie elf on the shelf."

"This storm is getting worse," Porsha mumbles, concerned. "Someone's posting about being stuck in the same spot on 285 for the past hour."

"Of course you finessed your way into me driving. And of course Stevie's mess got us out here being reckless."

She sucks her teeth, raising her phone. "Bruh, my car can barely drive in the rain, you think it'd survive a snowpocalypse?"

"Is that what they calling it?"

She scrolls through more posts. "Yeah. And people are literally trapped on the expressways."

"Do we really need this today? Ain't there enough going on?"

She smirks. "Extra-Special Hangry Kazeem."

I'm about to argue when I catch a whiff of something glorious.

Pizza. I smell it, and it smells like heaven. One more hour until sundown, then I can gorge myself on Ummi's aseeda, stew chicken, rice, and sweets. I can't wait!

We squeeze into GameStop and make our way through the swarm of children and sweaty parents.

"Ha! I remember when you used to build these," Porsha says, picking up a Star Wars LEGO set.

"Yeah. Then my dad told me if I was going to be a serious architect, I had to stop playing with toys."

"But even adults rock with these."

I shrug. "Children of immigrants don't have the luxury of being average. LEGOs are too easy. I built a whole city out of Popsicle sticks and cardboard, walking five miles in the snow to school."

"Okay, Grandpa." She nods over my shoulder. "Hey. There it is."

Behind me on the shelf is the LEGO roses set, for a pair of red roses.

"This the one?" I ask, grabbing a box.

Porsha checks the text message from Stevie. "Yeah, that's it. Must be some sort of inside joke or something. You can put that together, right?"

"Pssf! Please. A three-year-old could put this together."

"Great."

"Remind me why we're doing this again?"

"Love, Grandpa. We're doing this for love! It's so romantic, when you think about it. If some girl wanted my help finding your favorite video game"—she gestures around the store—"I would drive through blizzards."

"That's a lie."

"Maybe. But it felt believable."

"You're a good actress."

She grins and snatches the box out of my hands. "Told you I would've made a great Virgin Mary for the church play."

I shake my head. "Well, if it was you . . . I guess I'd just have to find one of those blue-and-gold gingerbread Advent calendars you had when you were six."

She spins around. "Wait, you remember that?"

"Of course . . . I remember everything about you."

She gives me one of her smiles again, and my chest feels so warm and fuzzy that I almost confess. But then a shopper weighed down with bags bulldozes her way between us, and one of her long wrapping-paper roll things slaps me in the face.

"You know, I never got flowers from a guy before," Porsha

says with a chuckle. "Real or LEGOs."

That's because Porsha hates flowers. Says they remind her too much of her mom's funeral. There were hundreds of arrangements sent to the house and Pastor Williams's church. Stevie's dad promised to send them all to an old folks' home.

But if I'd known that was all she wanted, I'd have picked up dozens of bouquets. Maybe I still can before tonight's dinner. Damn, does she like roses? Lilies? Wish I could talk out this change of plan with Sola. But I can't, like, call her right now about my love life when she's going through this breakup.

"Like, I know V-day is supposed to be the high-key romantic holiday," Porsha says as we drift to the cashier line. "But Christmas just adds an extra bit of magic to the love, you know? The special gifts, the parties, the lights, the mistletoe." She sighs. "And here I am. Single as hell, picking up romantic gifts for friends who found their person."

My heart is screaming "TELL HER, you dumbass!" But my brain won't let me do it. Not on some line at the Lenox GameStop. It has to be perfect. With cake, candy, and now flowers. Still, I can drop a little hint.

"Well, you never know. This year could be . . . different."

She snorts. "Yeah, right."

We make the purchase, and Porsha grabs some free candy canes as we head back for the escalators.

"Ooo! Can we get a frap?"

Porsha waves her candy cane toward the coffee-shop kiosk.

"No. No. See? That's why I didn't let you roll in here without me. You'd be in here for hours."

"Come on! I want that crumb cake."

The mention of food makes my tongue burn. I've been trying to stay focused, trying to ignore all the delicious smells around me. But I almost tackle a kid passing with a cup of Auntie Anne's pretzel nuggets. "Nah."

The bell on Porsha's Santa hat tinkles as she pouts, dragging her feet, walking slower than slow. She grabs her phone out her pocket and stops moving.

"OMG! OMG! It's him."

"Him who?"

"Dominick. He liked my last post! With an LMAO."

Dominick Reed. Porsha's had a crush on him since middle school, and he barely knows she exists. Or so I thought. And so what? He liked her post. Big deal. I comment on and like every post. Especially the pictures that I take of her because like a true best friend, I always get the best angles. Everyone thinks bro is so dope when really, he's just regular.

She pulls up all his social media pages with about seventy thousand followers.

Okay, yeah, so bro is like six-two, a buck eighty-five, and got the whole "my dad's a famous rapper" thing going on. Big deal.

Her mouth drops. "Kaz . . . he just DMed me."

Shit.

She bounces on the balls of her feet, having a complete freak-out.

"What do I do? What do I do?"

"Uh . . . I don't know. Maybe open it and see what he wants?"

Speechless, she nods. "You right, you right."

I blow out some nervous air, trying to keep it cool. He's probably just commenting on her picture. I mean, it was pretty dope, I should know, since I took it. And he's probably bored in the house, since we're the only fools driving around in a snowstorm, picking up fake flowers and arguing with hood-rich dudes over parking spots.

Porsha grips her phone, her eyes going wide with shock.

"Kaz. He invited me. To his house. For a Christmas party. THE Christmas party!!"

Every year, Dom's parents throw this lavish Christmas party that all the blogs and gossip pages talk about. He invites just about half the school. Clearly, we've always been in the other half. Until today.

"OMG! He just followed me." She spins around, wearing a stupid silly grin. "I can't believe it. I mean, I didn't even think he knew I existed, but wow. Just wow! Look!"

She shoves her phone in my face, and as soon as I read the message, my heart does some kind of sinking thing.

"The party is . . . tonight?" I mumble.

"Yeah!"

"But . . . but you have . . . I mean, don't you remember—"

"I heard girls get really dressed up for this party. Like flossy Hollywood style. What am I going to wear? I can't believe this is really happening!"

I sigh. "Yeah, neither can I."

"Let's bounce. I need to get home so I can get ready."

We ride the escalator back up to the main floor, weaving through shoppers, trying to hold my breath so I can miss the whiff of the mall food court. I could eat just about anything.

As we pass some fancy dress shop, Porsha stops short.

"Ooo, hold up," she mumbles, peering up at the window display, three faceless mannequins dressed for a New Year's Eve party.

She nods slow. "I need something to wear tonight."

"Bruh, are you really going to that party?"

"Yes! He invited me. I have to go!"

"No, you don't have to go!" I wanted to shout. "Because you HAVE to come with me!" But I don't say that. Why? I don't know. How do I talk her out of it without giving away my ulterior motives? I'm not about to pour my whole heart out in this damn mall.

"Come on. Help me pick out something," she says, backing inside the store.

"We should really—"

"We'll make it quick. I swear. Please."

Oh no, not the puppy dog eyes. She must know I can't resist those.

"Ugh. Fine. Ten minutes."

She beams with a happy clap. But inside, the store is mass chaos. Lines snake almost out the door as crazed shoppers scatter about with clothes piled in their arms. Sales associates, wide-eyed and red-faced, sweat over disheveled tables.

"It's the zombie apocalypse," I mutter.

Porsha doesn't hear me. Who can, over the terrible pop music blasting from the ceiling speakers? She attacks the first rack of clothes she sees.

"I need something that's cute but sexy but doesn't look like I'm trying too hard."

Across a table of folded shirts, two women argue over a size medium top.

"This is my worst nightmare," I say.

Porsha follows my gaze and swats at my arm. "Would you mind your business and help me!"

"Bruh, one of us needs to watch our ten and six. And why are you tripping anyways?"

"'Cause you know I don't know about parties or dresses or makeup or heels or nothing. I can't just show up in Jordans and a hoodie."

"Why can't you?"

"'Cause that's not what he . . . wants." Porsha purses her lips. "Okay. How about you stand in the fitting-room line for me while I pick out a few things?"

She points to a line weaving out of a back room. I stand for fifteen minutes, and the line has barely moved by the time Porsha joins me, her arms loaded with clothes.

"Just a few things, huh?"

"You weren't there to help me narrow down options. Here, what do you think of this one?"

"Is that a dress or a bathing suit?"

She laughs as she gently pushes my arm. "Come on! Be serious, Grandpa!"

"It's snowing outside! You'll catch pneumonia."

"Fine. I think I got a sweater dress in here or something," she says, throwing the rest of her items on a nearby rack before grabbing her phone.

"Now what are you doing?"

"I'm texting Stevie that we got the roses anyways, and that I got invited to the party. She is gonna freak out."

I inspect our purchase and smile. "You know, even though this get-Sola-back plan was wild, it's kinda nice, though. Being with someone who knows all the little things about you. Remembers all the details . . ."

I'm trying to drop hints, reminders like Sola suggested I do, but Porsha doesn't hear me. Too busy in her phone again. Not texting, but scrolling through Dominick's photos.

"I wonder what made Dominick, I don't know, hit me up? He's never said anything to me at school. Do you think he's just been creeping on my page all this time? Checking me out. Maybe you're right, Kaz. Maybe this year *will* be different."

I hold in a groan and shrug. "Maybe. I guess."

Finally we're up next, and Porsha disappears into a changing room. I sit on a bench beside a guy playing a game on his phone. I don't have time for games. I need to strategize. How am I going to talk Porsha out of going to that party? Yeah, dinner at my house would be dope, especially tonight, but nothing like a party at some rapper's mansion. Just have to play it cool.

"You know," I start, trying to think of a distraction. "You got a lot of stuff on that to-do list to check off."

"I know." She laughs from behind the curtain. "I can't believe how behind I am."

"And you said it yourself, the line at Honey Swine is gonna be long. Maybe you should, you know, skip the party. I mean, what's up with this last-minute invite? Sounds to me like he wasn't thinking of you at all."

Porsha doesn't respond. I keep pushing.

"Bruh, if I was you, I'd skip that party. Tell him you have plans. Like, you wanna look all thirsty, like you have nothing to do, like you were waiting around just for him? You better than that. Matter fact, you shouldn't say nothing. Keep him guessing. You feel me? Porsha?"

Porsha pushes the curtains and steps out of the dressing room.

"Okay. What do you think?"

Standing tall in silver heels, she tugs at the sleeves of a white knit dress that shows off her shoulders and collarbone, stopping right at her bare shins. An outfit fit for a snow princess.

"I . . . I . . . I . . ." I jump to my feet and drop my phone in the process. "Shit."

"Um, is that a good shit? Or a bad one?"

I pick up my phone, and my mouth, off the floor, yet still can't seem to pull it together.

"Well?" She lets out a nervous laugh, seeming unsure of

herself. "Aren't you gonna say something?"

I don't know what to say. I've known her for most of my life, and I've never seen her look so . . . beautiful. Yeah, she looks pretty all the time but this . . . THIS is something entirely different.

"You look . . . I mean, you look . . ." Stunning? Gorgeous? Hot? There are not enough words in the dictionary.

"Girl, you look cuuute!"

We spin around and find an older woman carrying an armful of clothes, watching us.

"Really?" Porsha gushes. "It doesn't make me look . . . silly? Do my legs look fat?"

"Not at all. Look at your boyfriend. He can barely speak a lick."

Porsha waves me off. "Oh, naw. He's not my boyfriend. He's my best friend."

The woman raises an eyebrow at me, like she can read my mind. "Hmph. You sure about that?"

I turn back to Porsha. "Uh, yeah, you look great. You, uh, should get a scarf, though, 'cause, you know, it's snowing. Um. You ready to go?"

Her face falls a bit, but she nods. "Yeah, just let me change."

I watch her walk back into the dressing room, because I can't take my eyes off her for one second. My knees give in just slightly, and I knock into a return rack of clothes.

The old woman chuckles, stepping closer to join me. "Mmm-hmmm. So what are you wearing to this shindig you clearly don't want her to go to?"

"Me? Oh, naw, I'm not going."

"Really? And you're going to let her go off, looking like that? Tuh."

The woman has a point. If I let Porsha go to that party, every guy in the spot will be checking for her. But if the thought of going off schedule for Christmas doesn't move her, then what will?

To our right, a girl steps out of the dressing room in one of those super-long flowery dresses . . . and a light pink hijab.

"Grandma, I think I better find another size in this."

We catch eyes, and the grandmother looks between us.

"This is my grandbaby, Nikki," the woman tells me. "Nikki, this is my new friend."

Nikki smiles up at me. "Hi!"

"Hey. I mean, assalamu alaikum."

She brightens. "Alaikum salaam!"

Grandma practically pushes her in my direction. "My Nikki is a junior, top of her class, plays piano, and can sing so pretty."

Nikki blushes. "Grandma, geez."

"Well, since you ain't going to that party, you doing anything tonight?" the woman asks. "Her parents are out of town, and we were just gonna cook some—"

"He has plans!"

We turn to find Porsha behind me, dress in hand. She clears her throat. "I mean, sorry, but we gotta go. Merry Christmas! I mean . . . yeah."

She grabs my arm and pulls me toward the cashiers.

As we wait in line, Porsha grabs a blue scarf hanging in the accessories section.

"What was that all about?" I ask.

She shrugs, avoiding eye contact.

"We don't know them like that. Lady looked like she was trying to marry that chick off." She shrugs. "And anyway, though, you told them bros outside we'd be back in fifteen. They probably looking for us."

"Or they just found another space. They can't be that gullible to just wait."

Porsha clicks her tongue as a bell rings overhead. An announcer's voice replaces the music.

"Attention, shoppers. Due to the inclement weather, we will be closing the mall in thirty minutes. I repeat, we will be closing the mall in thirty minutes."

"Damn," I mumble, checking the time.

"Is it really that bad out?"

"Let's roll before we get stuck trying to get out the damn parking lot."

As soon as Porsha has the receipt in hand, we rush out of the store, passing Santa and his elves, wrapping up his last visit. Outside, what little sun there was behind the snowy clouds has all but faded.

We race out the side entrance, back to our spot. The lime-green car is nowhere to be found.

"Told you they wouldn't be dumb enough to wait," I say, hopping inside Rita.

"Yeah, yeah, hurry up. I gotta figure out what to do with this hair before the party."

I sigh, resigning myself to my fate. Porsha is going, no matter what I say. I slip my key in and turn the ignition. It clicks over.

"What's wrong?" she asks with a frown.

"Uh. I don't know. It won't start."

She leans over. "What's that light over there. The kinda dim one?"

"Um. The gas light."

"Dang. Was that there before?"

Be cool, I remind myself. "It's fine. It's got enough gas to get us home."

I turn the car once more, and the engine rumbles to life.

"Whew! Thank god. Let's be out!"

I throw the car in reverse, and it feels like we're driving on rims scraping the road, barely moving. I slam on the brakes.

"What's wrong now?" she groans.

"I think . . . I think I have a flat?"

We glance at each other and jump out the car, running around to the front.

"Oh, shit," we say in unison.

One flat tire, I could call a fluke. Two, maybe bad luck. But three?

"Those dickheads," Porsha mumbles.

* * *

"My dad said it'll probably take him hours to get here," Porsha groans, hanging up her call.

"Yeah, and AAA just laughed at me like I got jokes."

Porsha rubs her arms, staring out at the emptying parking lot.

"Bruh, turn on the heat. It's freezing."

"Can't. Don't want to waste gas."

She digs into her shopping bag and snatches the scarf, wrapping it around her neck twice.

"Well, whadda we do now? There's gotta be a way to get out of here."

My stomach growls loudly. Porsha chuckles.

"Bruh, I wasn't talking to you. I was talking to Kaz."

I snort. "Yo, let's go back in."

"Back in the mall?"

"Yeah, we can stay warm while the traffic dies down. Plus I'm starving. I gotta find something to eat."

"Aight. Fine. But we have to figure out a way home. I can't miss that party!"

I roll my eyes. She's more worried about that damn party than the fact that we're stranded at the mall.

We walk back inside and find we're not the only ones stuck. Though the stores are all closed, a few stranded shoppers are camping out on steps and benches, trying to call Ryde to get home.

Wait, stores closed . . . does that mean . . .

"Aye, come on!" I shout, and take off running.

"Hey! Where are you going?"

I race through the hall at full speed, Porsha gasping to keep up.

"Kaz! Slow down! What are you doing?"

I rush down the escalators. To my horror, every stand in the food court is closed. The scent of chicken and fries still hangs in the air. My stomach cramps in response.

"You a runner and a track star now? What the—"

"Aye yo," I call to a guy passing by in a Popeye's shirt. "Y'all really closed? You ain't got any food back there? Not even a nugget?"

The guy shakes his head. "Naw, dawg. We shut down before the mall. It's ridiculous out there. My girl been stuck on 400 for hours."

"Dang, so *all* of the major highways are backed up," Porsha says.

"I'll pay you to let me back there, just to check it out."

"Kaz," Porsha snaps. "You are not about to eat forgotten chicken. Come on."

She pulls me back toward the stairs, and I go unwillingly. It's past sundown. No food. No water. No iftar. We drift through the halls in stunned silence, finding a free bench near the empty Santa Land, the trees still twinkling.

A security guard tries to corral a group of kids running around without their parents and get them away from the kiosks.

"Aye man, any word on how the traffic is doing?" I ask.

He shakes his head. "Think we 'bout to have a big ol' sleepover party."

Porsha groans to the sky, storming away, and I chase after her.

"What's up?"

"We ain't never getting out of here!" she shouts. "I can't believe I'm going to miss the party!"

"The party?"

"Yeah! This was probably my only chance and now . . . ugh. Why is my life like this? Can't I get a break?"

My fists ball and I turn away, steam rising up my throat. She has no clue, no clue at all.

"Kaz?" She hops in front of me. "Hey, what's wrong?"

"I was supposed to end my fast tonight."

She shrugs. "Yeah. So?"

"SO! I'm missing iftar. Missing Fake Eid. You know, *my* holiday you never come to."

Porsha frowns as if she has no clue what I was talking about. "Kaz . . ."

"You know, all year long, starting from the top, I'm always there. Valentine's Day cookie baking, Easter egg hunts, green soda on St. Paddy's Day, hot dogs and burgers on the Fourth of July. Labor Day potato salad contest. Halloween matching costumes, Thanksgiving Turkey Bowl, even though you don't like that holiday, and then it's Christmas, the Super Bowl holiday of them all. I don't miss one, not one. You won't let me. Not that I want to, because I want to be with you. I always want to be with you, so I put up with all your stupid holidays. And here I am, on the biggest holiday in MY life, and you're sitting here worried about some stupid party?"

She looks at me as if I've grown reindeer antlers. "Yo, where is all this coming from?"

"Can't you tell?"

The voice makes me stretch upright, and we turn. Santa stands, leaning against his sleigh. His regular red coat has been replaced with an army jacket; his hat is now a black beanie.

"Huh?" Porsha says.

"You've gotta be blind not to see that boy got feelings for you."

I jump up. "Aye, stay out of this, Santa!"

He chuckles. "All right. I'm just saying . . . only a man in love would do all that stuff."

Porsha frowns, eyeing him. Any other day she'd pop at the man to mind his damn business. But today of all days, she blinks and just stares at me. As if a light has come on.

"I . . . ," she starts. "I mean, I . . . shit."

Then she runs off.

"Porsha!" I yell. But she ignores me.

"I'd let her go if I was you," Santa says, now standing beside me. "You done dumped a whole heap of dog poop in her lap. Gotta give her a second to clean that off."

"Bruh, I don't know what your problem is—"

"No, but I know what yours is." He laughs. "And it's clearly that girl."

I want to argue. I really do. But I can't figure out what to say.

"How the hell do you expect a girl to know you like her if you don't tell her?"

"I was going to tell her," I blurt out. "I was! I had it all set up and ready. But then she got this invite to that party and . . . and I don't know. But I couldn't just tell her here, all regular, right?"

Santa chuckles and picks up his blue bookbag, heading for the door. "Sounds like excuses to me."

"Nah, I was just waiting for the right moment. It has to be special!"

"If you keep waiting for the right moment, it'll never come. Now, what if this storm didn't happen? You would've let her go to that party and blew another chance waiting for the right moment. Young man, sometimes you just gotta seize the day."

It's strange, walking around an empty mall. Seeing all the stores closed, yet still listening to Christmas music . . . without Porsha. She doesn't want me. Why else would she run? I can't believe I got this so wrong. I know I haven't eaten since yesterday, but I've never felt so empty and numb. Halfway through, I find myself in front of the locked-down GameStop and think of Stevie, probably struggling to figure out if all this stuff is going to help get Sola back while I've just lost the girl I want to be mine.

At our last Jack and Jill community service project, Stevie caught me staring at Porsha across the room, packing supplies for hurricane victims.

"Why don't you just tell her how you feel?" Stevie had said to me outside, as we loaded boxes into a truck. "You obviously really like her."

"You trying to have me out here looking dumb? I can't just *tell* her!"

"Well, you look dumb just staring," Stevie said, real matter-of-factly. "You have to do something."

I waved Stevie off. "I am gonna do something. Just . . . don't know what that is yet. But it has to be good."

Stevie shrugged. "I think I know someone who can help."

I didn't know Sola that well, other than the fact that we were in AP Chemistry together. But Stevie insisted that she was the queen of love and would know exactly what to do. And damn, she was right.

"Okay, we got our Fake Eid plan all set," Sola had said, as we partnered up for our midterm exam and worked on my Porsha game plan. "The cake is ordered and your speech is ready."

"All right. So I tell her, then what?"

"Once you tell her, ask to kiss her right away. She needs to know you're serious. 'Cause once you cross this line, there's no going back. So you have to kiss her like you want her."

"Of course I want her!"

"No. Like, WANT her, want her. Kiss her like it's the last time you'll ever kiss anyone in your life. Like you going off to war or something. Like in the movies. A glorious Hollywood kiss."

"Oh. Ohhhh."

Sola raised an eyebrow. "You do want her, right?"

"Yeah, it's just I never thought about . . . that."

Sola leaned forward, palming a soda can. "You know, maybe we're going about this all wrong. Maybe we should just keep it simple. Why can't you just tell Porsha how you feel? You two have known each other forever."

"'Cause I want it to be special."

"Or is it 'cause you're scared she doesn't like you back? Kaz . . . sometimes saying exactly how you feel, without all the fancy decorations, is special in a different kind of way. 'Cause when you really know someone, less is more."

My rumbling stomach drags me back into the half-deserted food court. Fasting can teach you patience and self-control. I had spent most of my fast thinking and praying about Porsha. I envisioned the moment I would finally tell her too many times to count. But if I was to keep it real, my "patience" was just another way of stalling. Because I'm shook. I know once I cross this line and tell her how I feel, I won't be able to take it back and I just don't know how she's gonna react, despite the way everything in me says we belong together.

I think of the LEGO rose. Still can't believe Stevie is doing something so wild just for Sola. Wild . . . and brave as hell.

A bolt hits me in the spine. I spin on my heels, jogging through the mall. I gotta find Porsha. I've been dragging my feet because I'm scared instead of . . . what did Santa call it? Seizing the day. I don't want another minute to go by without her knowing how I really feel. And if it goes bad, it goes bad. But at least I tried. At least I'll be able to tell Sola that much.

I run past Macy's. Near Santa Land and on the top of the steps, I spot Porsha. She has her phone out, focusing on some video. I reach the top and she closes her screen, clutching her scarf in her other hand.

"Hey," I mumble.

She takes a deep breath. "Hey."

"What are you doing?"

She opens her mouth, blushes, then relents.

"Looking up how to tie a headscarf. You know, like a hijab."

"Why?"

"Because . . . if we ever make it out of here, we need to go directly to your house. For Fake Eid."

I sit beside her. "Naw, Porsha. You don't have to. I get it. It's *the* Christmas party. You should go."

She shakes her head. "I always made you do all that holiday stuff and you never complained. All right, that's a lie. You complain the entire time. But never say no. You're always down. Now I feel stupid for forcing you to do stuff you really didn't want to."

"You didn't force me."

"I did . . . because I didn't want you to feel left out. When you first came here, and everyone was making fun of your accent and everything . . . Mom told me that I should help make you feel at home. So I guess I thought, what better way to help you feel at home than inviting you to be a part of American holidays? So ridiculous. And you're right. I love the holidays more than anything. But I also love them because you're a part of them. I can't imagine doing all that stuff with anyone else. Who's going to let me dress them up like a tree for the Christmas play?"

"Yo, never again, bruh."

She laughs, bumping me with her shoulder. "So yeah, it's *the* Christmas party. But . . . I wouldn't want to be there without you. And I guess I know, one day, soon . . . you're not going to be able to do this stuff with me. That you'll want to be with girls that know how to tie a hijab without having to look it up on the freaking internet. It's why I never wanted to go to Eid, because . . . I didn't want to make a fool out of myself. I was worried I'd say the wrong thing or mess up and then you'd see why I couldn't . . . I don't know. Be a good girlfriend."

I glance at the scarf in her hand. "Uh . . . you do know there are interfaith couples in the world, right?"

She squirms and covers her face with the scarf. "Ugh. This is so embarrassing."

I laugh. "You don't have to wear a hijab tonight. You can come as you are. Ummi loves you regardless. I mean, she calls you more than me. But if you want, I can teach you how to wear one. Just because."

She nods. "I think I'd like that."

"I'm sorry I didn't tell you how I felt and stuff. And that I blew up on you. I guess I just was waiting for the right moment, but I don't want to let another moment go by without you knowing that I love you. So there. I said it. I love you."

She nods. "On the steps . . . while we're stranded at the mall . . . in the middle of a snowstorm. Pretty romantic."

"I'm coming for Stevie's neck!"

Porsha shakes her head. "Here. I got you something." She pulls a granola bar and a bottle of water out of her coat pocket.

My mouth drops. "Where did you . . . how did you . . ."

"Traded with a kid for a few candy canes."

I munch into the granola bar and it tastes like the best thing I've ever had. As I chug down the water bottle, I look up and notice a green bustle tied with red ribbon hanging above.

"Ha, there's that mistletoe stuff."

"I know," she says coyly, at the floor. "I kinda sat here on purpose."

"Oh. Ohhhhh!"

We sit in silence for a few beats, twiddling thumbs, and she laughs.

"You can kiss me now, you know?"

"Oh, cool, yeah, I was just about to ask."

She smirks right as our lips touch. And in the middle of the mall, surrounded by cheesy twinkling lights and giant red bows, during the snowstorm of the damn century, I get to kiss that smile that I've been dreaming about since the day we met. Time freezes as we come up for air. I'm so lost in her eyes, I almost forget where we are.

"Uh . . . so . . ." I'm kind of at a loss. I mean, what do you do after you finally kiss your best friend?

She grins, beaming. "So . . . we should take a selfie!"

I chuckle as she leans on my shoulder and I wrap an arm around her waist, extending my other arm out with her phone.

"Ready? Three, two, one . . ."

She kisses my cheek and the picture is perfect, just the two of us. And wayyyy in the background . . . there is that damn Santa, on the first floor looking up at us. I turn around, and he waves.

"Aye! I knew y'all would figure it out!" he shouts.

Porsha and I bust out laughing as we watch him make his way back into Santa Land.

"All right," she says, grabbing her phone and swiping to Insta. "So what should be the caption?"

I think for a moment and laugh. "Hmmm . . . Holly jolly mall party!"

We laugh until our lips find each other again, and I wonder how I've survived this long without kissing her.

Porsha pulls away. "Um . . . Kaz?"

I lean my forehead against hers. "Hmm."

"How are we gonna get out of here?"

THREE

STEVIE

Virginia-Highland, 5:28 p.m.
Six hours and thirty-two minutes until midnight

"NOBODY CAN DRIVE down here when it snows," the Ryde driver mutters, causing the car windows to fog even more. "This is why we'll stick to these back roads. It'll be slower, but I've always found that taking roads less traveled works out best in the end."

When this car pulled up I thought it was a mistake. On the outside it's a bright red SUV with eerie green lights glowing from the bottom, like it's the star in a holiday installment in the Fast and the Furious franchise. Inside, there's a disco ball and red, white, and green string lights, and the driver has a big white beard and is blasting Christmas carols. "Is this a joke?" I asked as I climbed inside. But the driver just grinned at me in the rearview and said, "Only if you think it's funny. I'm ready when you are, hun."

"You know it's culturally insensitive to play Christmas music. What if your Ryder doesn't celebrate Christmas?"

He hit a button on his steering wheel and all of a sudden the lights turned blue and white, and the disco ball began to spin as a song in Hebrew emanated from the speakers. "Hanukkah?" he asked, with the right pronunciation and everything.

"Well, no, but—"

He hit another button and the lights went back to red and green, but the song playing sounded like . . . was that Swahili?

"Kwanzaa?"

"No, sir, what I meant was—"

He changed the lights and songs a few more times accounting for every holiday I could think of (even the winter solstice for all the pagans out there), until I said, "I can't think with all this noise!"

He nodded and muttered, "Well, why didn't you say so?"

So now I focus on the crunchy sound the tires make as they move over the snow, hoping it'll be the ASMR noise I need to keep my heart rate steady and my mind clear. There's so much traffic everywhere, taking the back roads doesn't seem likely to make a difference. I barely register the now overly chatty driver asking me question after question about why I'm going to the stadium during this snowstorm, and I feel a vague desire to tell him that one, it's actually not snowing right now; two, fewer than four inches have accumulated; and three, all this traffic is due to fear. But I don't. No time to correct his logical fallacy. Too much to figure out between now and when I get to Ern. Speaking of Ern . . .

E ERN

> You sure it's a good idea to try and come down here in this weather, Stevie?

S STEVIE

> I have to. It's the grandest gesture I could think of that—with your help, obviously—could be accomplished before midnight and be big enough to fix it.

Okay! This'll actually be good practice for Mr. Celebrity and his New Year's Eve proposal. Been planning this for months, but it's hard to test the storyboard when his future fiancée lives three blocks over.

But I've never tried to do this sort of thing in this type of weather, so I'll get started prepping and testing.

> Ern . . . What if it doesn't work?

Ah, come on, Stevie. You're a scientist, are you not? If an experiment fails, what do you do?

> Check the experimental design for flaws and then try again.

Exactly. This is that. Don't forget it, okay?

I flip open my observation log to a plan I'd been working on before I messed everything up.

EXPERIMENT TITLE: WOOING A WOOER

SCIENTIFIC QUESTION: Can you out-romance the most

romance-obsessed girlfriend in the world?

HYPOTHESIS: The right combination of romantic elements, proper planning, and adequate subterfuge will yield an outcome more romantic than anything Sola could ever dream of.

I'd been working on this one since Halloween, setting up a Christmas Eve surprise for her. It was my original reason for calling in favors from our friends, but now it might be all for naught.

The midnight ultimatum plays over and over again in my head. I imagine Sola sprawled across her paisley comforter, fairy lights leaving tiny freckles of brightness across her beautiful dark skin as she watches the baby grandfather clock I bought for her fifteenth birthday tick away on her nightstand. Knowing Sola, she'll count down every single minute, every single second until the deadline she gave me.

My heart squeezes, thinking about her burrowed inside her bedroom, tears soaking her pillow. Seeing her cry has always been the worst thing. She's one of those beautiful criers, where her eyelashes soak and elongate with tears, and her chin wobbles, and the tiniest little mouse squeak echoes from her throat. I could never handle it. Not even when we watched super-sad or super-sappy movies or when I knew she had had a bad day at school. The thought of her being in pain was always too much for me. I'd feel this urge to fix whatever was causing her tears, somehow, anyhow, immediately. Even though she'd say she loves crying—"A good cry clears the sinuses and the heart." And then she'd kiss me, all stuffy nosed and wet cheeked, to show me that she was okay. But part of me never wanted her to feel sad enough for tears.

Now I was the cause of it all. Which made me feel even worse.

I snatch a marker from my backpack and draw a big, wobbly X through that old plan. My hands can barely grip the pen, as if all the anxiety has piled up inside them.

"You don't have to be nervous, ma'am," the driver says, glancing at me in the rearview mirror. "It'll take a little time, but I'll get you there. Hopefully you won't miss much of whatever show you're trying to catch. Surprised whatever's going on hasn't been canceled already, with all the government alerts going on."

"Don't call me ma'am, bruh," I mumble under my breath.

"What was that?" His bushy eyebrow lifts.

"Nothing." I bury my nose in my observation log, hoping he'll get the hint. Stop trying to make small talk. Call someone. Do something else, anything else, but talk to me right now.

"You going to see someone special? I bet that's what it is." He chuckles as I sink deeper into the seat. "If it's a first date, then just be yourself. There's nothing worse than trying to wear a mask or perform for others. Any person would be lucky to have you. That's what I tell my girls."

Ugh, I bet Sola doesn't feel lucky anymore. I squeeze my eyes shut and can hear her voice whispering in my ear, cracking open one of the thousands of fortune cookies she collected to divine our future or determine just how auspicious our year would be.

* * *

The summer after ninth grade, Sola and I went to a leadership program at Barthingham Girls' Academy. One of the best—and luckiest—summers we've ever had. Our grand plan was to spend July and August together, away from our parents (especially *hers*) pestering us with questions about *why* we tried to hang out every day and *why* we stayed on the phone with each other on days we were apart and *why* best friends needed to spend so much time together.

While away, I'd work up the courage to admit I wanted to be more than just best friends, that there was something else between us . . . and I hoped she felt the same way. I had a big dream that we'd wind up going to boarding school—that was the whole point of the program. We'd room together, spending every waking moment between boring seminars on leadership skills and public speaking practice investigating the grounds, hanging out with Evan-Rose, and trying to figure out what was happening between us. Were we just best friends . . . or something more? Was there a bigger reason why we always felt like we needed to be together? Did she even have space to see me like that, like the love interests she wrote in all her novels or the ones in all the books she read? Was it all real or just in my head?

I draw a heart on the fogged-up car window, wishing I was back in those thick New England woods, overheated, sweaty, and grumpy, following behind Sola as we headed for the campus lake.

"How much farther?" I'd said, trying to hide my sheer hatred of the great outdoors from my voice as she skipped ahead, excited in her pretty dress and holding a basket full of snacks and a couple bottles of water so we could live our best Black-kids-and-cottagecore aesthetic. I didn't want my disdain to sour her day. I'd always tried so hard not to be that person, *that* best friend who was never up for the type of fun their person wanted to have . . . even though I'd rather be reading about the scientists I admired and their latest findings in my favorite quantum theory magazines, or curled up in the window nook of our dorm room watching all the kids on the quad play stupid games or watching one of her favorite sappy rom-coms while she threaded beads into my locs. Anything would've been better than the humidity, mosquitoes, and sneeze-inducing trees. But I always tried my best to not crap all over the things she loved.

"You okay back there?" She grinned, looking over her shoulder, ready to tease me.

"I'm fine. Of course I'm fine." I looked up at the trees to avoid eye contact, hoping the heat of my cheeks didn't show through the brown. The afternoon sun bore down on us, and my entire shirt was soaked through. I knew I probably had that weird outdoor smell and there were likely leaves and pollen in my hair. I tried to focus on the path ahead, making sure I didn't trip over any logs and branches and jutting rocks. Keeping my anxiety at bay.

"I can feel your thoughts," she'd chimed.

I sucked my teeth. "You know that's not scientifically possible."

"It's Solaology."

"You can't just—"

"Before you even try me, it's called a neologism. A newly coined word . . . or expression, okay? It's a writer thing. Go with it." She winked at me. "I have my own form of science now. Put some respect on it."

I laughed. "You're the future novelist, so I guess I should believe you." I rolled my eyes and reached out to tickle her sides. She always knew how to push me out of my own head and my stubborn resolve with the right kind of joke. Most people wrote me off as too serious, too obstinate, but not her. It always felt like she loved trying to make me smile or soften my hard edges. She had a way of reading me—keenly observing my quirks, knowing when I got stuck in one of my loops.

We rounded the millionth corner, and she held up the latest fortune cookie slip from the Chinese food the school had ordered in for lunch. "It says we're going to have a lucky day."

"I don't believe in luck. It's—"

"Not scientifically possible," she finished my sentence.

"But it's true. How does one even define luck?" I asked. "What are the variables we're considering?"

"Must we always make everything into an experiment or equation?"

"Shouldn't it be?" I tried to walk faster to keep up with her, and wondered how she wasn't covered in sweat and completely stressed out about these mosquitoes and gnats and pollen right now. "That way we know what is and isn't true."

"Some things can just be luck, or chance, or fate, or serendipity, *and* still be true. Or at least truthful." She raced to the end of the trail, pausing beside an enclosed bulletin board. She tapped the glass. A poster advertised a Barthingham Girls' Academy annual back-to-school bonfire. And it was mad old. The lake spread out behind her, the promise of a cold dip making me want to jump straight in.

"Convince me. What's your hypothesis? How will you test this theory of yours?" I'd asked, out of breath.

"What's bothering you?" Sola set the basket at her feet.

I stretched upright. "It's hot and sticky and we've been walking for hours."

"That's just annoying you. . . . What's *bothering* you? I can tell something is. You've been wound up all summer, and I haven't been able to figure it out. I usually can, but not this time." Her deep brown eyes scanned me, and I looked away, hating it, not wanting her to see how much of a coward I was, how much I'd buried inside, how afraid I was to tell her the truth. "You do all your science talk when you're worried."

"I do not."

"Oh yes you do. That brilliant brain of yours goes into overdrive. So you run back to your safe space, your experiments and your chemicals. Out with it."

"How do you know that?" I asked. My mom always said, "Feelings are a thing that all the experiments and hypotheses and data tables can't make sense of." And she'd push me not to swallow my feelings or make myself into a puzzle—especially not one that no one, even me, could solve. But I still didn't know how to say all the things I wanted to say. The words sat inside me, jumbled and locked away.

"I pay attention." She swept one of my locs away from my shoulder, her touch sending electricity across my skin. "I know *you*."

"It's nothing," I replied, but the words felt like lies. "Let's just get in the water. I'm too hot."

"Nope." She bit her bottom lip and wouldn't take her eyes off me. "You're ruining my Hollywood moment, my picture-perfect picnic, the memory we will retell over and over again, our romance novel turning point."

"What?"

She closed the gap between us, perched on her tiptoes, doing her best to be eye to eye with me. It was so cute that I felt myself smile through all the nerves and aggravation about the heat. She got closer and closer to me. I could almost taste the plum-flavored lip gloss she wore. "It'll be time to go back home soon and you're worried about us, but you shouldn't be."

My heart plummeted into my stomach. I tried to reply, but she took my hands and whispered, "I'm going to kiss you now, and you're going to be my girlfriend."

A nervous-excited tingle rushed down both my arms and into my fingertips. I opened my mouth to speak, but my voice squeaked.

She held up the fortune cookie slip in her hand. "I'd been waiting for the right day. The right card to show up in my tarot reading, the right astrology report to pop up on my app, and the right fortune cookie slip. I wanted it to be our luckiest day here to make this memory. I wanted us to never forget it. This would be the memory we'd come back to even if we were mad at each other."

I wrapped my arms around her, feeling the warmth of the sun in her skin. "I . . . I . . . love you," I stammered. "I always have. I always will."

"I know, and I love you too. And we're okay whether we're here . . ." She motioned at the lake. "Or home. And most of all, we're lucky. We found each other."

My pulse thundered. She leaned up and pressed her mouth to mine. The shock of it made me freeze. I'd dreamed for so long what it might be like to kiss her, to have her want me as more than a friend. And in that moment, the worries and questions I'd had drifted off. I felt so lucky that she had chosen me, that she'd known I'd been worried about what this summer together meant for us, about what would happen when we packed up tomorrow and headed back to Atlanta, back to all the things at home.

But there, behind that bulletin board, I'd had my first kiss . . . and I wanted it to last forever.

"You going to get that?" The Ryde driver's voice crashes through my memory. I'm back in the car, tiny snow crystals fluttering past the window, brake lights washing the seats in red, and my phone ringing over and over again.

Ern's picture flashes at me. An older version of Evan-Rose's smile. I pick up. "Hey, sorry."

"Dang, Stevie! You had me worried for a second! You good?"

"Yeah. I'm en route."

"Okay, cool. I was starting to think you'd changed your mind," he says. "This weather seems to be getting worse."

Which is when I notice he's right. The snow is *really* coming down right now.

"No, no. I'm coming. Just in a lot of traffic."

"Not sure how long it'll be, little lady," the Ryde driver chimes in, and I grimace.

"All right, so I've tested the first part of the storyboard, and I'm getting good reports. I already had the permits, but the police are annoyed. Luckily they don't have time to deal with me, with all the car wrecks on the highways." Ern laughs, and it reminds me of Evan-Rose's corny chuckle. It makes me miss her even more, and I can't wait for her to be home for winter break. "The whole thing is going to be beautiful, for real."

"It has to be perfect." My stomach squeezes, and I try to resist the urge to vomit.

"You're in luck, because perfect is my specialty. Don't worry. I got you."

Maybe this'll be the first time in my life when I have to rely on luck.

And I hate it.

NPR
The snow is falling . . . but is it safe to eat?
Meteorologists weigh in.

Atlanta Journal-Constitution
ATLANTA-AREA MALLS CLOSE EARLY DUE TO
INCLEMENT WEATHER: Why that last-minute
holiday shopping will have to wait.

Twitter
#SnowpocalypseAtlanta2PointOh is trending in
your area.

New York Times
New Yorkers poke fun at Georgia's reaction to
record-breaking snowfall, but scientists say climate
change is no joke.

NWS
The Atlanta metropolitan area remains under
a winter storm alert, making travel potentially
dangerous. State and local emergency officials urge
the public to monitor road conditions and avoid
driving unless absolutely necessary.

FOUR

E.R.

AS WE MAKE our way up the jet bridge—after an hour and a half of sitting out on the tarmac, waiting for it to stop snowing sideways so we could get to our gate, and me killing time scrolling through dozens of notifications—Savanna leans real close and whispers in my ear: "You sure we're not still in Massachusetts, Evan-Rose? I thought Georgia doesn't do 'this frozen tundra mess,' as you put it?"

"Oh, shut up." And I say this for good reason: her breath all up on my neck and ear is kind of a lot—it's warm, but also cool because she's always got a wintergreen mint in her mouth. Just . . . too much. I've got enough conflicting feelings swirling around in my head. No need to add hot and bothered to the mix.

God, she smells good.

Against my better judgment, I slide my palm against hers and interlace our fingers. She squeezes twice (a thing of ours), puts her head on my shoulder—while we're walking, mind you—and sighs.

What a mess.

"Ugh, you two are so cute, it's disgusting," comes a distinctly white girl voice from behind us. Then there's a jolting smack on my butt before a short girl passes by, head full of glistening blond tresses billowing behind her. Jameson Mabe, homecoming queen and student body president at the Barthingham Girls' Academy of New England. A place Van and I couldn't wait to get the hell away from for a couple of weeks. "Have an awesome holiday, lovebiiiiiirds!" she practically sings, without looking back.

"Wait," Savanna says, standing bolt upright. "Did she just . . . was that smack . . ."

"Yup."

"Oh, I'm definitely gonna kick her ass." Van tries to pull away from me. "I don't care if she does run our damn school, no Skipper-lookin' tramp is just gonna smack my girl's ass and get away with it."

"Chill," I say, tugging her back. Really tempted to correct the "my" part, but I'll resist. This time. "At least she didn't touch my hair. Also, a what-lookin' tramp? And could we maybe not use the word 'tramp'?"

"Umm, Skipper? As in Barbie's baby sister?"

"Ah."

"Homegirl ain't tall enough to be Barbie. And 'tramp' is way nicer than the word I really wanted to use. But I know how you are, so . . . yeah."

And there it is. One of my more notable qualms when it comes to this gorgeous girl: the semi-judgy way she sometimes talks about other girls. I pull my hand away under the guise of adjusting the bag on my shoulder.

We finally exit the bizarre retractable port-to-plane floating tunnel. (Who even invented the jet bridge? Gotta look that up later.) It's nice and warm inside the airport . . . but that has to be due at least in part to the sheer mass of bodies crowded inside. The place is absolute mayhem.

"Well, damn," Van says as she comes to a standstill beside me. Didn't even realize I'd stopped moving.

"You can say that again—ow!"

Clearly we didn't halt in the most convenient place. A guy with the height and build of a boat-sized SUV bumps my shoulder and knocks the long tube sticking out of my backpack into the side of my head.

"Oh, man, I'm so sorry!" he says, grabbing his wavy brown hair in panic like he just ran me over with a car or something. "Are you all right?"

"I'm good, sir." It's a struggle not to laugh at how distraught dude is. "I was standing right in front of the exit, so partially my own bad."

Now he's holding his hand over his heart. "You sure you're sure?"

"I am." (What even kind of question is that?) "Have a great trip!" And I pull Savanna out of the flow of Homo sapiens traffic.

"Girl, you are so much better than me," Van says as the man lumbers off into the masses. "I mighta swung on that guy had I been you."

"Somebody's feisty today."

And I'm annoyed. Why am I annoyed? It's not like she did anything for me to be annoyed about. . . . Why is this whole love-and-relationships thing so complicated?

Also why are there so many people here?

"Soooo, I've been quiet about it, but I have to ask now. You have a giant tube sticking out of your backpack because . . . ?"

So. Many. People. The air almost feels like it's vibrating. Which is making me itchy. "It's a sign."

"What's a sign? A sign of what?" Van looks around.

"No, silly. I mean in the tube. There's a poster. It came from that bulletin board at the end of the trail that leads to the lake on campus."

"There a bulletin board at the end of the trail?"

I smile. Apparently Stevie was right when she said, "Ev-Ro, I'm ninety-eight percent sure nobody even notices the thing."

"There is," I say to Savanna.

Honestly, though I knew the actual bulletin board was there, I was shocked to discover that the poster-style sign Stevie wanted still was. Cuz the thing is old. It reads:

**COME ONE, COME ALL, TO THE
BARTHINGHAM GIRLS' ACADEMY ANNUAL
START OF SCHOOL BONFIRE
LAKE ELLIOTT, EASTERN SHORE CAMPGROUND
AUGUST 28, 1981, 8:30 P.M.**

That's literally two days before my mom was born.

Which means it was locked up tight: poster's a little faded, yeah, but there's no water damage or bug-nibbled holes or anything. What should've been the easiest lock-pick of my life wound up taking more time and effort than I'm willing to admit.

And all because I'm clearly some kinda sucker for love or whatever. (Totally rolling my eyes right now . . . and trying not to look at Savanna.)

A family with three small kids passes behind Van, stroller *and* car seat on deck, and she's suddenly pressed up against my left side. And her coat is open. So I can feel her soft middle against my forearm. When she turns her head, her bob-length locs brush my cheek. Lavender, cedarwood, and coconut oil smack me on the inhale, and I'm instantly thrown back to the first time she fell asleep with her face buried in my neck. I'm tempted to slip my arm around her waist and pull her even closer.

I shake my head. *Gotta snap out of it.* "We should move," I say, taking her hand again and tugging her in the general direction of the concourse's main thoroughfare.

"So what's the sign for?" Van asks as we break into a (slightly) less densely populated space a few yards away from the gate area.

"My homie Stevie asked me to get it." I look left and right and left again in an effort to figure out which way we need to go to get to the plane train thing that'll cart us to baggage claim. "I've told you about my bestie from elementary and middle school. We completed one of those leadership programs at Barthingham the summer after ninth grade."

"Why doesn't Stevie go there?"

"Go where?"

"To our esteemed institution," Van replies. "Isn't that typically what those summer programs are for? To make it clear a girl wants to go to Barfingham and to prove she has the juice for the grueling academic journey?"

"Oh. Yeah, Stevie . . . decided to go in a different direction." I clear my throat. "After being there, Barthingham didn't feel like the best fit."

What I'm not saying, aka boldface lying about: Stevie attended the summer program with another good friend (turned girlfriend) Sola, and Stevie and Sola did in fact intend to go to Barthingham. And it was partially because of me. My freshman year there, Stevie was the only person back home that I talked to when I was dealing with my own . . . questions. About myself. And my, uhhh . . . attractions.

I told Stevie, who's been wide open about her preference for girls since we were eleven, that I felt like my "journey to self-discovery" (yeah, I really did use that phrase—ridiculous) was being accelerated because I was in a place where I saw girls being into girls at literally every turn.

That was all she needed to hear. Stevie told Sola what I'd said, and their plan was to escape to boarding school so they could be together without having to deal with questions and side-eye and people all up in their business. And they both applied and got in . . . but Sola's parents decided they didn't want their daughter so far away "at such a critical time in her development."

Sola stayed home, so Stevie did too. Now they co-lead the Marsha P. Johnson Magnet Genders and Sexualities Alliance.

Well . . . at least they *did*.

Another thing I'm very deliberately leaving out: the reason Stevie asked me to get the sign. She was trying to pull together some grand romantic gesture made of memory mile markers from her relationship journey with Sola. My job was to get the sign and bring it home . . . but it would appear my mission was futile. The whole plan is off because Stevie and Sola are broken up.

Just like me and the queen of a girl whose warm palm is the sole thing keeping me grounded as all these people move about. Between the cacophony of voices, the dizzying swirl of scents, and all the strangers getting way too close to us as they pass by . . . yeah, I'm a smidge overwhelmed. Despite the very clear contribution to my confusion, I'm really glad this technical ex of mine is beside me.

"Why are there so many people here?" I say, aloud this time, still trying to figure out which way to go so we can snag our checked bags and get the hell outta this place. I shot my dad a text as soon as we touched down, and he said he was en route. Really hope he's already here to get us.

"Well, if those screens are correct, there are no flights coming in or going out right now," Van replies.

"Huh?" I follow her eyes. A screen above us reads:

**Due to inclement weather in the
Atlanta area, the FAA has issued
a ground stop for Hartsfield-Jackson
International Airport. Your safety is
our highest priority, and we apologize
for any inconvenience.**

Beside that screen is one that lists connecting flights—all of which have an aggressively bold DELAYED in the status column. And beside that screen is a television tuned in to the news, where a well-bundled reporter surrounded by white is standing . . . on the highway?

"We're at a complete standstill out here on 75/85, Jo. And as you can see, though the snow has stopped coming down, quite a bit accumulated over a short period of time!" he shouts over the whistling wind. "You know I love this city, but I think it's safe to say peachy Atlanta is ill-prepared for a snowstorm of this magnitude. About twenty minutes ago, the mayor issued a citywide shelter-in-place order, and based on what we're seeing out here on the roads, it was a good call—"

Dude's voice trails off, and my vision goes white at the edges. This is not good.

"Oh, boy," comes a voice from somewhere beside me. I feel the weight of a hand on my shoulder, and a pair of fingertips gently press beneath my jaw, then Savanna's face slides back into focus. We're exactly the same height, so now I'm staring into her big brown eyes. "Your pulse is racing," she says. "And you look like you just saw that creepy-ass Chucky doll peeking around a corner or something. You need a hug."

It's a statement, not a question. And before I can rebut, her arms are wrapping around my neck. Mine, traitors that they are, instinctively snake around the waist I resisted grabbing not three minutes ago. She is so delightfully soft. The tension eases out of my shoulders.

But not for long. Because a horn blows, and we spring apart and out of the way as one of those little in-airport transport vehicles barrels toward us. The three passengers sitting on the back—an old man and the woman I assume is his boo, based on the hand holding, and a guy about our age who is white-knuckle gripping the handle of his walking cane—look genuinely afraid for their lives as they zip past.

And then: "So now our flight is canceled *and* there's no way for us to get to a hotel?" a man barks at a gate agent to my left. My head turns like I heard a gunshot or something. (Definitely not that serious, but all this stimuli is short-circuiting my brain, I swear.)

"Sir, I don't want to be stuck here any more than you do," the agent, a gorgeous dark-skinned woman with braids pulled up into a high bun, says. "But I am unfortunately not the brown-skinned, white-haired lady member of the X-Men. Sadly can't make it stop snowing." She shrugs.

My gaze drifts past them to the floor-to-ceiling windows beyond. Nothing visible on the other side but a thick white cloud with sparkling bits swirling around inside it.

I pull out my phone to call my dad. Hoping against hope he's not stuck on the highway . . .

But it's no use. Because three big, bold words now occupy the bottom of the TV screen where the news is still playing: SHELTER IN PLACE.

As in, don't leave.

Savanna takes my hand again, but it's not the least bit comforting this time.

We're officially trapped in the airport.

Since this is Van's first visit to Atlanta's good old Hartsfield-Jackson International, I make the executive decision to take her to my favorite place inside it so we can hopefully camp out both somewhere soothing and away from the masses. There's this frantic energy zipping through the air, and it's making me far jumpier than I'd like to be. "We're going to the jungle," I say, finally spotting a sign that makes it clear which direction is the right one. I take her hand then. "This way."

She presses up super close to me. Which is wholly uncalled-for and distracting, not in a good way at this particular moment. "Ooh, what's the jungle?" she practically coos right into my ear (again).

Definitely ignoring the chill that just shot down both arms into my fingertips. Which are now tingling.

I really can't stand her sometimes.

"It's, umm . . ." *Breeeeathe, E.R.* "It's this really pretty space down under the airport. You really only know it's there if you decide to walk instead of taking the plane tra—"

My watch begins to buzz. Which gives me an excuse to drop Savanna's hand and put some highly necessary space between us (for the sake of my sanity). I have to fish my phone back out of the pocket that she's practically smushed up against.

It's Stevie.

"What happened? She change her mind?" I ask as soon as I pick up.

"Very funny, E.R. I presume you made it?"

"Yeah, we did, but—"

"Good. Cuz there's a change of plans," Stevie says.

"Yeah, I know," I say. I take Van's hand and continue in the direction of the escalators. "Plan's off. I was in the group text, remember?"

"Ah yes. Well, there's a change to that change."

I snort. Gotta love Stevie. "Okay . . ."

"I need you to get that poster to Mo before you leave the airport."

Wait . . . "Huh?"

"Mo. As in Maurice. Your brother-in-law."

"I'm wholly aware of my brother-in-law's name, Stevie."

"Okay, well your brother said Mo's shift is about to end, so I need you to get the poster to him so he can bring it to me at the stadium."

"I . . . why are you at the stadium?"

"I'm not there yet, but I'll explain later. Can you get it to him?"

"Uhhh . . . I don't see why not . . ." *Do I tell her nobody can leave the airport right now?*

"Okay, great," Stevie says. "Thanks, E.R.!"

And we hang up.

"Okaaaay . . . ," I say, the device still clutched in my palm.

"Everything all right?" Savanna asks.

"Umm, I guess? Stevie just asked me to—"

The phone rings again. "I bet that's Stevie aga—" I start, but when I look at the screen, the rest of the statement unravels on the tip of my tongue.

"Who is it?" Van says as she eyes the device in my hand.

Look. I don't know who invented privacy screen protectors—which make your phone's face unseeable unless you're looking at it straight on—but I would like to give them a kiss. It's the sole reason Van can't see the big DO NOT ANSWER above the phone number lit up on my screen. She would certainly have all the questions.

"No idea," I lie, silencing the call.

"Ugh. Probably one of those spam calls where some computer voice tells you that your car's warranty is expiri—"

My phone rings again, and I inwardly kick myself for not thinking to turn the damn ringer off after rejecting the first call. I also know I have to answer now. This caller isn't likely to stop trying until I do.

I sigh.

"I'm gonna answer," I say to Van.

She shrugs. "It's your life."

If only she knew.

Deep breath. "Hello?" I say, putting the receiver to my ear. If nothing else, I can say it's too noisy, and I can't hear the call.

"Richie RICH!" comes a voice that sounds the way butter looks as it glides over the top of a warm biscuit. It's a nickname from my last name (Richardson), and this clown is the only person who uses it.

I hate it. (Because I maybe secretly low-key love it.)

"Uhh . . . hi?"

"Surprised to hear from me, I see," he says.

"Yes, that's correct."

He laughs. "Why you sound like you doing some corporate interview with a white man?"

Because I'd prefer that my ex(ish)-girlfriend not know I'm on the phone with the guy I maybe spent a lot of time with while she and I were on a break this past summer. "Is there something I can help you with?"

"Damn, it's like that? My apologies for thinking you'd be happy to hear from me."

He sounds hurt. Crap.

"Wait, no. Sorry, I . . ." *Crap!* "One sec, okay?"

I cover the mouth part and turn to Savanna. "I can't really hear. Gonna go over there where it's quieter." I walk away before she can ask any questions. Father on high, if you are real, please keep her from following me.

When I peek back over my shoulder, she's standing to the side of the main walkway, looking at her phone. Thank goodness.

I put *my* phone back to my ear. "Hello?"

"Rich, I gotta admit . . . the fact that I held on just now after you basically shattered my heart—again—is making me feel a little pathetic."

"I promise I wasn't trying to shut you down, Eric. It's just . . ." I peek around me. "A weird time. Loud. Lots of people."

"That's why I called," he says. "I was thinking that since we're both trapped in the Atlanta airport right now, we could maybe meet up and grab a bite to eat."

Umm . . . how the hell do you know I'm at the airport? is the first question to pop into my head, but I swallow that one down. "Why are you in the Atlanta airport?"

He laughs. "I mean, it is like the fourth night of Hanukkah and only four eves till Christmas."

Oh, duh, his grandparents live here. They're the reason we even met.

"Bagel the Beagle threw up or something, so my bubbe called your dad—who's apparently stuck somewhere called the cell phone lot, where he's waiting for you."

I almost stop him to explain that the cell phone lot is where cars park until you're ready to come out, so your ride doesn't have to keep circling the terminals since they're not allowed to stop and wait by the exits, but then it hits me: Dad did make it here. That's good news, at least.

"When Bubbe told him that I'm stuck in the airport too—I shot her a message as soon as I peeped the words 'ground stop' and she told me Pawpaw was en route, but in traffic—he told her to tell me to hit you up. Small world, ain't it?"

"You can certainly say that again." I shut my eyes and shake my head. Eric Ryan Castle being stuck in the same place as Evan-Rose Richardson while the latter is with Savanna Estelle Divine (yes, that really is Van's name, and yes, it is Too Much just like she is).

This is going to be more of a disaster than a snowstorm in the "ill-prepared" city of Atlanta.

First day of ninth grade, I step into one of the hallowed halls—aka super-old, over-large, anticlimactically basic classrooms—in the Wharton liberal arts wing at Barthingham Girls' Academy.

Disgusting how pretentious it all sounds, isn't it?

Anyway.

Front row, there's a clear go-getter of a girl with beautiful glowy brown skin, big brown eyes, and long brown locs . . . wearing brown lipstick. And when she saw me she totally did a double take before dropping her eyes to her desk.

Savanna Divine.

It was a certified moment.

A moment that passed even more quickly than it had come. It would be weeks before Van and I actually spoke to each other. And that only happened because we got paired for a project.

Thus began the most confusing year and a half of my life.

It's not that I hadn't *noticed* girls in that way before. I just never thought much about it. There had been boys. Quite a few of them. In the couple of years between my first kiss (at the beginning of seventh grade) and leaving for my all-girls' high school at the end of the summer after eighth, there were a number of journeys between first and second base on different boy playing fields.

But from that very first day at BGA, noticing Van seemed to kick the "Wow, girls are far more appealing than boys!" door right off the hinges. Like, it was suddenly so obvious! From their varying shapes to the softness of their skin to the way they smell and sound and feel. Way overgeneralizing here, but my point is that I was suddenly overwhelmed by all the girl glory around me. Stevie heard from me frequently during this time.

By the end of ninth grade, I had come out as gay—at school and to Stevie, at least. And Savanna, who'd had her "first girlfriend in first grade" if you let her tell it, was at the center of it all. The sun in my sapphic solar system (learned that word in Gender and Sexuality Studies). I didn't want to admit it, because that meant admitting I'd been wholly knocked off my square, and it scared me to think anyone had that kind of power over me. But the knotted stomach and sweaty palms and racing heart and daydreams and inability to put together a coherent sentence (at first) were difficult to brush under the rug. I was super into her.

But so was, like . . . everyone. Which became increasingly evident the further we got into the school year. What's more, word on the street was that there were a number of former-flame girls back in her hometown who still pined after her.

She and I became . . . "friends." In quotes because it was a weird-ass friendship. Very electric, if that makes any sense. Like there was always this buzz of something more than friendly zipping between us. And this is even with her dating other people. Because she certainly did throughout freshman and sophomore years. None of those relationships lasted more than a couple months, but my blood would boil for the duration.

(Not that I told her that.)

Anyway, a month before the end of sophomore year, she went through yet another breakup. Came to me crying. So, I'm sitting with my arm around her shoulder, genuinely ready to fight somebody, when she drops the ultimate bomb on me: she wasn't crying because some girl—Shay, in this case—had broken her heart. No, her tears were the result of "knowing I'm never going to have a healthy, lasting relationship here because I'm too wild about you."

As in me. Evan-Rose Richardson.

Obviously the feelings I'd been harboring for her basically exploded and covered me in shimmering confetti. . . . But Van's confession had a second, unexpected effect. Because when I let myself *go there* and, like, actually imagine how it might feel to be with her, I realized just how separate I was keeping world-of-school from world-of-home: I wasn't even out to my family.

Now I'll admit . . . I can be quite the coward. Definitely a problem, and I'm hyperaware of it and trying to do better. That being said, because it was so close to the end of the school year, I pulled an "I'm into you too, but we probably shouldn't start this long-distance, right?" (Savanna lives in Maryland.) So we agreed to kick it in the friend zone for the summer and revisit the idea of us at the beginning of the next school year.

Except when I went home, I . . . couldn't do it. I couldn't tell my family. And I felt real dumb about it, too. Because it's not like they would've been opposed or had qualms or something. Hello? I'm supposed to be delivering a poster to my brother's husband.

Anyway, since I didn't tell them anything, when Daddy—Robert Richardson the Doggy Doctor, as people call him—mentioned that the grandson of one of his "dog moms" was visiting from DC for the summer and could use a tour guide, I rolled with it. It's not like I was even attracted to boys anymore.

Except I apparently was.

Am? Yes, am.

Ugh.

"So how 'bout we grab a bite?" Eric is saying into my ear (through the phone). "Catch up a lil bit. I was hoping I'd get to see you, so this is kinda perfect."

My heart beats a little faster.

This is the thing about Eric: *he* is damn near perfect. Well, according to my estimation, at least. He's tall. Like six-four. Cliché, yes, but at five-eight myself, I prefer tall boys. He's delightful to look at—eyelash game is on infinity and he's got these really full lips and his light brown skin is basically flawless. And he's super smart: got a full-ride offer from MIT last year after winning some sort of engineering contest. As a high school junior, mind you.

But that's not even the kicker. The kicker is found in what Eric refers to as "emotional intelligence." Homie can read me like a Judy Blume book. Which is saying a lot. Because I, Evan-Rose Richardson, am a certified expert at masking what I'm truly feeling. Even from myself, at times.

The only other person who's ever been able to do this? You got it: Savanna Divine.

Eric and I . . . got involved. In fact, the only reason we stopped being involved is because he had to go home.

And I'm not proud of it, but once I got back to school, I didn't breathe a word about Eric to Van. She and I just . . . started dating. A few months in, she decided that instead of going to the Bahamas with her parents like she typically would for Christmas, she would come home with me. Meet my family. We broke up a few weeks ago because . . . well, I needed a breather—living in the dorm room next door to your girlfriend equates to a lot of time spent together, and things got real intense real fast. It's a miracle we've never gotten caught . . . doing stuff.

And anyway, as terrible as it sounds, it sort of worked out in my favor. Yes, she still came home with me. But now I'm not lying when I refer to her as my "friend."

"Uhh, hello?" Eric says. "You still there—"

There's a *booop!* in my ear. Another call coming in.

"Hey, E, one sec. I need to answer this."

"As you wish, Richie Rich."

I tap over without even looking to see who it is . . . which means I'm not ready. "Ummm, E.R.? You done with your weirdo phone call yet?" Savanna's voice says. "You sorta left me in a very unfamiliar place with, like, thousands of people milling around."

Crap.

"I know, I know. I'm so sorry," I say, squeezing my eyes shut.

Phone *booops!* again.

"Van, hold on one sec, okay?" I say, though I don't wait for her response before pulling the phone away from my ear to actually check the screen this time.

Eric. Which . . .

I tap over. "Hello?"

"Hey, sorry, the call dropped. Didn't want you to think I hung up instead of holding like I said I would."

I palm my forehead. "Okay, stay there."

Back over to Van. "Hey, sorry about that."

"You're frazzled, E.R.," she says. "I can feel it coming off you in waves. What's going on? Where are you?"

Really not interested in being read like this right now. Especially not over the phone.

Man, what was I thinking, bringing Savanna home with me? She doesn't know I'm not out to my family and that they think she's just my boarding school best friend. In fact, I'm pretty sure *she* thinks I'm my hometown's queen of the teen gays.

And I'm certainly not out to Eric. Who I might still be into? But who am I into MORE?

How did I even get here?

I need some time and space to think.

"I'm not too far from where I left you," I say to Van. I move onto the wide walkway and look back toward the gate where I told her to hang tight. "Step out into the aisle and look," I say.

After a beat, she appears, and I lift a hand in the air. She waves back. Seeing her from a distance—in her fitted gray jeans tucked into matching fur-topped suede moccasin boots and cream-colored turtleneck beneath her long puffer coat—does a number on my wildly confused heart.

"Listen, I've got Maurice on the other line." (Yep. Part of me just died lying to her like that.)

"Ummm . . . who is Maurice?" Oh boy . . . she sounds the way she did when Jameson smacked my behind on the jet bridge. How am I supposed to tell her about Eric, knowing how she is about this kind of thing?

"My brother-in-law," I reply. "Sorry, forgot you don't know his name. If you're cool with it, I wanna run and meet him right quick so I can get rid of this poster. Shouldn't take more than, like, fifteen minutes. I think he said he's in the international concourse."

"You . . . don't want me to come with you?"

Ugh. "I mean, you could. . . . But I think it'd be a waste of your time and energy. I need to move pretty fast and I don't want to trigger your asthma." *God, please don't strike me down dead here in this airport.* "Maybe you can keep an eye on the screens and text me if they lift the shelter-in-place order and we can get outta here?"

For a few beats, she doesn't respond. And as much as I wish I could say I'm primarily concerned about her well-being over the course of these stretched seconds, I'm really thinking about Eric and how long I've kept him waiting.

"Okay," she finally says. It's got resignation draped all over it, and the knife in my heart from looking at her gets a solid twist. When she speaks again, I feel like she's staring into my dirty rotten soul. "I'll be right here," she says. "Waiting for you."

Another twist.

"Okay. Be back as soon as I can." I wave and make my way to the escalators as I switch back over to the other call.

"Eric?"

"Hmm?"

"Oh, good." I exhale. "You're still there."

He laughs. "Why in my right mind would I hang up, E.R.? I really want to see you."

I shake my head. "Yeah, about that . . ."

"Here we go," he says. "You're about to break my heart again, aren't you? And during Chrismukah at that!"

Shake it off, Evan-Rose. "Nothing like that," I lie again. "Just need to find my brother-in-law so I can give him something," I say, using the same excuse. *(Cowaaaaard.)* "I'll, umm . . . I'll call you back."

"Okay," he replies. "I'll be waiting. Semi-patiently."

* * *

How?

This is the question running circles around my brain as I descend the escalator to the plane train by myself. How did I wind up in this . . . predicament?

The whole Eric thing really wasn't supposed to happen. It started by accident. I was working at the front desk at Daddy's veterinary practice, and I heard this laugh from outside that caught me so off guard, I knocked over a cup of pens. Door opened, and in strutted an adorable little old white lady with a big halo of burgundy hair. She had a beagle tucked under one arm and a brown-skinned teenage boy on the other one. "Bubbe, you wild, bro," the boy was saying to her.

It was one of the most confusing scenes—yet adorable and also heart-wrenching . . . I'd lost my own grandfather just a few months prior—I'd ever witnessed.

And I was staring, apparently. Because when the guy looked up, we locked eyes, and dude stopped dead. Like whole face changed. He even dropped the lady's arm.

"Oy, he's fallen in instalove with the dog doctor's daughter," she said.

Which was enough to crack the eye contact. My face got real warm.

"Yo, Bubs, chill with all that," he said. "And I'm not even on that app, so whatever you just said is impossible."

"Bah," the woman replied, flicking his response away with her hand. "I said instalove. . . . Clearly *somebody* doesn't read enough young adult novels."

I chuckled (while very much keeping my head down).

And then he was in front of me. "Sorry about that," he said. I looked up (and basically died). "My grandmother has a twelve thirty appointment with Dr. Richardson—"

"I don't have an appointment, ya goof. Bagel does." She held up the very old-looking dog.

"My bad, Bubbe, dang."

I couldn't help but smile then. "I see Bagel's name here on the schedule—"

"And what's yours?" the boy said.

"Huh?" My chin snapped up.

He shook his head. "Sorry, got too excited. What's your name?"

"Oh," I replied. "I'm—"

"Evan-Rose." From the grandmother. She made her eyebrows do one of those ooh-la-la dances. "Her pa never stops bragging about her. And look at that, you both have E.R. initials!" she said. "This is Eric Ryan."

"Ah. Well, lovely to meet you both," I replied.

As soon as they went to the back, I decided to leave for the day.

Which would've been all well and good. One-and-done type thing. Outta sight, outta mind, nothing at all to dwell over being confused about.

Except my phone rang two days later, and it was him. Telling me he'd heard that: one, I'd agreed to show him around town (definitely forgot about that), and two, I was into "fashion as art." He asked if I wanted to accompany him to a private preview of an haute couture urban apparel exhibit the following week. An exhibit that I'd been looking forward to for, like, a month.

How had he gotten my number? He'd asked my dad for it.

I said yes, and it was downhill from there.

What compounded the complications was the fact that my family absolutely adores him and his grandparents. Bubbe (or Bubs) is Russian and Jewish, and Pawpaw is a Black man from the South Carolina low country, and I have to admit, they're both hilarious and amazing. And the way Eric loves them? *Pshhhh.*

So there I was, confining myself to the proverbial closet, and totally using all-admired Eric to block the door. Was I talking to Van daily and still bonkers over her? Absolutely. I just, like . . . couldn't seem to tell my family the truth. And the longer I kept up what I thought was a ruse, the more I leaned into it. To the point where pretending to like him and how I actually felt about him started to blur together.

The wild part? We never even kissed or anything like that. In fact, my relationship with Eric wasn't too different from the one I had with Savanna before she told me she liked me. He and I were friends, but, like . . . sort of more? Feelings-wise, at least.

Anyway, I knew something was going on with my wayward-ass heart when I found myself sobbing in my room for three solid days after he went home. Once I returned to school, I told him I needed to focus on my work and not get distracted (complete bullcrap), and then

I threw myself headlong into Van's lovely bosom. Almost literally.

There's zero denying that she's got a hell of a hold on me . . . but is this weird super-cliché fluttery thing I've got going on beneath my ribs a sign that he has a grip too? Or is that just guilt over using him?

I need some room to think.

I'm about to step into the airport jungle—an art exhibit between concourses A and B that features treetop-shaped sculptures hanging from the ceiling, backlit by a variety of greens and teals—when I stop. I told Van I was going to bring her here. Yet here I am by myself.

Because I lied to her.

I sigh and pull out my phone. Call Maurice to see where he is so I can get rid of this poster. It's starting to feel like a tube full of bricks. Stevie is just so committed to Sola. It's beautiful. That's why I was so quick to agree to the task—I may not have a clue how to get my love life together, but I want to see my besties thriving.

Mo answers on the first ring. "Baby sis! I was just wondering when you would call."

I smile. "Hi, Maurice."

"I'm guessing you're ready to make the drop?"

"Geez, Mo. Way to make it sound illegal."

He laughs. "Not sure where you are now, but come down to concourse E. Right after you step off the escalator, you'll see a set of display cases ahead of you on the right; I'll be standing there. Hopefully they lift this shelter-in-place order soon so we can get outta here."

I exhale. It would seem that instead of striking me down, somebody upstairs in the heavens is hearing my heart. The relief I feel at the thought of being rid of this poster practically floats into the air.

"Okay," I say. "Be there shortly."

Full disclosure: my brother-in-law is a total babe. Tall and fit, with a shiny bald head and a glistening and perfectly groomed black beard. He also smells like fall—warm and earthy with a good dose of spice. His favorite spot, as it turns out, is a series of display cases holding Reverend Dr. Martin Luther King Jr. memorabilia.

When I walk up, he's staring at the one that contains a suit jacket. And though I open my mouth to speak, before I can get a peep out, he says, "He really wore this. Can you even imagine? Here you are in your suit jacket, doing what you do and changing the whole course of history without even realizing it. The decisiveness that man had to embody is staggering."

Decisiveness. I gulp.

He turns to me then. Smiles and spreads his arms for me to step into. Which is when I notice how much less hustle and bustle there is around us. Interesting.

"How goes it, baby sis? You got the contraband?" he says as he wraps me up. It's nice.

"Sure do." I lower my backpack from my shoulder and pull out the tube. "Here it is. And just so we're clear, it's not really contraband, Mo. It's a poster."

"Ah, loosen up, kid," he replies, taking it from me. "This have anything to do with Stevie's little stunt?"

"Huh?"

"I got a message from your big-headed brother, telling me Stevie's got him up to something at the stadium. He was supposed to just be there setting up for that whole engagement gig. His company is growing. But you know anything about that?"

"I don't know what she's up to. But definitely curious now . . ."

"Shame what happened between Stevie and Sola." He shakes his head. "You whippersnappers don't have a clue how good you have it."

A growing sense of dread spreads through my middle. "What do you mean?"

"The space you have to love as you wish, for the most part. You probably don't know this, but your brother and I were super into each other when we were your age, but neither of us felt comfortable making a move. Eighteen years ago, our attraction to each other wasn't the least bit acceptable."

I'm too stunned to speak. I didn't even know Ern and Maurice had gone to high school together. My brother was headed into his freshman year of college when I was born. (I was our parents' "unexpected blessing," as they put it.) I just knew that when I was nine, we went to visit Ern in Boston, where he was a graduate student, and he told us that Maurice, who I had assumed was his roommate, was actually his boyfriend.

"I mean . . . not that I'm suggesting relationships are easier now," he continues. "Guess I just wish you young people had a bit more fortitude in the hang-on-to-your-love department." He looks at me like he knows something—about me—and a shiver dances down my arms.

"Ah." Because what the heck else am I supposed to say?

"That's an old song, by the way." He winks. "Sade. A whole classic. Look it up."

I nod. "Okay."

"Actually, I'll text you a link. Be sure to really listen to the lyrics. I know I sound like an old-head right now—"

I laugh. "Won't lie. You really do."

"If the shoe fits." He shrugs. "Anyway. I guess what I'm saying is that I wish you all would fight a little harder to hold on to love once you've found it. As cheesy as that probably sounds."

No idea what my face is saying, but it has to be something, because Mo cocks his head to one side and narrows his eyes. "Side note: Where's your guest? I could've sworn Ern said something about you bringing a friend home from school. . . ."

My heart beats a little faster. "Oh, ummm . . . she's on another concourse." I swallow. "Speaking of which, I should probably get back to her."

"That might be exactly what you need to do, Evan-Rose," he says then, giving me a light boop on the head with the poster tube. It makes me smile.

"See you at Christmas Eve dinner?" I ask.

He hmmphs. "Hopefully we'll be outta this airport by then,"

he says. "I'll let you know when the drop's been made." He lifts the tube to his temple, and with a wink, he turns back to the MLK display.

As I return to the down escalator, I decide to look up the lyrics of the song Mo mentioned. But I only get through the first couple of lines in verse one before my phone buzzes with an incoming text.

V   VAN

> You alive out there, Solid Flower?

And now there's a clenched fist in my chest, and my dumb eyes are getting damp.

Shortly after Van and I decided to be open about our feelings for each other, my grandfather passed away. He'd been sick for a long time, but there's a huge difference between knowing somebody will die soon and having that death become reality. I *thought* I was ready for it—Grandaddy was suffering quite a bit—but . . . yeah, I wasn't.

After my mom called and told me, I was so shell-shocked, everything else vaporized out of my brain. To the point where I blanked on a picnic lunch I was supposed to be having with Van.

So she came looking for me. We're not allowed to lock our dorm doors at school, so she found me on the floor beside my bed in the fetal position. Silently weeping.

I heard the words, "Oh, honey." And then I was being helped up onto the bed itself. Savanna pulled my head into her lap and slid her fingers—the nails of which were polished orange, my favorite color—into my mass of curly hair to massage my scalp. And she started humming.

At first I was freaking out a little. Literally *no one* had ever seen me that . . . vulnerable before. I couldn't have put up a guard if I tried.

Yet it felt *good* to be tended to. Loved on. Accepted precisely as I was in that moment, with zero judgment. "You know what you are?" she said looking down at me. I'd never seen eyes that kind. "You're a solid flower." She wiped a tear from my face with her thumb.

And I snorted and sat up. "*What* now?"

"Well, Evan means 'rock,' and 'rose' is obviously a flower, and you really *are* the most solid soft person I know," she said with a shrug. "Strong and steady, but also supersensitive. You're totally an empath. I can tell."

It was odd being read so fluently.

"You're also really pretty," she continued. "So, it totally fits. You, Evan-Rose Richardson, are the most perfect solid flower." She touched the tip of my nose.

I caught her hand. Held it and looked her right in her big brown eyes.

Then I kissed her like I'd never kissed anybody before. Just thinking about it makes me want to kiss her now.

I read the message again, and then I go back to the lyrics.

Like, what am I even thinking? Would I really just *walk away* from the one person who makes me feel like it's okay to be a whole person? Who has created and held space for me to feel?

And for what? Because I have some irrational fear that my parents will be disappointed that both of their kids are queer?

"Damn," I whisper aloud.

I have to tell her the truth.

Eric too.

I text him first.

E E.R.

> Sorry for the wait . . . and also the fact that it's going to be a little bit longer.

> I need to find my girlfriend.

E ERIC

Girlfriend?!?!

> Yeaaaah . . . long story.

> But I'm going to tell you the whole thing, I promise.

Holding you to that, Richie Rich!

Especially considering the giant knife I now have sticking out my heart!

I cringe but shake it off. Gotta get back to Savanna.

E E.R.

> Hey! Yeah I'm good. Sorry for the wait.

> I'm headed back. You in the same spot where I left you?

> I need to tell you something.

V VAN

Moved to Concourse B. There's this cool bookstore/restaurant spot called Café Intermezzo.

Meet me here. It's right in the central atrium near the escalators.

I ran into someone I want you to meet.

From back home. An ex if I'm being honest— but in town to visit family for the holidays and stuck here too. So I figured why not link?

A fire ignites in all the spaces between my ribs. Here I am avoiding Eric like he's carrying some pandemic virus, but Van is just kicking it with her *ex*?

Well, this certainly doesn't feel good.

My mind gets to churning with all the stories I've heard around school about the string of desperate girl hearts Van left behind when she came to Barthingham. Her roommate once told me there's even an ex-girlfriend who *still* sends Van a weekly love letter.

What if she's tired of my crap and this girl she's with now is perched in the wings, waiting to win her back? It *should* be unlikely—but *I* was just contemplating ditching Van for a semi-former flame, wasn't I?

Shit.

As I step onto the plane train, I think about what I'm going to say to her—absolutely in front of this ex, so homegirl is *fully* aware that Savanna is not available for a rekindling.

And then there's the explanation I owe Eric. Which reminds me, I also have to tell Van *about* Eric. And *then* I need to tell my family that I'm *with* Van, and will therefore not be interacting with Eric like that anymore.

This break is about to get interesting.

Once off the train and back up from underground, I spot the restaurant when I step into the atrium. As I approach, Savanna catches sight of me and waves me over. The ex sitting across from her is wearing a hoodie with the hood pulled up.

Once she shifts her focus back to the conversation she's having, I roll my eyes. A girl from Van's past *would* be some too-cool-for-school chick who wears her hood up indoors. Probably also got sunglasses on.

I take a deep breath, force a smile, and head over.

"Hey, babe," I say, lifting Savanna's chin and leaning over to give her a very public kiss on the mouth.

As I stand back upright, her eyebrows lift. "Oh, okay! I see somebody's in a better mood. . . ." And she looks me over, head to toe to head.

There's that tingle.

"Just happy to see you, is all." I lower my backpack to the floor and pull out a chair to sit. Time to face the past—who hopefully got the message about the *present* nature of Van's and my relationship. "Hey, I'm Evan-Ro—"

You have *got* to be kidding me.

"'Sup, Richie Rich?" Eric says, grinning like he just won the gold medal for subterfuge. There's that twinkle in his eye that used to drive me bananas.

"Wait . . ." Van's voice embeds itself into the tension. "You two know each other?"

"Uhh . . ."

"Evan-Rose's dad is my grandmother's dog's veterinarian," Eric says, breaking our eye contact.

My gaze drops to the table. Couldn't look at Van if my life depended on it. And let's be honest: right now, my life—as I know it—really *might* depend on it.

"Hold up, so have you known who she is this whole time, Ryan?" Savanna says. And of course my traitorous head lifts. *Ryan?*

Eric shrugs. "I mean, Evan-Rose isn't a *super* common name, so when you said it, I kinda figured it was this queen right here. Especially when you mentioned your school."

And he *winks* at me.

"Ryan!" Van reaches across the table and smacks him on the shoulder. "Why didn't you say something?"

"Well, for one, I wanted to be sure," he says. "And for two . . ."

Now he turns to me and makes his eyebrows bounce. "I thought it'd be a fun surprise."

That loosens my chest. A *fun surprise*? Really? "Eric, I—"

"Wait, you call him *Eric*?" Van interjects.

"That's what my grandparents call me," he says. "So most people I know here in Atlanta do too."

"Weird," Van replies.

Eric smiles at me. "I go by my middle name back home."

"Yeah, I gathered as much," I force out of my now desert-dry throat. "So what I—"

"Evan-Rose and I hung out a lot this past summer," Eric says, speaking directly to Savanna. "She was definitely the highlight of my six weeks here."

Oh god, oh god. "Ummm . . ."

He leans forward and lowers his voice. "You wanna know the best part about all the time she and I spent together, VanVan?"

VanVan?

Crap, I have to *stop* this—

"It was how much she talked about you," he (loudly) whispers.

"Eric, I—" *Wait* . . . "Hold on. What now?"

Savanna's beautiful loc-covered head has whipped in my direction, but for the life of me, I cannot read her face.

"Granted, she wasn't using your *name*," he continues. "And frankly, I don't think Evan-Rose even realized how frequently she would talk about her best friend at school. Now that I know it was you, everything she said makes perfect sense."

"And what exactly did she say?" Van doesn't take her eyes off me.

"She talked a lot about how sweet and soft you are, and was always saying she wanted to be more like you."

Dear God: if you're not too busy, I would like to evaporate, please and thank you.

Because now Eric is looking at me too.

He goes on. "There was this one time I was talking to her about something, and I started crying—"

Van smiles at that. "You always were a crier."

"Kettle. Pot," he says, pointing to himself, then to her. "Anyway, once I'd gotten it all out, Evan-Rose was looking at me like I'd just shown her the key to unlocking the multiverse or something. So I said, 'It's important to feel your feelings. They there for a reason, aren't they?' And she replied—"

"'That's what my best friend always says,'" I fill in, completing the story.

"I gotta tell you, VanVan. Homegirl is *high*-key obsessed with you."

"Oh my god!" And I smack him in the chest with the back of my hand. It's enough to break the tension . . . but then I hear Savanna sniffle. *She's* crying.

"Told you you're a crybaby too," from Eric (Ryan?).

"Shut it, Ry!" Van says.

Now I'm laughing. Because it's all so ridiculous.

Savanna is still staring at me, tears streaming down her face with her lower lip poked out and quivering. Probably not the most appropriate time for the thought, but I'd really like to bite it.

"Yo, y'all seen this?" Eric says, shattering the moment Van and I were just having.

Boys.

"There's apparently some weird light activity going on above the stadium," he continues without waiting for a response. "The internet is going nuts over it! 'The A-T-L Sees Snow . . . and Aliens?' That's the headline on the Shade Room. Current image looks like a ladle or a music note."

"Wait . . ." What did Maurice say about Ernest being up to something at the stadium for Stevie? "Is there—?"

The phone starts ringing in his hand.

"Oh, dang. I gotta take this," he says. "Doing a project on Frank Der Yuen with a classmate. I'll leave you two lovebirds to your business."

"Frank *who*?" Van says, clearly unable to resist asking.

"Dude who invented the jet bridge," Eric says.

"Umm . . . random?"

"It's really not," from Eric. "He was an aeronautical engineer who went to MIT."

"Ah. *Your* dream," I say.

"Precisely." He swipes a thumb across the screen and puts the phone to his ear. "Sean, my man! You found that info?" He gathers his stuff.

And then he's gone.

Man, I have a lot of explaining to do.

Without a word, I reach over and brush a fresh tear from Savanna's face. Totally still got my fingerless gloves on. She made them for me.

She sniffles. "You said nice things about me?"

"Oh my god, you are *so* dramatic." I put my face in my hands. Because I am embarrassed. A secret lover of love who is uncomfortable with love's manifestations. Gotta get a handle on that.

"Whatever," she says. Then she sniffles again and pulls a small pack of Kleenex from her bag. ("A crier must always be prepared," she told me once.) "You totally love it."

I sigh. "I really do." It's quiet for a moment, and then I peek through a crack between my fingers before lowering my hands and looking at her dead-on. "I also love *you*," I say.

"I mean, duh." Van rolls her eyes and blows her nose. "You're definitely a crabby little asshole every now and then, but I see how you look at me and feel how you care for me. Sometimes words aren't necessary."

Now *I'm* about to cry. "Van, will you be my girlfriend?"

"I'm already your girlfriend, E.R.," Savanna replies. "We both know that whole break thing was a joke. Literally nothing changed between us."

I laugh then. "Touché, baby girl."

She gets all blushy. Totally loves when I call her that, and I love how she reacts.

So here we are.

"Sooooo . . . can we go to that jungle thing now? I googled it, and it looks pretty amazing," Van says. "Perfect little spot for a quick makeout sesh. Because you obviously *have* to kiss me now. And I'm not gonna wanna stop."

She's eyeing my mouth as she says this, and I have to look away. The *things* this girl does to me without actually doing anything are a little overwhelming. "Sure," I say. "It's right downstairs."

"Fantastic."

We get up to leave the cute little bookstaurant, as Van is calling it, and discover that Eric already paid the bill. So we shove out into the throng of people in the concourse B atrium to head back downstairs. Pressed together, palm to palm, and fingers entangled.

Stevie is going to be thrilled.

Just as we break through to the other side, my phone vibrates in my pocket, and I instinctively pull it out to check the message.

The whole way down the escalator, I can't help but smile.

ERIC

You're welcome, Richie Rich. 😉

B BESTIE CHAT: J & S ♥

6:40 p.m.

Sola

It's over. I just know it.

Jimi

Didn't you give her till midnight?

Sola

Yeah, but . . .

Jimi

Then chill. Wait to see what happens.

Sola

I thought she'd, like, rush over or whatever.

Jimi

I get that, boo. But maybe Stevie IS rushing around. Maybe she's working up the nerve to apologize. Maybe you should give her a chance.

Sola

You're supposed to be on my side.

Jimi

I'm on whatever side that means the two of y'all are back together.

Sola

I don't even know if I can forgive her.

Jimi

But isn't it worth a try?

FIVE

SOLA

Sola's house, Inman Park, 7:17 p.m.
Four hours and forty-three minutes until midnight

EVER WONDERED WHAT sound a heart makes when it's breaking? If there's a melody to it? Or a pulsing rhythm that comes as it ruptures? Or a cadence as each fiber disintegrates? It's that whole "if a tree falls in the forest" crap. Does it make a sound? But seriously . . . if I took Baba's stethoscope and put it to my chest right now, could I hear my heart cracking in two?

Even though Baba says it's medically impossible to hear heartbreak, when it gets really, really quiet, like tonight as the snow falls and the neighborhood goes sleepy and silent, I can hear my own. I've been wearing the kiddie stethoscope he bought me for Christmas when I was eight. He'd been preparing me to become a doctor. Or at least trying to plant those seeds in my head, no matter how much I tried to keep them out.

Now, as I press the cool metal against my skin, I can't help listening. I look for evidence of heartbreak the way Stevie looks for evidence of . . . everything. I wonder what Stevie would say if I asked her to explain the piercing silence of my pain. What would her scientific explanation be?

I have to do something, anything, to make it all hurt a little less. I yank on my boots and shout for my cousin. "Gbemi! You coming?"

She lumbers into the mudroom holding five shoeboxes, and her limbs look all bulky, like she's got on four layers under her clothes.

"It's not that cold," I say, barely able to see her cute round cheeks.

She sucks her teeth. "It's snowing."

"Yeah . . . so?"

She stares at me and then looks pointedly out the window. "In Atlanta."

"I mean, I do have eyes."

"I'm aware. But unlike you, I don't live in a fairy tale. You're gonna be cold as hell in that dress." She zips her coat up the final inch so the collar covers her mouth. I trade the stethoscope for a lacy white scarf and try not to take my anger out on her. It's not Gbemi's fault I'm in this mess. That honor goes to my soon-to-be ex-girlfriend, Stevie.

Stevie loved this dress. So it's only fair I say my final goodbye to our relationship while I'm wearing it.

"You sure you want to do this?" Gbemi asks.

"Absolutely."

"You know you're being a drama queen, right?"

"Takes one to know one. I heard you on the phone with your friends earlier." I glance down at her. "Talking about Jabari." I sing his name and waggle my eyebrows because teasing her is the only thing keeping my tears at bay.

Gbemi rolls her eyes. "I'm in seventh grade. All I have is drama. And I don't like him; he likes me," she clarifies, putting the boxes down to gesticulate in my direction. All the women in our family talk with their hands. "You're a senior in high school, and my mama says you're a walking Nollywood movie and need to go to church more." She pinches her nose, mimicking her mother. "'Adesola is full of wickedness and witchcraft. She needs to get right with the Lord,'" she says, in a perfect rendition of Auntie's accent.

I feel my shoulders tense up. Her impression of my aunt brings me right back to that Sunday. The terrible night. I take a deep breath and start stacking the boxes to bring them outside. "Have you ever even been in love, Olugbemi?" I ask.

"Uh, no. Yuck. I mean, I like people, but I don't want to be in loooove. That's why I keep rejecting Jabari. He's too thirsty. I like hanging out with him and everything, but I have goals, okay?"

I smile a little. "Okay," I tell her. "But love doesn't always have to be a distraction." She looks back at me like she isn't so sure. As I say it, I wonder if I'm wrong. What if I've been a distraction for Stevie this whole time?

I clear my throat. "Help me with these."

I was already in love with Stevie in seventh grade. I just didn't know it yet. I didn't know that the overwhelming desire to be in her presence all the time went beyond wanting to be her best friend forever—that it was the beginning of something . . . more. In classes

I always grabbed a seat beside her, and in the cafeteria we always shared a table. Even after school when Stevie lurked inside the science lab or brought me with her to aquarium exhibits, I'd bring a romance novel and keep her company just to see her eyes light up. I loved being the reason Stevie went bright and shiny around her edges—it was in those moments I knew Stevie loved me as much as she loved her complicated concepts, experiments, and books.

But now I wonder if what I felt, what I thought she felt, was real.

"One day, you'll understand," I say to my cousin, trying to convince myself too.

We pack up my childhood wagon with the shoeboxes. It took a collection of thirteen white, pink, and yellow boxes to fit the entirety of Adesola Olayinka and Stevie Williams's relationship, so it's good my shoe collection is as extensive as it is. But thirteen is an unlucky number. Maybe it's a sign we weren't meant to be after all. The thought adds another tiny crack to my heart.

I take a deep breath and grab both of Baba's shovels. Gbemi follows, tugging the wagon. "Follow me."

We tromp outside. The sound of Gbemi's groans and grumbles and the noise of our boots feel louder than they should in the silent neighborhood. The quiet leaves too much space to think—too much room to feel.

I lead her behind my childhood tree house, the one my little brother begged our parents to build right after we moved to Atlanta from Chicago. "Don't look up, don't look up, don't look up," I mumble to myself, but my eyes betray my heart. The first time

Stevie and I spent time together outside of school, it was in this tree house. We read together until it was dark, our feet tangling under a quilt, flashlights in hand because I'd read about a pair of lovers doing just that in a novel. Stevie teased me about the sweet love stories I was obsessed with, reading parts over my shoulder and giggling until I shoved her away. I knocked on the hardcover of her physics textbook. "You were supposed to bring something you wanted to read for fun," I said.

"This is fun for me, bighead," Stevie replied.

"Nerd," I muttered.

"You love it," she said back.

"I do," I whispered. Stevie heard me and smiled.

I squeeze my eyes shut, trying to erase Stevie's little-kid face. She'd skipped fifth grade and still had so much baby fat in her cheeks. She had too much hair for her to keep it tamed despite her mom's best efforts, and thick glasses that never fit properly, so she obsessively pushed them up the bridge of her nose. I shove down the warmth of the memory and tell myself I'll erase it—and Stevie—as soon as I can.

"Your phone keeps going off," Gbemi says, out of breath from trying to keep up with me. I guess I'd started walking faster, wanting the tree house and its memories behind me.

"I know."

"Aren't you going to answer?"

I don't bother taking my screaming, pinging, incessantly buzzing phone from my pocket. I know it's filled with all the messages Stevie has sent. But I can't bring myself to read what she's said or to write back. Not yet.

Nothing like this has ever happened to me, to us, so I had no idea I could get this angry. That I could be this hurt. I didn't know I could avoid Stevie's texts or ignore her calls. That I could be this hardened against a person who before only made me soft.

Maybe my heart isn't broken. Maybe instead of it being the warm gooey mass it's always been, swelling and pumping and swooning from love both real and imagined, it's gone cold. Frozen. Maybe it's as solid as ice. A simple "I'm sorry" text message three days too late won't be enough, and I can't imagine anything short of her standing in front of me and professing her love like they do in the movies melting my heart.

But the thing is, I know Stevie would never do something like that. And that's how I know we're over.

The sadness turns quickly to anger. I've been flip-flopping back and forth between those two emotions for days. I point to the snow-covered ground. "Right here will work," I tell Gbemi. "Let's start digging." I'd promised her twenty bucks to help me. She begrudgingly picks up a shovel.

"For the record," my cousin says, even as the blade of her shovel cuts into the snow-dusted grass, "I still think this is super unnecessary."

I ignore the judgment of a seventh grader and proceed. Soft snowflakes drift all around us as we dig a shallow hole behind the biggest tree in my yard. I hope Mama doesn't stop all her cooking (and fussing) and glance out the kitchen window at us tearing up her yard. The sky is a big stretch of white, thinning out in places just enough to see a few stars and a big bright moon. The cold moon.

I resist the urge to look up my horoscope again. It was full of "You're going to have a tough journey on the winter solstice, the longest night of the year" warnings. Not what I want to hear after I'd given my girlfriend an ultimatum hoping she'd fix everything, but having very little faith she'd come through. It's snowing in Atlanta, so my horoscope is more of a horrorscope. Plus, the fortune cookie I got at lunch didn't have a slip inside. It's a doomed day. A doomed night. A doomed freaking week.

I dig harder and harder until my hands are all sore and my knit cap is soaked through. I try to focus only on the sound of crunchy earth and snow beneath the shovel. The bottom of my dress is getting dirty, but I can't stop now.

I grit my teeth and tell myself to forget Stevie, forget everything. If she was really sorry, she'd be here by now. Part of me knows ultimatums are never good in relationships. I've listened to enough couples-therapy podcasts, read enough books, and watched enough rom-coms to know better, but I'm too mad. Too sad. I'm always so patient with Stevie, and most of the time, it's impossible to be upset with her. I need her to show up for me, just this once.

Gbemi starts to hum a song our grandmother always sings, and I think of her face from that night. The deep frown that pierced Grandma's already wrinkled brow as the dinner party came crashing down; the way she shook her head and sucked her teeth.

The loss of warmth in her smile. My grandmother always told me that anger grows like a weed in the soul, and now it threatens to stretch throughout my arms and legs and torso, consuming my entire body.

"Is it deep enough yet?" Gbemi whines. She's shed her coat, the digging clearly heating her up.

"No. Keep going. Six feet. That's how deep I want it. My relationship is dead, so we're digging it a grave."

"Ummm, I'm five feet and you're not much taller. Six feet would take us forever. Let's just make it deep enough for the boxes to fit," Gbemi replies.

"Whatever." I keep pushing the shovel in and slinging the dirt aside, trying to let the crunch of the snow and soil get loud enough to shove the memory of that night further and further away. But every time it gets too quiet, the details fill my head like a waking nightmare instead of the fairy tale I'd hoped for.

I'd spent all weekend preparing the house, dealing with every one of Mama's complaints about me decorating her dining room my way, with fairy lights and woven place mats, wildflowers and mason jars. She had no idea that this wasn't a regular Sunday dinner—our usual after-church meal. This was the dinner. The dinner where I'd tell everyone that Stevie wasn't just my "little friend," but my girlfriend, my soul mate, my person, and that we planned to go to Howard University together next fall. Mama didn't have a clue how important that night was to me, but when I began taking out the good china, she knew something was up.

"I don't know why you're making all this noise in here, running around like this," Mama said as she set the nice silverware on the dining-room table for me. I loved when she pretended to be annoyed but helped anyway, despite all her fussing.

"Everyone comes in like an hour," I said while adding old-fashioned lanterns and centerpiece garlands I'd made myself. Everything needed to be perfect. "Don't you want it to look nice?"

"You never been this excited to see them before." Her perfectly manicured eyebrow lifted. "What's going on?"

"Can't I do something special for you all?" I said, trying to hold on to the half-truth for as long as possible. "And we haven't seen the family since before the pandemic. Haven't you missed your mom, your sisters—and your brother?" I knew this would get me an eye roll, but I had to try it. Deflection is the name of the game. They'd all arrive in an hour: Auntie Adesua flying in from New York with Gbemi; Uncle Tosin driving down from DC; Baba's brother, Uncle Wale, arriving from Chicago; and Auntie Adelayo bringing Grandma all the way from Lagos to visit until after the New Year.

With that, Mama turned on her heel to go check on her egusi soup and left me to my own devices in the dining room. I set out tiny name tents on each plate, lit gorgeous candles I had hand-dipped myself, and folded the lacy cloth napkins. I was trash for a dinner party, and Stevie always thought I'd make a killing as an event planner for weddings and engagements, creating moods straight out of people's wildest dreams.

I placed Stevie's name tent on a plate beside mine, then arranged and rearranged it a dozen times before tearing myself away to go get more of the winter stars I had made to liven up the tablecloth.

The front door swung open, and the house filled with the sounds of family arriving. Aunt Adelayo was already complaining about how bad the traffic was from the airport and how Mama needed to turn the heat up in the house, otherwise they'd all catch a cold. Uncle Wale bumbled in with his arms full of suitcases and gift bags and headed for the Christmas tree. Uncle Tosin cracked jokes with my younger brother, Femi, about how scrawny he still was, and Mama ran back and forth from the kitchen checking on the food while Baba tried to get Grandma settled into the armchair in front of the fireplace.

I cracked open the dining-room doors, peeking out, watching the chaos, hoping they'd settle down before Stevie arrived. Nerves tumbled through me. The more fussy and amped-up they were, the worse dinner could be. The more nitpicky commentary. The more questions. The more room for them to be unimpressed— or pretend to be. But Stevie was impressive, I'd reminded myself. Had much better grades than me and had colleges and universities sending her letters, wanting her to enroll. Still, I worried.

I texted Stevie. No answer. I thought maybe she was just running behind as usual. I sent her another message to make sure she wasn't freaking out about the dinner. Her nerves had been a mess lately— and we'd had a big fight the night before about her experiment.

I got dressed in a vintage number I knew Stevie would love, did the rounds of hellos and hugs like the good daughter of a host, then waited nervously by the front door for Stevie.

But as time ticked forward—ten minutes, twenty, thirty—there was no sign of her.

"I'm not going to let the food get cold, Adesola. Time to eat." Mama swept me out of the foyer and into the dining room, where my aunts, uncles, and cousins sat around the table I'd dressed, critiquing and commenting on every little thing.

"You've got a real eye for this," Uncle Tosin said.

"Who are we even waiting for?" Auntie Adesua complained. "The whole neighborhood can hear my stomach by now—"

"Adesola's friend Stevie is joining us," Baba interjected.

Auntie Adelayo pressed a shocked hand to her chest. "You let her have boys over here, Tiwa?"

My stomach knotted. I willed away the nervous sweat.

"Stevie isn't a boy," Gbemi chimed in.

"What kind of name is that?" Uncle Wale asked.

"It's Stephanie, but that's what we call her," I added.

They all expressed their opinions about whether or not Stevie should call herself *Stevie* because it's very confusing. Gbemi launched into a speech about names, gender, and how everyone needs to be more open-minded. I blocked it out, the nervous hum of my pulse flooding my ears. "C'mon, Stevie. C'mon, Stevie," I muttered, and continued to text her.

The doorbell rang. The ping of it rattled inside my chest. I shot up from my chair like someone had put a firecracker under it. I snatched open the door. Stevie stood there, swaying, covered in weird powder and stinking of the lab.

"You're late."

"Sorry. Got caught up in trying to make the magnesium—"

"Get in here." I yanked her into the foyer. I scanned her head to toe. I sniffed her. "Did you just pull this on over your lab shirt?"

"Yeah, sorry. Didn't have time to change."

Her voice sounded strange, the words all stretched out and slurred, way more than her Southern accent usually drawled.

"What's wrong?"

"Nothing."

I leaned forward to look into her eyes; the usual light brown of her irises was barely visible, so blown wide were her pupils, and the whites of her eyes were bloodshot. "Are you okay?" I said, starting to feel genuinely nervous. This wasn't like her. "Did you stay up all night in the lab?"

"I had a neck cramp after dealing with the lab equipment. I was also feeling tense, so I took a couple of muscle relaxers. It's no big deal."

"Stevie." I stepped closer to her and lowered my voice. "You look . . . high." A hot anger creeped up my neck. Why would she do this tonight? A night when everything needed to be perfect. A night where good memories were supposed to be made. A night where one mistake could ruin everything.

"I'm not."

"Adesola!" Mama's voice echoed in the hall.

I pulled her forward. "We don't have time for this right now," I whispered. "Pull it together."

I took a deep breath and stepped into the dining room with her. My loud Nigerian family got quiet. Their eyes scanned over Stevie, taking in her disheveled sweater, her chipped nail polish, her almost waist-length locs, the constellation of freckles on her nose, the way she nibbled her bottom lip and fiddled with the piercing there. Stevie hadn't even remembered to remove it before coming over. I tried not to panic even more.

I slowly introduced her to the out-of-town family members she hadn't met and felt Mama's glare as we slid into our seats.

The rest of dinner felt like a storm in slow motion: my aunties grilling Stevie with questions, my uncles cracking jokes no one laughed at, Baba trying desperately to cut the tension, Mama not saying a word. Stevie's anxiety had turned into arrogance, fueled by the muscle relaxers and her desperation to impress.

I felt each and every one of the stress hives that started climbing their way across my chest as Stevie talked.

"I'm no expert on the Yoruba language, but I believe it's pronounced . . ."

"No, that's technically incorrect, but not to worry—lots of people don't understand the science behind the issue."

"You should use the term 'climate change' instead of 'global warming,' because the latter is just one aspect of the former . . . of course not everyone is as familiar with the intricacies of . . ."

"Oh well, don't take my word for it, though I'm actually a certified genius. . . ."

I tried to squeeze Stevie's knee under the table as she made more and more of a fool out of herself: trying to use the Yoruba words I'd taught her or challenging Uncle Wale's theories regurgitated from the newspapers, reminding everyone of her high IQ and genius intellect. I tried to interrupt her long, rambling, slurred soliloquies. I tried to whisper to her to calm down, to just be herself . . . but nothing worked.

We hadn't made it to dessert before Mama stood up abruptly. "Enough!" The single word she'd uttered since Stevie's arrival.

The table went silent. My cousins stopped eating mid-chew, Grandma shook her head, and my heart froze.

"I will have no more of this foolishness at my table. Not on this Sunday, not ever. Stephanie—" Her eyes narrowed at Stevie. "I'm not sure what is going on with you—or frankly, what you might be on—but I've had enough of this show for today. I must ask you to leave."

Stevie stared at Mama, eyes hazy. "Please don't call me that," she said.

"Excuse me, young lady? Don't call you what?"

"Or that," Stevie said. She moved her leg so that my hand fell from where it had been resting on her knee under the table.

"Adesola," Mama said. "You better get your little friend."

"She's not my friend," I muttered, thinking no one would

hear, as everything about this disaster of a night filled me with embarrassment and sadness.

"What did you say to your mother?" Uncle Tosin asked.

I glanced up at him, and back at Stevie. "I said, she's not my friend. She's my girlfriend, okay? That was why I wanted everything to be perfect."

"Ohhhh," Gbemi said. "That's why this table looks like a cottagecore catalog threw up in here! It's your coming out dinner?" She grinned and clapped and started playing "Born This Way" on her phone.

"Gbemi, enough," both my aunties said at the same time.

Mama looked at me, then at Stevie, then back at me. She pointed her long brown finger at Stevie.

"You need to go."

"But Mama—"

Her hand went up and I swallowed the rest of my sentence. Baba cleared his throat, which always meant no more talking.

Stevie awkwardly stumbled to her feet, causing the aunties to frown even more.

"Are you okay to drive, young lady?" Baba asked as I held my breath, swallowing down the tears that threatened to fall.

"I'm fine," Stevie mumbled, not bothering to correct him again. Then she skulked out of the room before anyone could say anything else.

My feet itched to move, and every part of me wanted to jump up and race after her.

"Don't even think about it," Mama said as if she could read my mind.

I slumped back in my chair and gave up fighting the tears that streamed down my cheeks. The table conversation moved on, and Gbemi reached her small hand beneath the table to hold mine. Her soft grip was the only thing keeping my hand from shaking and me from completely dissolving right there. I stared at my glass until my eyesight went blurry, watching the snowflake-shaped ice I'd created for the night melt and the watery liquid fuse with the tea lights.

My relationship with Stevie felt like that snowflake, a fragile thing losing its shape, melting into nothing.

"It's gotta be deep enough now." Gbemi's voice snatches me out of my memory. Her little brown cheeks almost shine, slick with sweat.

I step down into the pit, then look at all the shoebox coffins lined up beside it. "I think it will fit. Hand me one of the boxes."

Gbemi obliges. "You sure?"

"I have to be."

I can't resist peeking inside, only to find all the items that represent Stevie's and my future together: all the fortune cookie slips about happiness, brochures from Howard, a floor plan I'd made of the apartment we'd eventually share there, designs for her dorm room and mine, postcards with the names of the children we'd have, a notebook full of my favorite stories about all of our best dates so we'd never forget them, playlists of the songs I'd chosen for our wedding. A future that wouldn't exist now.

I'm so deep in remembering I don't hear Baba call my name at first. I whip around.

"Yes, Baba."

"What are you doing, my sunshines?"

I drop the shovel.

"She made me do it, Uncle. I swear," Gbemi snitches, running back toward the house.

"You're not getting that twenty bucks!" I holler after her.

He laughs, and his warm smile and concerned eyes greet me. There's more white in his beard now, from the pandemic and all the hospital shifts and lost patients. "I see your partner in crime has abandoned you."

"That traitor," I reply.

He chuckles until his eyes meet mine. He goes all still and serious. "So tell me. What are you doing?"

I sigh. "Herein lies the death of my relationship with Stevie Williams. It is survived by nothing. I want to erase it all. Would you like to attend a funeral? It'll start in about ten minutes."

Baba's face scrunches. "We've been to too many funerals these last few years. I don't want to see or hear about any more death."

I instantly feel terrible.

"I thought we discussed you spending more time with the family while they're in town, and less time"—he rests a hand on my shoulder—"obsessing about all of this."

The noise of my big, loud—and visiting—Nigerian family escapes the house as Gbemi opens the back door, their laughter and jokes and fussing echoing all throughout the yard. They're arguing about some movie, eviscerating every plot point, every bad wig and terrible makeup job. I've been avoiding them since the dinner with Stevie. I didn't want to hear the commentary and all the jokes. I didn't want to hear the told-you-so perils of dating someone who wasn't Nigerian, and Yoruban specifically. I didn't want to hear about the son of this auntie's friend or the member of this uncle's church, ready to date me. And most of all, I didn't want to hear that it was somehow wrong for me to date—and love—Stevie.

He shrugs and steps close to me. I glance away as a few little snowflakes nestle in his hair. He has the type of eyes you can't look into without breaking down. The corners smile and they have a special shape, the kind of reflection that makes you tell the truth. How could you let down those eyes? How could you ever want to see disappointment in them? How could you ever lie to them? Maybe this is why his patients love him so much.

"I just . . ." The words sputter out.

"It's okay, sweetness. Tell me what's on your mind," he says.

"I'm burying my relationship. I'm putting it six feet under. Ish. It's dead and I want to forget all about it—all about her."

"I'm not so sure forgetting is the answer," he says. "Besides, just because something, or someone, dies, it doesn't mean we forget."

I squirm. He's right. The memory of that night washes over me again.

"I'm so mad, Baba."

"It's okay to be upset. It was very upsetting to experience, to witness. But the Olayinkas and Fayemis can be a tough bunch. Though Stevie isn't new, how you're talking about her is new for all of us." He takes my hand in his; the size of it always swallowing mine, forever making me feel like a little girl who's skinned her knee and is in need of her dad's comfort versus being almost eighteen. "We don't make it easy."

"But Stevie shouldn't have behaved like that." I take a deep breath. "She shouldn't have come to the house like that." I kick one of the boxes. Its contents tumble out into the snow: tiny moon jelly plushies she'd given me.

A quiet settles between us. I wonder if Baba can hear how my icy heart has fractured, the lightning-bolt crack branching out further as I fight not to comb over every single detail of that awful Sunday night again. It's been playing on a loop, one that hasn't stopped for days. My heart will be completely shattered by midnight.

I close my eyes. "Got a prescription for heartbreak?"

Baba chuckles, then smiles. "Time . . . and forgiveness." He squeezes my hand, then kisses my forehead. "Have you spoken to her?"

"No. I told her that if she didn't really, really apologize to not just me, but all of us, by midnight, then I'm never speaking to her again."

"An ultimatum?" His bushy eyebrows lift.

I nod.

"That's not how love works, sunshine. Life isn't a romance novel or a movie."

"It should be," I grumble as my phone lights up. Messages pour in from Jimi, and a few more from Stevie.

"Is that her?"

I shrug. "Mostly Jimi."

"I'm pretty sure Stevie called the house earlier. Probably trying to work up the courage to apologize to your mama, which, let's be honest, is the hardest thing in the world. 'How DARE you!'" he says, mimicking Mama's mad voice and how she gets so stirred up about manners and decorum.

We both laugh until a tiny tear escapes my eye. He uses the pad of his thumb to wipe it away.

"Are you going to listen to what she has to say when the time comes?" he asks. "Even if she doesn't meet the deadline?"

A surge of anger explodes through me. "I need to feel it, Baba."

"I know how much you love her."

Hearing Baba say it aloud makes my heart squeeze, and I swallow down the cry working its way up my throat. "You . . . you . . . knew?"

"Of course I knew."

"How—and why didn't you say anything?"

"You were always together, and somehow you forget I have known you your whole life. I can tell by the look in your eyes when you love something or . . . someone." He laughs a little. "But I was waiting for you to be ready to tell me—to tell Mama—whatever it was you wanted us to know."

Tears stream down my cheeks. It all tumbles out. The feelings

I've been holding in, everything I've tried to swallow. I'm a deflated balloon and almost crash into the snow when I finish.

Baba listens and nods. He takes a deep breath, starting several times before actually speaking. "I am a scientist by training, just like Stevie, my sunshine, so I connect with her on a lot of things. We are natural skeptics. We want to believe like you do. We want to get lost in the fantasy of it all, but our brains tether us to certain details. We can't let them go. We have to understand how something works, its mechanics, its patterns. Everyone is just trying to make sense of the world around them. This is us."

He cradles my chin. "Many of your complaints about Stevie are the ones your mama has with me. Oftentimes I wish I could be more like you. A lover of the impossible. I wish I could've been a child like you—one who believed that a vampire lived next door just because old Ms. Wyndham never left her house in the daytime or who investigated every tree stump looking for fairy houses or who left letters on your windowsill for visiting aliens each time you saw a comet streak across the sky. Your imagination is so big. It's one of your most noble qualities."

I bite back more tears and stare up at the sky to keep them from falling. I've wasted enough tears on someone who doesn't believe in love, who did a whole experiment on how love is nothing more than a chemical reaction of the brain. The clouds have thinned out, and bits of dark blue peek through. The longest night of the year. The worst night of the year.

"Sola, give it some time. Remember the things you love about her and give her an opportunity to at least explain. Don't let your anger burn out the light between you. Okay? Do that for me?"

"I still believe Ms. Wyndham was a vampire. She was almost see-through, too," I say, to keep from crying, and to try to harden the anger inside me.

He laughs, kisses my head, and picks up a shovel. "Now, let's put this yard back together before your mama gets nosy and comes out here. If she catches you, we both will never hear the end of it."

We put the dirt back into the hole, and he helps me collect all the little shoebox caskets I'd packed up with everything Stevie has ever given me.

"You ready?" He tucks a few boxes under one arm and drapes his other around me. "It's going to be all right, my darling, I promise. One foot in front of the other. You'll find a little magic again."

I don't believe him, but I'm too cold to argue. I drag myself forward, tights soaked through and my skin numb. Is this how I'll feel forever without Stevie?

"What's that?" Baba pauses, pointing up. The sky lights up, the darkness turning turquoise blue.

I groan. Must be fireworks. But who's setting them off after a snowstorm? Makes no sense.

"Did you see it?" he asks.

"See what?"

Gbemi bursts out of the back door, out of breath. "Did you see it? Did you see it?"

"What?" I poke at her.

"There's a word in the sky," Baba replies. "I'm almost certain of it."

The sky explodes with colors. My favorite ones—pinks and turquoises.

"I saw your name!" Gbemi shouts. "The fireworks are doing that."

My heart thunders.

"Those are drones," Baba corrects.

It can't be.

Stevie?

E ERN

How goes, kid?

S STEVIE

Not terrific. I've moved literally a mile and a half in the past two hours. And this car I'm in is all decked out for the holidays. My driver even LOOKS like Santa. I can't decide if the universe loves or hates me right now.

Haha. Well, at least the snow stopped. For a minute the lights were impossible to see due to clouds. Let's hope it clears up even more.

I'd give you an ETA, but I don't have one. I'm sorry, Ern.

Cut that out. As I mentioned, this is superb practice for Mr. Celebrity's big night. Thrilled I could help.

Okay.

You just make sure Santa gets you here safely, all right?

WTOP ATLANTA RADIO REPORT

7:59 p.m.

In addition to the snow that brought the Atlanta
metro area to a halt, there are now reports of
unauthorized air traffic.

We're hearing from listeners that there are
strange objects illuminating the clouds. The
#AtlantaUFOs hashtag is trending on all social
media platforms, though the mayor's and governor's
offices have yet to make an official statement. Some
report sightings of musical notes, while others
report words.

Stay tuned for updates and the latest breaking
news.

SIX

JORDYN

I-85 S at the south Peachtree Street Bridge, 8:01 p.m.
Three hours and fifty-nine minutes until midnight

SOCIAL AWARENESS HAS never been one of Omari St. Clair's strong suits. If it were, he would've noticed hours ago how my jaw tenses and my grip tightens on the steering wheel every time he changes my radio station.

It may not seem like a big deal—it's just the radio—but it's the principle of the matter. Since it's *my* car and *I'm* driving, shouldn't *I* control the radio or at least have some say in it? Not that Omari St. Clair cares about how I feel.

There's also a chance I'm just frustrated because we've been in my car for more than eleven hours now, a few of which we've been stuck in gridlocked traffic on I-85. It also doesn't help that I'm stuck with the friend I haven't really talked to since we kissed a year ago.

The snow coating the ground has turned my beloved Atlanta into an unfamiliar planet. Though the white stuff is no longer falling from the sky, I've watched tires skid, watched cars creep at one mile per hour, and watched drivers pull over to the side of the road to be safe. After just one semester in DC at Howard, I've gotten a little used to driving in snowy conditions, but this whole drive I've replayed Daddy's instructions in my head. *Jordyn, drive slow. Jordyn, accelerate slowly and brake slowly. Jordyn, don't threaten to throw that boy out of your car because he keeps turning your radio.*

He didn't tell me that last one, but he should've. If this boy turns my radio one more time . . .

But Omari St. Clair doesn't just turn it once more. No, he turns it several more times. A Christmas song plays. *Click,* he turns. Jazz. *Click.* Trap music. *Click.* A voice says, "Six inches of snow have accumulated across Metro Atlanta and officials have—"

Click.

"Whoa!" I turn the dial back. "We need to hear that."

"—state of emergency. Traffic on several interstates is currently at a standstill due to road conditions. Emergency officials are working to remedy this but currently have no ETA on when roads will be safe again. Thousands of drivers may be spending the night in their cars—"

"What?" I shout.

"She said thousands of drivers may be spending—" Omari notices the glare I give him and stops. "Chill, Twenty-Three. I was only trying to lighten the mood."

Omari has been calling me Twenty-Three ever since he found out that my dad named me Jordyn after Michael Jordan. "There's no way to lighten the mood when we may be spending the night in my car," I say.

"It could be worse. We could be spending it *outside*. Then we might freeze to death."

"Not helpful since people can freeze to death in cars," I say, and open my GPS app on my phone. Six inches isn't a lot of snow compared to what DC gets, but it's a Southerner's worst nightmare. This is the equivalent of a blizzard down here.

That's exactly why I wanted to leave the Howard campus no later than eight a.m. It was the only way we could beat this mess, but Omari took his sweet time coming down from his dorm. I bet he was late to his own birth. We left around nine a.m. Had things gone as I originally planned, I would've pulled into Omari's driveway at six-thirty p.m., then I would've made it to Jimi's show, given her the stuff I brought from school, and ended my night in the warmth of my home, watching Christmas movies with my granny and my sisters.

Instead, it's 8:10, and my plans seem to be ruined.

Plans are kinda my thing. Granny Vee tells me all the time, "If you wanna make God laugh, tell Him your plans." My therapist, on the other hand, calls plans a double-edged sword. They definitely help with my anxiety, but thanks to this thing we call life, they don't always go as, well, *planned*. When they don't, it throws me out of sorts. This snowstorm has thrown me, spun me around, and turned me upside down.

Omari looks at the snow on the ground, his eyes gleaming with awe. Pretty brown boys with hazel eyes and wavy haircuts used to be a weakness of mine. *Used to.* I wonder if golden-brown fat girls with dark eyes and braids were ever a weakness of his.

"When I was little, I thought snowflakes were big like the ones we'd make with construction paper," Omari says. "When you think about it, it's wild that they're so tiny and so unique. There may be millions of them in Atlanta at this very moment, and none of them are alike. Mother Nature is legit."

"Yeah, legit," I mumble as I change my GPS app to show walking routes instead of driving routes. We're on I-85 near the south Peachtree Street Bridge, not far from Mercedes-Benz Stadium. The shortest route to our destination—the Fox Theatre—would've involved getting off on North Avenue two exits ago, but it and the exit after it were both closed. I can see the (open) Courtland Street exit ramp just ahead of us, but we haven't moved in over an hour.

Omari and I both live in Inman Park, a ten-minute drive from here without traffic, which is impossible in Atlanta, so let's say a twenty-minute drive. Thirty if it's rush hour.

The Fox Theatre is now north of where we are, and even if *this* traffic miraculously started moving, it would probably take us thirty minutes to get *there*.

However . . .

I stare out the windshield and narrow my eyes. That *is* the south Peachtree Street bridge in front of us . . . and the Fox is *on* Peachtree Street . . .

I feed the info into the map app. It's a fourteen-minute walk. Not bad. I switch to the weather app. It's currently thirty degrees, so I search, "Can you get hypothermia in thirty-degree weather?"

Omari stretches his neck to look at my phone. "You're thinking about walking?"

"Absolutely. I can't let Jimi down, Omari. Not again."

Feels like that's all I do lately. Jimi, my little sister, asked me to bring some stuff from school for this kid named Stevie, who's dating Jimi's best friend, Sola, and if I was "interested," to come watch her band play outside the Fox. Initially, the merch—some Howard sweatshirts and a Howard banner—was supposed to be part of a Christmas present. Sola and Stevie visited Howard a while back and made a pact that they'd go there together.

However, according to the call I got a few hours ago, I need to get the stuff to Jimi stat, because Stevie and Sola had some big blowup and the gifting has been accelerated. "Just bring it to me at the Fox," she'd said. "Hopefully it'll help Stevie win Sola back."

In my own way, I hope to win my little sister back. This was my first semester at college, and I haven't been the best big sister to Jimi or Jayla, our baby sister, these past few months. I could easily blame my anxiety. College life and being away from home were super overwhelming. But either way, I wasn't there for them like I should've been.

But nothing's worse than my Thanksgiving break screwup. Jimi and her band booked a gig, and I promised her I'd come. She'd already been bummed after our deadbeat mother didn't show up to one. Except I somehow got the days wrong, and I hung out with my best friend while my sister searched the audience for me. I could easily blame my anxiety for that, too. It makes me get dates and times mixed up. Regardless, I let Jimi down.

I have to keep my word to her this time. That means getting this stuff to Jimi so she can get it to Stevie before midnight. I'll walk to her if I have to.

But this weather doesn't wanna let me be a better big sister. The first result of my search says that a person *can* get hypothermia while walking in thirty-degree weather. Fairly quickly too. "Crap. Okay, if we bundle up—"

"Nah, Jordyn," Omari says, shaking his head. "We shouldn't try to walk in this. We're safer here. We've got food and water in that emergency kit. I bet it's all kinds of stuff in there."

"Heated blanket, portable phone charger, lots of water and snacks," I admit. My dad got it for me. He's the definition of a prepper. Plus, he's a couponer. He keeps his man cave stocked with stuff he buys. When everyone else couldn't find toilet paper and cleaning supplies in stores at the beginning of the pandemic, Daddy was the plug.

"Then we're good," Omari says. "It's dangerous out there, Twenty-Three. I bet if the streets are icing over, the sidewalks are too. I'm not trying to get hurt."

My leg bounces. I hear him, but . . . we can't stay here. *I* can't. Beside us, a red SUV with bright green underglow lights zooms past in the emergency lane blasting Christmas carols. For a second,

I consider tailing him—it feels like a sign. But I don't have the nerve.

It's not just that I wanna see my sister, and *she* wants to get this stuff to Stevie before midnight, but this car is too small. The temps are too low. We could freeze or starve. What if we run out of oxygen and—

A hand lands on top of mine. "Hey."

My eyes meet Omari's.

"Breathe," he says.

I inhale deeply, and Omari does it along with me. We exhale together.

"Did you, um . . . did you take your medicine today?" he asks.

I frown and pull my hand away. "Don't do that."

"It was only a quest—"

"The insinuation is demeaning," I say. "A pill isn't some magical cure, Mari. Anxious people can have panic attacks even on our meds. Plus, we're stuck on a highway. Who wouldn't panic right now?"

"My bad. I just want you to be okay."

I shift away and bite my tongue to keep the "I didn't think you cared" from tumbling out. That's not a conversation I want to have.

Lil Kinsey's song "0 to Dark" comes on the radio. So weird that Jimi's old middle school crush is now this big-time rapper. For once, Omari doesn't change the station. He nods and mouths along, as if he can rap . . . and as if he knows the words. Omari never knows the lyrics.

"Thanks again for the ride," he says.

"It wouldn't make sense for you to spend money on a plane ticket when we're going to the same place. Plus, flying home days before Christmas in bad weather is a recipe for a canceled flight. And with all these nasty people who still don't wanna do right, bringing their germs on the plane and not covering their mouths when they cough or sneeze without a mask on . . ." I cringe. "Why do you think I refuse to fly?"

Omari smirks. "I hear you, Ms. Germophobe. Still, I was surprised you let me come."

I kinda was too. Omari and I have known each other since kindergarten, when he and his little brother, Mason, first moved to Inman Park. We weren't best friends—for me that title goes to my girl Mira—but Omari and I were always cool with each other and hung out with the same people.

Over the years, he became my "person" in our friend group. You know, the one who liked the same stuff that I did. We both loved horror films, the bloodier the better, so I could always depend on him to watch one with me when nobody else would. We both hated roller coasters, so we always sat them out together when our friends would ride. We both wanted to go to Howard, so together we'd look up pictures of the school and imagine ourselves on campus.

We got our acceptance decisions the same day. We texted each other and agreed to meet up at the park in our neighborhood and read them together. We loaded the portal on our phones, then he read mine, and I read his. We both got in.

And in the midst of the excitement, all these *feelings* overtook me, and I didn't resist the impulse: I kissed Omari St. Clair.

But I quickly learned that you can't act on feelings. It can lead to the boy you kissed telling you he's sorry, which is usually what's said before someone explains that they don't like you the same way you like them. I didn't let him finish. I ran home and decided I couldn't be friends with Omari St. Clair, not when I felt something for him, and he felt nothing for me.

Now here I am, stuck with him on the Christmas break road trip from hell. I look ahead for some sign that traffic may be moving, but all I see are red brake lights. "Can't they salt the roads?" I ask. "That's what they do in DC."

"I doubt Atlanta has salting trucks," says Omari. "And it's too late for that. Everybody's stuck already."

"They've gotta do something! They can't expect people to sleep on the interstate."

"People did in the last big snowstorm in 2014, remember? We slept at school."

"Don't remind me," I say as my phone plays the ringtone that I set for Daddy, "Papa Don't Take No Mess" by James Brown. Nobody uses songs as ringtones anymore, but Daddy insisted that I make that song his. He hit a split at a family reunion talent show one time—one time!—and now he swears he's James Brown's long-lost cousin twice removed.

I answer the call with a warning, "Hi, Daddy, you're on speaker."

"Aw, man. You mean I can't call Omari a big-headed dork?"

"Dang, Mr. Robinson," Omari says. "A man has feelings."

Daddy chuckles. "I'm playing with you, kid. How are you guys doing? Has traffic moved any since we last talked?"

I sigh out my nose. "No. It's at a complete standstill."

"I figured. We've been getting calls left and right," he says. Daddy is a fire captain at one of the stations downtown. I used to love going to work with him just to slide down the fireman's pole.

Now that I think of it, it may be a better idea to walk to the fire station than to walk to the Fox. "Hey, Daddy? Do you think we could walk to the station and—"

"No, absolutely not," he says. "You're not walking anywhere, young lady."

"But I promised Jimi I'd get—"

"Jimi will understand if you can't keep your promise," Daddy says. "I know staying in the car isn't ideal, but it's the safest bet. You have a heated blanket, water, and other necessities in that emergency kit I bought you. Which is more than she can say. Hopefully she's *inside* that theater and not out on the street freezing her behind off. You. Stay. Put."

Omari mouths, "Told you."

I ignore him. "Yes, sir," I mumble.

"Omari already told you that, didn't he?" Daddy asks, and Omari busts out laughing. "Hey, I know my girl."

I ignore that. "How are Jimi, Jayla, and Granny Vee?" I ask.

"Jimi's phone keeps going straight to voicemail, but don't worry," Daddy says, before I can. "I know she *made* it to the Fox, and she's supposed to be recording a song with her band. You know your sister. She gets caught up in the music and ignores her phone. I'll keep calling. Jayla and Granny Vee are safe and sound at home, making Christmas cookies."

I'm sure Jayla loves that. After our mom left when we were younger, Daddy moved us in with Granny Vee so he could have some help. Jayla and Granny have been thick as thieves ever since. The only thing my baby sister would love more than being stuck at home with Granny would be being stuck at Granny's nightclub, Vanity's Aura.

"Stop worrying about them, Jordyn," Daddy says. "Stay put until it's safe. Okay?"

"Fine," I groan.

"Good. Hey! I've got a joke for you," Daddy says, and I almost groan again. Besides swearing he's James Brown's cousin, he also swears he's a comedian. "What is it called when a snowman has a temper tantrum?"

"I don't know, what?" Omari asks.

"A meltdown!" Daddy says, and cracks up at his own joke.

Omari snorts, but I glare at him. "Don't encourage this," I say.

"Encourage it, Omari," Daddy says. "Encourage all the dad jokes. I'm gonna call Jimi again. I'll check on you guys later."

"Later, Daddy."

"Later, Mr. Robinson."

We hang up, and I sigh. I'm eighteen years old, technically an adult, and all I want right now is for my dad to come rescue me.

"All right, Atlanta, that was the hometown boy Lil Kinsey bringing the heat on this cold evening," the radio DJ says. "I hope you're safe wherever you are. I gotta tell you, this is an odd day. Something weird is going on in the sky. It looks like a light show happening out there. Somebody's taking the Christmas spirit to a whole new level."

A light show? I try to look out through my front window. It's dark, and the sky is gray and starless. "I don't see any lights," I say.

"We'll keep an eye out," Omari says, and reclines his seat a little.

Guess he's decided to get comfortable. I refuse. According to my watch, it's nine o'clock now. Three hours until midnight. Three hours to keep my promise to Jimi.

"So, how was your first semester?" Omari asks.

I look at him. "Huh?"

"We haven't talked all semester. I'm trying to catch up."

And why haven't we talked? I almost ask, but I don't. Confrontation isn't my thing. The very idea of it makes me nauseated.

"It was fine," I say. "My roommate is great, thankfully. I've heard horror stories."

Omari raises his hand. "I happen to be one of those unfortunate souls with a horror story. Dude they originally put me with hated showers, smelled like Fritos and garlic, and snored like a hyena. I requested a move ASAP. It pays to be a legacy kid."

"The privilege."

"Hey, white kids do it all the time." He looks over at the lime-green SUV next to us on his side. The headlights dim and then go dark. "You may wanna turn your car off completely, Twenty-Three. The battery could die if we just sit here like this."

"I wanna hear the radio. Besides, I got my battery checked out before we left. The mechanic said it's in great shape. We should be okay."

Omari puts his hands up. "Fine. Your car, do you."

I snort. "Tell that to my radio."

"Huh?"

"Boy! Do you realize how many times you've turned the radio station since we've been in this car?"

"Oh," he says, and it's clear he didn't realize. Self-awareness isn't Omari's thing either. "My bad. Why didn't you say something?"

Because that's not *my* thing. "It wasn't a big deal," I lie.

"You're sure about that? It seems like it was a big deal for you."

"It obviously didn't mean much to you. Let's just drop it."

"How do you know how I feel, Jordyn?" he asks, sounding kinda mad.

Which just makes *me* mad. "Actions speak louder than words."

"Are we still talking about the radio?" he says, over me.

Heat rushes into my cheeks. I hate the way he's looking at me, because he's not looking at me, he's looking through me. They say the eyes are the windows to the soul, and Omari St. Clair somehow knows how to break the glass panes of mine.

My phone dings. Thank god for text messages.

I look away from Omari and focus solely on my texts. I've got two unread messages. One of them may stay unread forever. The sender deserves nothing less.

The other is from Jayla. She just sent me a picture of her latest baking masterpiece in progress: Christmas cheesecake. My baby sister can't just make cookies and leave it at that. No, she's turned Christmas cookies into a crust for a red-and-green cheesecake. Once she gets it in the oven, she says she plans to cook some lamb chops with duchess potatoes for dinner tonight. Jayla likes to cook and bake when she's bored. Luckily for us, she's good at it.

"Is Jayla okay?" Omari asks. He was looking at my phone again.

I connect it to my charger. "Yeah, she's fine. I'm glad she's at home with Granny and not stuck at her school like we were that time."

"Being stuck at school wasn't so bad. I consider Snowmageddon the coolest day of school ever."

"What?" I say. "That day was awful, though this storm is worse."

"C'mon, Twenty-Three. It wasn't that bad. Remember how Coach Harris organized a faculty talent show to keep us entertained?" Omari laughs.

I fight a smile. "Mrs. Walton did the moonwalk, and everyone lost their minds."

"Yooo! That was wild. The highlight of third grade. The video is still online."

I shake my head. "Of course it is. The internet is forever."

"Hey, a historic moment like that needs to be preserved. Didn't Mr. Robinson come pick you and Jimi up in the fire truck? Or did your mom get you?"

"It was Daddy. She had left by then."

"Oh."

"Yeah," I mutter, and stare at the 1 next to my text icon for the one unread text.

"Love on Top" by Beyoncé starts to play. One of my all-time favorite Bey songs. I'm about to do the little hum with Beyoncé at the beginning, but Omari has the audacity to turn the station. What the hell?

My mouth falls open. "Uhn-uhn! You did not just turn off Beyoncé!"

"Oh, I forgot you're a Beyoncé fan," he says, so casually.

"Um, it's Beyhive all day, every day, twenty-four seven, three-sixty-five. You have some nerve turning the queen off."

He shrugs. "That's just not my favorite song of hers."

"You know what? You are proving my theory completely right."

"Theory?" Omari says, and turns to face me completely. "What theory?"

I turn to face him too. "I'm convinced there are two kinds of people in the world."

Omari's eyebrows wrinkle. "Only two? Isn't that kinda limiting? That's my issue with Hogwarts houses, besides the author, of course."

"Let's not get into that," I say. (Though: just say no to transphobia.) "Anyway, my theory. I think there are two kinds of people in the world. There are people like you, who change to another radio station the second a song comes on that you're not vibing with and proceed to keep changing stations until you find something you like. And then there are people like me, who go with the flow and understand that if we wait, something good will come along."

"Interesting theory," says Omari, rubbing his chin. "So, you're basically saying I'm impatient and you're patient?"

"Obviously."

"But this also means you're a control freak."

"What? How?" I ask. "You're the one who keeps changing the station, not me!"

"The fact that you noticed that I keep changing the station and got bothered by it says you're the bigger control freak. It could also be said that I'm okay with change and you're not."

"I'm fine with certain changes," I say. "Like the seasons. For instance, I will be thrilled when it's spring again."

He laughs. It gets a small smile out of me. Omari St. Clair's laugh has that effect.

"But you're not okay with big life changes?"

"After what my mom—" I lose my voice, but I clear my throat to get it back. "Change hasn't been a good thing in my life."

Omari quietly nods. He turns the radio again, but this time he goes back to the previous station. Back to "Love on Top."

I almost smile at that, but as I stare at my phone, smiling is impossible. A sinking feeling hits my gut when I think about the unread text, and I don't know if it's dread or fear. I wish it was anger, and although there's lots of that in me to go around, it's nothing compared to the fear. "She texted me."

Omari does a double take. "Wait, who? Your mom?"

"Don't call her that. Mom is a title you earn. She lost that the day she walked out on us. Egg donor is more appropriate."

"All right then, your *egg donor* texted you. What did she say?"

I shrug. "Don't know. I haven't read it."

"How did she get your number?"

I sigh as the tip of my fingernail finds my scalp under a braid and scratches. "Jayla. Last year she signed up for every single social media app—and found her. She and Jimi were talking to Erica for weeks behind Daddy's back. I found out when Erica sent all three of us gifts. I threw mine away. Then, two months ago, Erica asked to talk to me. Jayla gave her my number. She texted me, but I refuse to read it."

"She sent that two months ago?" Omari asks.

"Yep. She's called me a few times too. I don't answer. You'd think she'd get the message that I don't want to talk, but apparently she's as bad at picking up signals as she is at parenting."

"Dang, Twenty-Three," he says. "I'm sorry."

My leg bounces again. "You know, it's the audacity for me. You leave your husband and your three daughters to pursue an acting career. That fails big-time, and you wind up waitressing in Los Angeles. You remarry some truck driver, have two more kids with him, and then have the nerve to want to 'patch things up' with the kids you abandoned? It doesn't work like that."

"How do you know she's a waitress, got remarried, and had two more kids?" he asks.

"Jayla isn't the only one with a Facebook."

"Gotcha."

Silence makes itself comfortable in the car. I stare at the sticker on the window of the minivan to our left. It's a little stick figure family of five, holding hands and smiling. Once upon a time, that was my family, until Erica decided it wasn't.

I look at my watch again. Less than three hours to get this stuff to Stevie somehow. If I don't keep my word to Jimi, am I any better than Erica?

"You ever thought about talking to your m—egg donor?" Omari asks. "If she's calling and texting, she must really want to talk."

"Mari, there's nothing she can say to me."

"Yeah, there is. 'I'm sorry' would be a good start. You deserve that, Twenty-Three."

"Did I deserve it after our kiss?"

"What?"

"Nothing," I say, and pick up my phone again.

Omari tugs it down. "Hold up. What are you talking about? Jordyn, talk to me."

I bite my lip. Do I really want to have this conversation with him? I've successfully avoided it for a year. Can't I just avoid it for one more night, at least?

Suddenly my radio goes silent, my headlights dim off, and the hum coming from the vents shuts off, taking the heat with it.

"Welp," Omari says (wholly unhelpfully). "There goes your car battery."

* * *

In the middle of the jam-packed highway, Omari pops the hood of my car as if he knows what he's doing. Omari St. Clair is good at faking it.

I blow into my hands and glance around. On one side of us, a couple is huddled up on the back seat holding a phone together, the glow of the screen lighting their faces. They laugh at whatever is on the phone. I kinda envy anyone who can laugh during this day from hell.

Beside us, the minivan sits with the engine off. A snaggletoothed little girl with afro puffs stares at us from the back window. She blows on the glass and writes *Hi* with her finger in the condensation, but it's backwards and looks like *iH*. I wave back.

Omari holds the back of his head, his fingers scratching through his waves. "It looks normal, so that's good?"

"But it's not acting normal," I say. "Crap!"

"I won't say I told you so—"

"Then don't," I snap, then I immediately sigh. This isn't his fault. "Sorry."

"All good. That *was* an asshole thing for me to do."

"One hundred percent," I say, and he looks at me. "What? I'm not cutting you slack."

He smirks. "Never. Do you have Triple A? Knowing Mr. Robinson, you do."

I look up and down the highway. Traffic is at a standstill as far as I can see in both directions. "Yeah, but that's useless. I doubt they could even get to us in this. What are we gonna do? I have to get this stuff to Stevie before midnight, Omari. For Jimi."

Omari waves at our little spectator in the minivan. She covers her eyes and ducks. It's funny how little kids think if they can't see you, you can't see them.

"We could ask the driver of the minivan if they have jumper cables. One of these other drivers might have some also," he says.

"Maybe," I say, wishing I hadn't cleared out the stuff Daddy put in my trunk, including the jumper cables. If that were the case, though, wouldn't the other drivers notice us looking under the hood of my car and offer some help? That's usually how it is in the South. But everyone either doesn't notice or is pretending not to notice. I can't really blame them. In a mess like this, it's every man, woman, and person for themselves.

What if we're stuck like this, even once traffic gets moving? What if we end up getting hit by another car? Or what if we hold traffic up worse and have other drivers mad at us? What if my car is stuck here for good?

"Hey," Omari says, and I meet his eyes. "Don't overthink this. It's gonna be okay."

Overthinking is like breathing for me, and what-ifs are the oxygen. I try to take in a deep breath of actual air. "You think someone will really help us?"

Omari takes my hand, as if it's a normal thing that he does all the time. Our hands fit together surprisingly well. It's like this is a normal thing for them too.

"Only one way to find out," he says.

We go around to the driver's side of the minivan. Our spectator ducks again on the back seat and covers her eyes. Little kids are weird.

Omari knocks on the window. The mom—I'm assuming she's the mom—blows into her hands before lowering the window. She immediately smiles at us, though I can tell she's concerned too. She reminds me of the moms I would see in the school carpool line, picking up their kids after school . . . the ones I used to wish were my mom after she left.

"Are you kids okay?" she asks.

I have to remind myself that although we're eighteen, to some people we're still kids. At a time like this, that's actually a relief. I don't wanna adult right now.

"For the most part, yes, ma'am, we're okay," Omari says. "But our car battery died. Do you happen to have some jumper cables?"

"I wish I did, sweetie. I'm so sorry," she says. "Someone is bound to have them. If you manage to find some, you're more than welcome to get a boost from me."

"Thank you so much!" Omari says, as if that's the best thing he's heard, and pulls me along with him.

"Why are you so happy?" I ask. "She doesn't have jumper cables."

"But we can get a boost from her. Even if someone far away has cables, we can come back, use those cables, and give your car a boost from her. The glass is half full, Twenty-Three."

Of course he's a glass-half-full type. Me, I just hope the glass doesn't tip over.

Omari leads me over to the lime-green SUV that's on the other side of my car and gently taps the window with his knuckles. The glass is tinted, and at first all we can see is a billow of smoke pouring out as it rolls down. I fan some away. I'd rather not get a contact high right now.

"What it do, dawg?" a guy with cornrows says.

"You got some booster cables, homie?" Omari asks, and points his thumb back at my little Corolla, which is tiny beside the SUV. "My girl's ride went dead, and we wanna be able to get up outta here once this stuff clears."

His girl? I hate how my heart flutters.

"I gotchu," the driver says, and sets his, um, recreational activity down.

I get out. The driver, whose name turns out to be Kentrell, gets his jumper cables out and tells us all about how he ended up stuck in the traffic. He was at Lenox Square Mall, trying to get a last-minute Kwanzaa gift for his grandma, but he wasn't able to find a parking space before the mall closed early due to the storm. "This dude in an old truck took my spot," he says, face going dark for a split second. "It's cool though. Took care of that."

Okay then . . .

On his way home, he got stuck in traffic just like we did. "Really sucks too. I been *craving* my grandmama's sweet potato pie."

"That's how I am about my mom's pumpkin pie," Omari says.

Kentrell and I look at him like he became an alien right in front of us.

"Pumpkin pie and sweet potato pie are not in the same league," I say. "Don't even mention pumpkin in the same breath as sweet potato."

"Facts, shawty," Kentrell says. "Let me get this battery going for y'all."

Kentrell has me get in the driver's seat of my car, and he gets in his. In no time, my battery is back working, and I'm so happy I almost hug a complete stranger.

"All good, baby girl," Kentrell says. "Keep the car running for a while. You got a good lil dude here, looking out for you."

"Always," Omari says.

Our eyes meet, but not for long. I quickly look away. I can't let him see through me right now, because I'm not really sure I even know what's going on at the moment.

Kentrell hops back in his ride, leaving me and Omari on the road. All these cars and people, yet it feels like it's just me and him.

"So . . . ," I say.

Omari stuffs his hands in his pockets. "So, what now?"

"We wait for traffic to get moving again, I guess."

"All right—wait a second," he says, and bends to look at my front tire. "What's that?"

My heart drops. "Don't tell me I have a flat—*arghh!*"

Something heavy, wet, and cold smacks against my cheek. Snow. In a freaking snowball.

I look up, and Omari St. Clair is wearing the biggest smirk, his hands tucked innocently behind his back. "What was what?"

I think I may kill him. "You jer—"

Another snowball hits me, this time on my chest, the snow splattering me in the face.

Omari grins. "Just trying to help you chill, Twenty-Three."

"Have you lost your ever-loving mind?" I shout.

Omari bends and scoops up more snow. "Today sucks, I get that. Being stuck in traffic sucks. Spending the night in the car might suck. But that doesn't mean we can't have fun."

I watch him make a ball with the tiny amount of snow he scooped. "Don't you dare—"

He throws it at my leg, then winks at someone. The little girl in the minivan hides her snaggletooth behind her hand as she giggles.

"C'mon, Twenty-Three," he taunts, "give me what you got."

"Omari Ramon St. Clair, I am not getting into a snowball fight with you."

He scoops up more snow. "She used the whole name. I think she might be mad."

"You hit me again and I'll—"

The biggest snowball yet flies at me, and lands in my hair, splattering into my braids.

Oh, hell no.

It's on.

I scoop up a handful of snow and form it into a ball quick, then I get in the same pitching position I used in my softball days.

Omari's eyes get big. "Uh-oh."

Word to the wise: never challenge a former softball pitcher to a snowball fight. I throw it like it's a fastball and hit Omari dead in his face.

Our little spectator laughs so hard, she falls over her seat, out of sight.

Omari blinks a few times and spits snow out. "I . . . I wasn't expecting that, to be honest."

I get more snow. "You started it. Now finish."

And right in the middle of a gridlocked interstate in Atlanta during a snowstorm, Omari St. Clair and I have a snowball fight. We duck behind cars, we ignore other drivers (who watch us like we've lost our minds), we laugh so hard it hurts.

And for a few minutes, I forget that we're stuck in gridlocked traffic. I forget all the what-ifs. It's a good way to be.

"Okay, okay, okay!" Omari says, coming from behind a souped-up Jeep, his hands in the air. "I surrender! You win, Twenty-Three."

"Of course I do."

"For now." Something above us catches his eye. "Hey, look."

I glance at the dark gray sky, and lit up brightly is the word "changes." I guess the radio was right about the light show.

"What in the Tupac?" Omari smirks. "Get it? Tupac? His song 'Changes'?"

I purse my lips. "You just made my dad's joke sound great."

"Quit hating. That was a good one," Omari says. "I wonder what it means?"

I wrap my arms around myself. Now I'm colder than I was before. "Maybe it's"—my teeth chatter—"a message or something?"

Omari immediately takes off his coat and wraps it around my shoulders, "C'mon, let's get you warm."

We go back to my car and hop in the back seat. There's only one warming blanket inside my emergency kit. We put it over ourselves, and we're closer than I thought I'd ever get to Omari St. Clair again, shoulder to shoulder, leg to leg, foot to foot.

My heart pounds. This is how it started before.

I'm not going there again. I grab my phone off the front seat and look at the clock. It's 9:12 now, and traffic hasn't budged an inch. It's looking less and less like I'll keep my promise to Jimi. "Crap! This stuff isn't gonna get to Stevie in time."

"Why are you so caught up on that?" Omari asks. "She's your little sister's best friend. It's not that big of a deal, is it?"

"I promised Jimi I'd do it, Omari."

"I know Jimi. She'd understand. Not like you can do much in these conditions."

"But if I don't come through, I'm . . ." I swallow. "I'm no better than our egg donor."

That's the first time I've said that out loud. But ever since I ghosted on Jimi at Thanksgiving, I've been wondering if I'm the apple that didn't fall far from the tree. If I'm like Erica. Granny

Vee always says you can easily become the thing you hate, and the thought of being anything like my egg donor terrifies me.

"You're nothing like her, Jordyn," Omari says.

"I haven't been there for Jimi and Jayla lately—"

"Because you're adjusting to college," he says. "I haven't been there for Mason like I used to be. Cut yourself some slack, Twenty-Three. Now, let's say you decide to be hardheaded and trek out in this snow just to keep your promise to Jimi. What if you got hurt, or worse? Jimi would be devastated."

I hate it, but he's got a point. "I just wanna be a better big sister," I murmur.

"Then stay safe in the car so you can be around to do that," Omari says.

I sigh. Again, he's got a point. I open my texts and write one to Jimi.

> **J JORDYN**
>
> I'm stuck on the interstate. I don't think I'm gonna make it. I'm sorry. I know how much this means to you and your friends. I promise I'll make this up to you. Love you.

I hit send, hoping that's enough.

In seconds, my phone buzzes. There's no way it's Jimi already. . . .

It's not. It's a new message from Erica, to go along with the first text I never read.

I sigh. "She texted me again. The egg donor."

"You should read it, Jordyn," Omari says.

"Omari—"

"That doesn't mean you have to answer," he says. "Just get reading it out of the way."

I'm not sure I can. I hold my phone toward him. "Here. You read it."

"You sure?"

"Yeah. I trust you."

"You do?" he says.

I replay what I said in my head. It came out before I realized it, but the more I think about it . . . "Yeah. I do."

The tip of Omari's tongue wets his top lip. I almost think he's gonna say something, but he doesn't. He takes my phone.

I'm quiet as he reads the texts. I'm sure it's full of I'm sorrys and excuse after excuse for something that's inexcusable. There's nothing she could say to make up for leaving us.

"Wow," Omari says. "Well, she starts out by apologizing."

Figures. "Not enough."

"She said that too. She also said there's no excuse for what she did to you, Jimi, and Jayla, and you have every right to never speak to her."

"I do. What else?"

"That's about it. She didn't write a lot. She said this is a conversation better had over a phone call," he explains. "Her latest text was just her checking to see if you were safe. Jayla apparently told her you were stuck in traffic."

I need to have a talk with my baby sister. I don't appreciate her telling Erica my business. The less that woman knows about me, the better. "That's it?"

"And she loves you more than you know."

I stare at my boots. "She has a heck of a way of showing it."

"Listen, I won't tell you what to do, Twenty-Three. I can't imagine how you feel. But I will say this: sometimes people hurt people they love, and it has nothing to do with the person they hurt. It's about them. They're the ones who are the problem. They say things they don't mean or don't say enough. They may not have intended to hurt someone, but intentions don't mean a lot when it comes to heartbreak. They still have to find a way to make things right."

This doesn't feel like it's about Erica anymore. "You sound like you know about that."

"I do," he mutters. "It's what I did to you."

My heart races, but I swallow. There's no way he's talking about what I'm thinking about. "What do you mean?"

Omari St. Clair puts his hand on mine under the blanket.

"I mean what happened between us last year, Jordyn. Our kiss."

My breath hitches, and my stomach knots. "Omari . . . I . . . I don't—"

"We didn't get to talk about it," he says. "You avoided me after that. It's been a whole year since . . ." He swallows. "Why did you stop talking to me?"

I tug my hand away. "You really have to ask why? Omari, you immediately apologized after we kissed. So I thought you . . . I made the first move, I thought that your apology meant—"

"That I didn't like you in that way? Because I do, Jordyn. I have for a long time."

I don't really know how to respond to that. "Then why did you apologize?" I ask, my voice cracking. It's the question I've wanted to ask for a whole year. "You know what that felt like?"

Omari cups my cheek, brushing his thumb along my jaw. "You never let me finish. You ran off and refused to talk to me afterward. You didn't give me a chance."

I stare at my phone and at the text message from my mom that awaits a response. "Can you blame me?" I whisper.

Omari lifts my chin so I have to look him in the eyes.

"I understand that you're scared," he says. "But not everyone is gonna hurt you the way your mom did. I won't."

The tears fall. "You already did."

He brushes them away. "And I'm so sorry. I didn't realize I had. I replayed that kiss in my head at least a thousand times, trying to figure out what went wrong. I thought you regretted kissing me or that you didn't mean to do it and were embarrassed. I wasn't gonna push you.

"But one day, it finally hit me that you probably took my apology the wrong way." He gives a half smile. "Self-awareness isn't my strong suit, you know."

"I know," I mutter. "You're not too socially aware either."

He smirks. "Definitely not. That day, Jordyn, the only thing I was sorry about was that I didn't make the first move," he says. "I'm sorry that I didn't tell you I liked you sooner. I'm sorry I didn't tell you that I think about you all the time. I'm sorry I didn't tell you that when you smile and your eyes light up, it makes my entire day. I'm sorry I didn't tell you that I hate horror movies and would only watch them to get alone time with you."

"Wait, what? Seriously?"

Omari laughs. "Yeah. I'm a big scaredy-cat, honestly. Horror movies give me nightmares." His lips curl up a little. "But it was always worth it just to be with you."

"Hold on," I say, trying to process this. "You hated *Get Out*? And *Us*?"

"I didn't hate those, but I was uncomfortable and didn't sleep well for days afterward."

"But it's Jordan Peele," I say.

"The only Jordyn I cared about was you," he says. "Was that too corny?"

A smile tugs at my lips. "A little. But I like that about you. I like everything about you."

"Even when I change the radio station?"

"Except then."

Omari laughs, and I do too. He cups my cheek again.

"Maybe I can make up for that."

This time, Omari St. Clair kisses me.

Omari St. Clair is good at kissing.

Omari St. Clair makes me smile.

Omari St. Clair drives me up the wall and makes my heart flutter at the same time.

Omari St. Clair is perfectly imperfect.

And even though I'm not perfect—certainly not a perfect big sister—I'm pretty sure Omari St. Clair is perfect for me.

O OPERATION SOLA AND STEVIE SURPRISE

9:12 p.m.

Porsha

> Check in. Y'all got everything? Kaz and I are headed to the stadium now. Or at least trying to. These back roads are a mess.

E.R.

> Still stuck at the airport, but we might be able to grab MARTA? I'll let you know if it's running.

Ava

> I think I'll be good. Anyone heard from Jimi? Should we add her big sister to the group chat?

> I bet Mason can get it from Omari.

Porsha

> Yeah, add Jordyn. We only got a few hours left, and who knows if we'll make it in time.

> Best to know how everyone is doing.

Jordyn has joined the chat.

Ava

> Hey, Jordyn! Heard from Jimi?

Jordyn

Hey, y'all. I haven't heard from my sister in a while and I'm still on the damn highway.

I have the Howard gear tho.

And I know where Jimi is. If I get outta this, I'm gonna swing by and scoop her.

Porsha

Cool. Okay. See y'all soon. 👍

SEVEN

STEVIE

Mercedes-Benz Stadium, 8:42 p.m.
Three hours and eighteen minutes until midnight

I ALMOST BACKFLIP out of the Ryde, so happy to escape the overly chatty and semi-nosy driver, his too-cheerful lights and seasonally diverse music. I'm across from the gate two stadium entrance.

"Good luck to you, my dear!" the driver says before easing off into the darkness. I wave goodbye, trying to force the scowl from my face. Several hours of forced human interaction zapped my ability to socialize. But he never gave up on completing my ride, so part of me is grateful. I'm one step away from this plan actually working. From potentially getting my girlfriend back.

I look around, rubbing my hands together to try and hold on to some warmth. Now I'm missing the heat of the car. The empty streets feel eerie, streetlights bathing the snow in pale yellows. The roads are quiet, and there isn't another person in sight. A prickle of fear works its way up my spine. I need to get inside quickly. I dart across the street while texting Ern.

S STEVIE

I'm almost to gate two.

E ERN

Gate four.

Crap, okay, will walk around.

Call me when you get close and I'll send my
assistant down.

Cool. And thank you again.

Got you.

I stuff my cold hands into my jacket and take the long trek
around the stadium. The few inches of snow sit like Sno Caps on
the lampposts and trash cans. Not even a foot of snow, and this city
is crushed.

Sola would say the storm made the whole place look more
beautiful, more romantic. A winter wonderland. When she first
moved here, she used to complain that the city of Atlanta had
no romance, not like Chicago or New York or Paris or even gray
London. The only thing she knew about the city was that racist-ass
book and movie *Gone with the Wind* and the Coca-Cola factory,
but I always thought it'd be a challenge for us. It'd be our city of
love, where we began.

If she were here, she'd force me to lie in the empty road right now and make snow angels until a car came whizzing past, and we'd have to race out of the way. She'd make up a word for the entire torturous endeavor, and call it thrill-seeking memory-making or something out of that *Notebook* movie. We'd laugh until we almost peed and we'd be flushed with heat. I'd cup her hands and warm them with my breath, and it would be one of the forever moments she'd write down in one of her observation logs to keep safe.

A headache works its way into my temples as the feeling of missing her and the feeling of what I did wash over me again. The quiet lets it all in, and somehow I miss that annoying driver right about now. His stupid conversation kept the thoughts away, at least.

I gaze up at the sky one more time as thick clouds stretch overhead, nimbostratus ones, ones that might ruin the rest of my plan. "Stay away, stay away," I whisper, my breath creating its own vapor. "I just need clear skies for a few hours." If I believed in a god like my parents so desperately want me to, I'd ask it for that. Just the one thing. A stretch of cloudless sky for approximately fourteen minutes.

I walk faster, panic settling in as we get closer and closer to midnight. My phone is a mess of texts and missed calls and voicemails. Three from Dad and two all-caps angry texts from Mom about why I'm not picking up the house phone and how they know I have somehow gotten ahold of my cell. Ugh. I mentally calculate how long I'll be grounded this time around. Maybe until graduation. Maybe until college move-in day. Maybe they'll find a way to restrict me even when I move out.

My stomach squeezes. Even if I fix things with Sola, I probably won't get to see her until we head to Howard . . . if that same future still exists. So much for prom and senior week and all our summer plans.

I call Ern.

He answers the phone, out of breath.

"You okay?" I ask.

He dives into how he's been racing around, redoing the storyboard and making sure everything is in place. "This was actually just what I needed to try out a new feature."

"Was it hard to change the storyboard? I know these shows take months to plan."

"You and Mr. Celebrity have the same amount of words or symbols requested. Ten. Yours is way more poetic than his: '*Will you marry me right now, Sara. Love you, shawty.*'"

I laugh for the first time tonight.

"Took me a few hours to reconfigure—and proved how versatile and adaptable my light drone tech is. Also, now I know they're weatherproof in case more snow is headed our way for New Year's Eve. I have something to report back to Mr. Celebrity to prove this added stadium time he paid for is worth it." He starts yelling strange degree measurements, then says to me, "Get to the security door and my assistant will let you in."

The line goes dead before I can respond. It should make me feel better, but my stomach is still a bundle of nerves. I can't get the feeling to go away.

I run all the way to gate four now, my heartbeat thundering in my ears. I think of him behind his dashboard like an obsessed flight engineer. I remember being at the Richardsons' family party after he got his wings as a certified pilot a few years ago, and then again, when he pioneered new software for light drones and started his state-of-the-art company. There was a whole write-up about the software patents in *Science Weekly*, and his company was on the news as one of the fastest-growing Fortune 1000s. I knew then that I eventually wanted to be just like him.

I duck inside and head for the security door. Then knock and wait, nibbling my bottom lip and checking my phone—all my text messages to Sola are still on read. I squeeze my eyes shut to hold back the tears and the cold. "Just hold on," I say, imagining the worst.

The door springs open and a short white man stares back. "Stevie?"

"Yes," I reply. "That's me."

"I'm Paul, Ernest's assistant. Follow me."

We slip inside, and I'm grateful for the warmth, and for the fact that we walk in silence. Paul has no idea how much I need it. I feel like if I talk, I'm going to vomit. I just need to get to Ern and make sure that when he stops with the message test run that the real version will most definitely and without a doubt be seen near Sola's house in Inman Park, which is about three miles from here. I want to see his visibility reports. Maybe seeing that everything is going to work will get my heart to slow down.

Our footsteps echo as we navigate the huge, sweeping halls. We pass booths and closed concession areas, and I almost laugh, thinking about all the times I've been here with Sola. The memories crash into me. This is a place of firsts for the two of us. My heart squeezes as I remember when we were here last, racing through these halls, trying to get to our seats before Jimi and her crew took to the Battle of the Bands stage.

We'd been looking for an alternate route to our seats because a person had fainted and the paramedics had blocked the whole section off.

Sola was in full whining mode because her feet hurt. Her baby toes kept pinching because she'd once again worn the wrong kind of shoes trying to match her outfit in service of the perfect look for a concert date, knowing full well that she could wear a potato sack and I'd still think she was the most beautiful person.

Pop music poured through the speakers, and despite what she *said* was "the worst foot pain ever on this plane of reality," Sola sang every single song at the top of her lungs as if she was trying to make sure the masses could hear.

"You sound like a dying cat," I'd said.

"Let's not *derogatorize* the death of the most wonderful, the most amazing, the most splendid creature ever to be put on this planet aside from moon jellies." Sola stopped her terrible song rendition to correct me, then listed all of the noble qualities of the three cats she owned plus the ones at the shelter where she volunteered.

Then she *hmmph*ed and went quiet. Mission accomplished: eardrums were saved.

After a few seconds, Sola draped her arm around me, shifting her weight from one leg to the other. I bit my tongue, trying to will myself not to whisper in her ear, "I told you so," about those too-tight shoes. They might've made her feet look beautiful, but there was a cost.

"Here." I pulled off my sneakers and removed my socks, handing them to her before sliding my bare feet back into my shoes. "Take those off and wear these for a while. Live your best almost-barefoot white girl life until your feet feel better."

Her beautiful face lit up as she unclasped her T-strap sandals. "They really do walk around with no shoes on outside. It's wild." She leaped into my arms. "Thank you for rescuing me."

"Your feet, you mean."

"You like my feet," she teased.

"I like everything about you," I replied as she got on her tiptoes and leaned up to hug me.

She swayed left and right on me, trying to force me to move in sync with her to the music pumping through the speakers between sets. Jimi's band, Rescuing Midnight, was up next. I froze, feeling like people were watching me fail to find the beat.

"We've never slow danced together," she'd whispered in my ear.

"That can't be true. You're exaggerating per usual."

"Any dance we go to, you sit at the table or sneak off to the science lab." She rolled her eyes.

"We've danced together, for sure. Like in your room or mine."
I tried to quickly comb through our relationship, thinking about
all the times she played her father's Nigerian music for me or we
listened to all her moody-ass playlists. We definitely, probably
danced together. Maybe we can't remember it.

"No, we haven't!" she protested with a poked-out lip. More
dramatics. I brushed my lips against hers to try to get her to stop
sulking.

"I don't like to dance. It's not my thing."

"Correction: you *hate* dancing but won't even really give it a try."

"Incorrect. I dislike dancing. There's a difference."

"It's romantic."

I rolled my eyes. "Here we go. . . ."

"It's a way people connect with each other," she said, launching
into a diatribe about the history of courtship and dance as a vehicle
for partnership. She sounded like my dad in his pulpit more than
anything else, especially when she started listing all the supposed
health benefits of dancing, "both cardiovascular and cognitive,
because it releases all these happy chemicals in the brain," as
though learning this would get me to dance with her instantly. It
was cute . . . and *almost* successful. She knew me so well to link it
to chemistry and science, but the heat of embarrassment crawled
its way up my neck as she pressed against me, trying to show me
how to slow dance. I already knew how to, but my hands went all
clammy and my feet filled with lead.

I couldn't get my limbs to move. What if I stepped on her toes?

What if I hurt her? What if I made fools of us both? The spiral of questions kept me stuck in place, the head bop to the beat my only contribution to the world of dance.

"Please," she said with the voice I couldn't usually resist.

"I don't like attention. I suppose that's why I don't love to dance."

"I know. And it makes you nervous."

"I can admit that." I kissed her forehead, hoping that would suffice.

"And it makes you feel out of control," she added.

"Okay. Dr. Olayinka, therapist, reporting for duty. How much will this analysis cost me?"

"All right, all right!" a voice boomed through the speakers. "Next up to the stage, we have one of Atlanta's youngest and finest! Put your hands together for *RESCUING MIDNIGHT*!"

"OMG, OMG, it's them!" Sola squealed. "LET'S GO, JIMI!"

I cringed as her shriek stabbed me in the eardrums.

"Anyway, like I was saying: it's true, and it's okay." She leaned her head into my neck again, the warmth of her forehead sending a shiver down my arms and legs. "Just promise me that if we ever get really, really mad at each other, we will just dance, like this . . . slow and steady . . . until it passes. My grandma used to say, 'When the music changes, so must the dance.'"

"What does that even mean?" As the music started, the phrase rolled around and around in my head as I tried to make sense of it, hating the way language had so many layers and interpretations.

I opened my mouth to ask more questions, but Sola kissed me, pushing them away and somehow imparting an answer. Then she hummed along with the ethereal singing voice of her best friend, her lips lightly fluttering against mine, and the chaos all around melted away. It was just us, swaying and turning. In that moment, finally, all the worries drifted off, and we danced for the very first time. If I stepped on her toes, she'd just laugh. If someone watched, they'd get a great show. If we made fools of ourselves, then we looked stupid together.

I never wanted not to be dancing with her.

Ern's lanky form sharpens in the distance, and the memory of my first dance with Sola tucks itself back inside me. His smile is wide, and his eyes are filled with confidence and excitement, just like Evan-Rose's usually are, and it almost makes me lose it, wanting my other best friend here to help with my nerves as I try to fix this ultimate screwup.

"Hey, hey," he shouts, ushering me into a tech room. "Glad you finally got here. I have so much to show you. The test run is complete, and I recalibrated for max distance and brightness. You ready to tell Sola to look out her window?"

I have to be.

EIGHT

JIMI

Fox Theatre, 9:24 p.m.
Two hours and thirty-six minutes until midnight

I PLAY LIKE no one's watching.

I close my eyes, feel my way along the fingerboard, and strum Delilah, my lucky guitar, so hard I drop my pick. But I don't let it slow me down. I sing from my belly, my chest, using my whole torso to make my voice big and bright as it exits my throat, hoping it will carry far beyond the lighted awning I'm standing under.

I glance down Peachtree Street, praying for the people I've been waiting for to show, but it's oddly muted by the snow, the streetlights making everything sparkle like a disco ball and the pink lenses in my glasses making the whole world blush. It's achingly pretty, so I swallow hard and squeeze my eyes shut again, imagining the rest of my band appearing here, because if it can snow like this in Atlanta, I can surely be forgiven. I'm hoping my sister shows too. I belt out and hold the final high note in this song longer than I ever have before, but when I open my eyes I'm still alone.

"Thank you so much," I say, forcing a smile in the direction of the small, applauding crowd in front of me. A guy in a yellow beanie tosses a couple of wrinkled bills into my open gig bag, but I don't want money. I'm just trying to keep my fraying hope alive.

I cup my hands to my mouth, blow on my icy fingertips, and warmth billows out in a soft cloud that fogs up my glasses. I wonder how much longer I should wait. I glance down the empty street, let out a defeated sigh, then I check my phone again.

No new messages.

I scroll up to reread the end of my band's most recent . . . disagreement.

Jimi

> **Look. You know how I feel about love songs.**

Then comes the angry flurry of texts from Kennedy and Rakeem. (Things were said that I won't be repeating.)

Jimi

> **Let's take a few days. See how we feel after we all calm down.**

But Kennedy had immediately replied.

Kennedy

> **Nah, I don't need a few days. I'm out.**

And minutes later Rakeem weighed in.

I don't think I can rock with you anymore, J.
What kinda musician hates love songs?

ME, I wanted to text back. *I DO.* The urge to clap back was strong, but New Year's Eve was too soon. My Granny Vee pulled some strings so our band could play at her club, Vanity's Aura, on the thirty-first, and I didn't want to let the opportunity pass us by. Despite how badly I wanted to tell them why love songs are trash and have no business on our set list, I wanted to be on stage more. Granny Vee always says, "No one has ever choked from swallowing their pride, Jamila." So I bit my tongue. Vanity's would be our biggest venue to date.

After my mom left and we moved in with Granny Vee, I spent countless nights at her club holding on to the hems of her long dresses, following her around and meeting all her musician friends. Those nights are core memories that play like a catchy bassline in my head, just like all of Granny Vee's sayings. We were terrified the club wouldn't survive the slow pandemic years, but somehow we made it. And now I have a chance to perform on the stage I used to dance around on after hours as a little kid. The only place I've dreamed of playing more often than Vanity's is here, at the Fox Theatre.

I keep scrolling.

Jimi

> **If I let this go . . . will you still play the Vanity gig?**

An hour went by before Rakeem replied for them both.

Rakeem

> **We'll think about it.**

We'd made previous plans to meet here tonight, to record Stevie and Sola's favorite song of ours, so I suggested we still do it—that if they wanted our band to stay together, they should show it by showing up. But my most recent message floats, a single blue bubble at the bottom of my band's group chat, still unanswered for the third hour in a row.

Jimi

> **Y'all coming?**

It's freezing out here.

I check the time. Only two and a half hours till midnight—Stevie's new Sola-imposed deadline. My sister Jordyn was supposed to be here to hear me play and then drive me to Stevie's to deliver some Howard gear—another part of the Christmas-turned-apology gift for Sola. I have feelings about the whole thing (I hate love songs for a reason), but the longer I'm out here—alone—the more I begin to accept what I've been trying to deny for the last couple of days, if not longer. Just like Stevie, I really messed up this time.

Though I love music with every bone in my body, my anti–love song lifestyle is incompatible with just about everyone, and my band, Rescuing Midnight—my third in recent years—might be breaking up because of it. What's more, my big sister is too busy for me. And also likely pissed at me for talking to our birth mom.

If I keep breaking everything I touch, does that mean there's something broken about me?

I want to call Sola and ask her this question—to have her kind voice in my ear telling me I haven't ruined everything. But she's in the middle of her own crisis, and heartache tends to rule her sun and moon when she's in the thick of it. When Sola's sad, she doesn't have room for anything or anyone else. It's why I have to do what I can to get her and Stevie back together—Sola lets her pain eclipse everything else, and I lose her for a while whenever she's hurting. Stevie is the only person who gives her balance. And especially with Jordyn being so MIA lately, I need my best friend back.

The tears that fill my eyes are as sudden as they are surprising. But I only let a single one fall from each eye before wiping my face and bending down to retie my combat boots. I grab my guitar pick from where it landed between my feet and tuck one of my fat fuchsia yarn twists behind my ear. I feel heat creeping along my scalp—something that always happens when I'm pissed, and I clench my fists before kicking at the inches of snow collecting all around me. It is wholly unsatisfying, like kicking a sheet or something else just as insubstantial, but I keep at it until I'm so warm I'm verging on sweaty. A second later, just as I'm about to pack up my things to leave, someone trips over my gig bag, sending crumpled dollar bills and spare change flying.

"What the—" he shouts. He hits the ground hard, his right hip, elbow, and shoulder banging into the snow-dusted pavement in front of me in quick succession. His sunglasses fly off and land behind a parked car several feet away.

I wince.

"That had to hurt," I say, stepping closer to him. "You good?" I reach out a hand to help him up.

When he lifts his head, I freeze.

"Téo?" I whisper, though I know it's him. He's totally different than he was when we were in middle school, but I'd recognize his new look anywhere—Killmonger-style locs with a fresh fade, sparkling grill, and tattoos—because my little sister, Jayla, has been one of his biggest fans since he became who he is now.

Lil Kinsey.

Top-of-the-charts rapper by day, legendary party boy by night. He's done collabs with everyone from newbie indie pop stars to rap legends since he was discovered at a local freestyle contest the year we both turned thirteen. Daddy is always screaming at Jayla to turn down "0 to Dark," Kinsey's hit single, since it came out this past summer.

He's become a bit of a fashion icon too, though today he's just in ripped jeans and an oddly shiny puffer coat. He actually walked in a few Fashion Week shows last fall.

Despite all that, to me he'll always be Téo Santiago-Watkins, the first boy I ever kissed.

As I stare, our history comes flooding back to me:

We met in the poetry club in seventh grade. He was the only boy at our after-school meetings, and though other guys in our classes teased him mercilessly for it, I loved how little he cared about what they thought. I was also obsessed with his moody, dark poems and the way his locs (they were longer then) fell into his eyes while he read out of beat-up composition notebooks. After he read one comparing an unnamed girl's hair to storm clouds, he'd slipped me a note saying it was about me. I'd gently stroked my afro puffs the rest of the afternoon before cornering him in the hallway. And when we kissed—my first kiss ever—it was dizzying, dazzling, damn near perfect. The moment our lips touched, I was sure I loved him.

Sola, who was a romantic even then, told me that I should tell him that the kiss was everything; that I should come clean about how I really felt. We decided I could put all my feelings into a poem the same way Téo had. But a line from one of the stanzas hit my ear like a refrain from a song, and I'd just started getting good at guitar. Without telling Sola I'd decided to, I added music. It took weeks to get right. When I finally recorded the song and sent it to him, he never replied. And the week after, he wasn't in school. I begged Sola to go to his house, worried he was sick, or worse—that he hated the song so much he didn't want to face me. Sola said when his grandmother answered the door, she just looked at Sola with the saddest eyes beneath her tumble of black curls and said, "He's gone, amor."

I was convinced he hated the kiss, the song, and maybe even me so much that he'd transferred schools and moved away. And a year later when he appeared on TV as Lil Kinsey, I was terrified me and my song would end up as something he joked about in interviews.

That was the year my hatred of love songs started. From then on, every time I heard one, it made me feel sick.

Now Téo sniffs, rolls his eyes at my outstretched hand, and stands up without any help. He walks away to grab his glasses and I pull back, frown, and cross my arms.

"Oh, it's like that?" I say. "Wow. Okay, then."

I watch him, trying to figure out why the hell he still goes by Lil anything. He towers over me, which is hilarious. When we were kids, I was taller than him. He's over six feet now, and not skinny like he used to be. Despite his height and, um, thiccness, I can still see the kid I grew up with underneath. He has the same round baby face.

I inspect my bag and it looks okay, though my extra picks have spilled out and the Rescuing Midnight button pinned to the front pocket is scratched; some of the red is scraped off the cape a full moon wears in our logo. When I start picking up my change—a small consolation for being stood up by both friends and family in the snow—I hear a deep, rhythmic voice say, "Maybe you should find somewhere else to do your lil show, shawty." I turn to look at Téo as he puts his sunglasses back on even though it's dark out.

My frown returns and deepens. "Excuse you?"

Téo chuckles. "You heard me. You out here, in the middle of all this ice and snow, putting lives—including mine—in danger."

"First of all, Téo, you should watch where you're going. Just because you think you're hot shit now doesn't mean everyone is required to make room for you like you're some kind of hip-hop royalty. And second, I cannot believe you're fixing *your* mouth to talk to me like I'm one of your lil groupies," I say, almost all in a single breath.

"Hold up," he says. "Did you just call me Téo?" He squints.

Oh. Maybe he isn't just being a dick. I do look pretty different from middle school Jimi. I step closer to him, pull my bright twists away from my face, and take off my rose-tinted glasses.

"Imagine this gorgeous face with braces," I say. "Plus a bubblegum-pink backpack with nothing inside it but a well-loved journal, big purple headphones, and cherry cola lip gloss."

His eyes widen.

"Jimi?" he says, like he can't believe I'm real.

"Yes, *Téo*," I repeat. "I know you're Lil Kinsey or whoever now, but that don't mean you can talk to people like you're better than them."

I let my hair fall and put my glasses back on. I lift my guitar over my head, place it in its bag, and zip it up while Téo watches, still looking astonished. Since Téo, I haven't had much action in the romance department, to be honest, thanks to my overprotective father, his team of intimidating firefighter besties, and the pandemic. Besides, music takes up most of my time, and I'm okay with that. From my experience, people always leave anyway. Especially the ones you love.

I'm not used to boys staring at me (except on stage). The hairs on the back of my neck prickle.

"Can I help you?" I say, with a bit more attitude than I intend.

Téo's face shifts, and he smirks. "Nope," he says in a voice that sounds different than it did a minute ago. Amused. Less guarded, maybe. He pulls his hands out of his pockets and puts his palms together, like he's ending yoga practice. Instead of exhaling a "Namaste," though, he looks me in the eye and says, "You right. My bad, Jimi. Sometimes I lose track of where Kinsey ends and Téo begins. It's been a brick since I've seen anyone who knew me before. If Vovó was here, she'd say, 'Ei, Téo Lorenzo, pode baixar a bola.'" His voice goes all high-pitched and his accent is so spot-on it's disorienting. I can't help but grin.

It's surprising how quickly an image of Téo's gorgeous grandmother appears in my head. I didn't even know there were Black people in Brazil till I met her. It's also funny that he's thinking about what his grandma would be saying right now the same way I'm constantly thinking about mine. He looks like her: deep brown skin, high cheekbones, plump lips. . . .

"And that means . . . what exactly?" I ask, pulling my eyes away from his face and focusing on my guitar again.

"Oh, it's just something she says to me all the time. Basically means 'You ain't all that.' Point is, I'm sorry, J. I'm a idiot."

All of his bravado has fallen away, and it's endearing how quickly his whole posture changes. It's rare you see a guy with neck tattoos and a grill showing any kind of vulnerability. And there's a whisper deep inside me too that I'm trying to ignore: when he looks down like that, I can see the cute, quiet boy from middle school he used to be. The one I used to like.

I get up and shift my weight from one foot to the other. "It's cool," I say.

It's stopped snowing and only a few people are out, smoking cigarettes or walking toward Ponce de Leon. A noisy snowplow crawls down Peachtree—didn't know we had those in this city, but looking around me now, I'm glad we do—wildly scattering rock salt like a horizontal hailstorm in its wake. A few of the salt chunks hit the curb and one even bounces off my shin. We both take a step back and I clear my throat. "So. Besides all the getting rich and famous stuff, how you been?"

Téo blows out a big breath and shakes his head a little. It's so cold that it looks like he's vaping. "It's been . . . weird, I guess. Surprising. Dope AF and scary as hell all at the same time. Kinda like bumping into you."

"Why is bumping into me scary?" I ask.

"You serious?" he replies. When I nod, he bites one corner of his bottom lip and looks skyward for a second. He chuckles softly. "Yo. I can't believe I'm sayin' this. But when we were kids, I was terrified of you."

"Wait, what?" I ask.

"Yeah," is all he says, and he doesn't elaborate. He looks over at my bag. "Why you out here anyway?"

Now it's my turn to look down. I rub the back of my neck, grateful I'm too brown for him to see it going red with the heat of humiliation. Dark skin is such a blessing. "It's, uh, kind of a long story."

He looks around at the empty streets, and the wintry weather speaks for itself. "You got somewhere to be?"

I groan. "My band was supposed to be meeting me out here if they wanted to . . . you know, still be a band." I rub my hands together and blow on my fingers again, bouncing up and down in place. "We're also on the hook to record a song before midnight for a friend of ours, but that's another, separate, very long story." Téo takes off his sunglasses, and his dark eyes sparkle in the light from the marquee.

He glances around. "Why they ain't here?"

"I mean, I'm hoping it's because of the snow? But I also kinda lost it on them," I mutter. "Right when they were telling me about a new song they'd been working on."

"Not the chillest thing to do," he says. "But bands fight all the time. That don't seem bad enough to make 'em ghost you."

I cringe a little. "Well, I . . . said some things."

"Like?" Téo asks.

I start pacing. "So, my band is just the three of us, right? Kennedy, Rakeem, and me. At our last practice they tell me they're writing a song together, and while I was a little in my feelings about them working on something without me, I said cool. But then they tell me it's a *love* song, and when I said, 'Ew, why?' they looked at each other and smiled this little conspiratorial smile. Turns out they've been dating. For a while."

Téo chuckles. "And let me guess. You took that personally."

I stop pacing and put my hands on my hips. I don't like the way he can see right through me. "Um. Of course I did! They'd essentially been lying to me and hooking up behind my back for who knows how long, and then they spring this fucking *love song* on me, knowing I *HATE* love songs, and I could just imagine us performing it and them making googly eyes at each other while I'm just standing there in the center of the stage like an idiot. And then who knows? Maybe they decide they don't need me at all. Maybe they leave, start their own band without me. Since I'm basically like a third, unnecessary wheel in their relationship, maybe they'd decide I was unnecessary to the music too."

I'm breathing hard when I stop speaking. My throat is tight and achy, and I don't want to cry, but I feel like I might.

Téo nods, like he's taking it all in. "You have heard of tricycles, right?"

That makes the threat of tears I felt building evaporate. I glare at him and say nothing until he puts up both his hands like he's under arrest. "So . . . did you say all that to them?" he asks.

"Not exactly. I said they shouldn't have lied."

"True," Téo agrees. "But they also didn't have to tell you at all. It ain't really your business."

My eye twitches. "I told them, we're a band, so we should write stuff together."

"Also true," Téo says. "But weren't they bringing the song to you to get your input?"

"Maybe," I allow. I cross my arms and look away from him. "Then I said, 'It's never gonna work.' Because most relationships don't. That when they inevitably broke up, they'd get why love songs, and love *in general*, ain't it."

"Woooooow," Téo says, twisting the tip of his shoe into the snow. He looks back up at me and shakes his head a little. "Damn, J."

"Yeah," I say. "Not my finest moment. So now they're pissed. Problem is, we have a gig on New Year's Eve. A big one."

Téo looks thoughtful. "Y'all gettin' paper for this gig?"

I shake my head. "Probably not. You know how it is. We're new so we gotta pay our dues. Or maybe you don't know how it is. . . ." I mutter the last part so low I don't think he hears me.

"So, lemme get this straight. You shat on their song instead of being honest about how their lie *of omission* hurt your feelings?"

"Umm," I mutter.

He leans forward and cocks his head to the side. "And then you basically gave them an ultimatum, to meet you here or you're through? Band is donezo?"

"Your point?" I say, feeling heat climb up my neck, for a different reason this time. I can't tell if I'm mad, embarrassed, or feeling something else entirely.

"My point?" Téo chuckles. "My point is, that's some bullshit,

Jimi. And that's not how any of this works. What's your beef with love songs anyway?"

I don't want him to know that *he's* the reason I can't hear the word "love" in a song without having a visceral reaction. Sola calls it "affection rejection." That, when I think about the song I wrote him, how he ignored it, how he walked away from me and never came back after I bared my soul, I have involuntary full-body cringes. It seems ridiculous, and I feel like I should be over it. But it was my first-ever song. And he was my first-ever love. And he left after my first-ever kiss. My mother leaving is baked into my bones, so every other abandonment lingers too. His clings to me like the snow clinging to my twists.

Something inside me hardens and seals shut, the way locks won't let your key in when it's too cold.

"Why would I take advice from you anyway?" I say, sidestepping his question. "You got discovered when you barely had any facial hair."

Téo takes a step back, and I realize I've gotten all up in his face (as much as a five-five person can be in the face of someone nearly a foot taller than they are). I remember him saying he was afraid of me when we were kids, and while I was curious before, now it just makes me feel powerful.

"You don't know what it's like to have to really fight for what you want. I need to know my band wants to make it as desperately as I do. That they won't let a dumb disagreement threaten our future. That they won't just *leave*. We're gonna have much bigger challenges than this. Especially as a Black band playing what everyone thinks of as silly white girl music."

"But . . . silly white girl music has always been your thing, right?" he asks.

I scoff and pivot away from him to collect myself, because visions of me getting into an all-out brawl with *Lil Kinsey* on the mean streets of ATL fill my head in vivid detail. The headlines, the posts that would fill every feed, the way I'd look, wild-eyed and hungry as I tried to wrestle his giant ass into a choke hold, in blurry cell phone photos passersby would capture—though hopefully lens flare from the shining lights would stop me from being recognized.

"I gotta go," I tell him, because Granny Vee always says the only way to get out of trouble is to stay away from it in the first place. If I stay here, I know I'm going to do or say something I'll regret.

I open up the Ryde app, but there are literally no cars populating the map. I close and reopen it, thinking maybe it's a weird glitch because I've never seen the map completely empty, but then I realize that my efforts might be in vain anyway. I'm sure prices will be surging because of the storm. It wouldn't even be worth it to put a request in with the wait times I'd probably be offered, but I pretend to anyway just because I want Téo to know how much he's pissed me off.

"Oh, come on, lil mama," he says. "I didn't mean liking silly white girl music is a bad thing."

I ignore him, pick up my bag, heavier now that it's weighed down by Delilah, and step closer to the street. I look down Peachtree as if I'm expecting someone to come to my rescue any second, and as I lean forward, I slip and stumble off the edge of the curb. I catch myself and try to play it off by stepping farther out into the street, like I'm right where I want to be.

Just then I hear the screech of tires to my left, followed by the sound of a car horn blaring. I turn toward the noise in what feels like slow motion, only to see a red SUV with green underglow lights illuminating the snowy road beneath it, fishtailing, careening in my direction as it spins out of control. I don't know why I don't run, but it's like I'm watching a girl who looks a lot like me do nothing to save herself. For a brief moment, I wonder if being hit by a car would make Kennedy and Rakeem forgive me. Luckily, before that unhinged thought can gain any traction, I'm being full-on tackled by Téo Santiago-Watkins.

He grabs me around the waist and yanks me backward, pulling me out of the path of the oncoming vehicle. Our legs tangle and we land hard, close to the ticket booth in front of the theater, a small snowdrift cushioning our fall. But it still hurts like hell to have his huge body coming down like a boulder on top of mine.

He immediately shifts his weight, so that it isn't pressing down on me, and braces himself on his forearms. His face is only inches from mine, but he doesn't move away.

"You good?" he whispers, breathing hard.

He doesn't look at anything but me until I nod, and since I'm a little breathless from both the fall and his closeness, it takes a minute for me to respond. "I think so," I whisper, swallowing shallow inhales because he smells a little too good to be true—like wood smoke and honey.

He scrambles up and looks down the street to where the truck has regained control and slowed. But when the driver doesn't stop, doesn't get out to check and see if we're okay, Téo jogs forward a bit like he's chasing after them and shouts, "You serious, bruh?" Then he gives the driver the finger just before the truck turns a corner and disappears.

I lie there, sprawled and wincing on the ground, until he comes back and offers his hand. He pulls me forward and I stand slowly, dusting off my jacket and jeans. My hands are shaking, and my hip feels bruised, along with my ego, but all I can think about is Delilah. I unzip my gig bag and lift the guitar out to examine her, holding my breath and begging the universe for mercy. Two strings have popped, and her body is a little scratched, but otherwise I think she's okay. I want to kick myself for not using my hard-shell guitar case today.

My mother got me Delilah for my birthday last year. She got my sisters special gifts recently too, after almost a decade of radio silence. Jordyn got a worry stone and a mindfulness journal that she promptly threw away—Mom thought it would help with the anxiety I told her Jordyn has—and Jayla got a set of cookware because that girl stays in the kitchen. Even though Jordyn says she'll never forgive Mom for leaving, and that these gifts are her attempt to *buy* our forgiveness, I still think it means something that she's been reaching out, trying to make things right.

Delilah's been with me through every practice, every gig, every show I've played this last year or so. My bands have come and gone—Reigning Stardust, Seven Suns, and now Rescuing Midnight—and I haven't seen my mother at all since the day she left. But when Delilah was with me, it felt a little like my mom was too.

A few people have rushed over, asking if we're okay, and a few others gawk at us from afar. I try my best not to cry, but between being ghosted by my band, the almost hit-and-run, my damaged guitar, and my bruised ass, I feel the hot sting of tears at the backs of my eyes again.

"We're cool," Téo says. He aims his face down toward me as he speaks instead of looking at anyone else, and I see that his glasses are gone again, which is when I realize mine are too. Both must be lost somewhere in the snow. His lashes are so curly they nearly double back to touch his eyelids, and I suddenly remember the way his eyes would go wide whenever I read one of my poems in middle school . . . the way they went big right before we kissed. I look away from him, down at my boots, attempting to hide my brimming tears, but Téo must see. "Give her some room."

He walks me behind the line dividers that block off the entrance to the theater and I look around, nervous that we've crossed a threshold we're not supposed to. Téo seems unconcerned. He helps me sit down again and I prop myself up on the other side of the ticket booth, cradling Delilah like my dad would cradle me when I was sick as a kid. I look up at nothing, blinking and fanning my face. I take a few deep breaths.

"Seriously. You sure you're okay?" he asks again.

"Yeah," I tell him. "Delilah, on the other hand, not so much."

"Jimi. You're shaking." He reaches out and wipes my cheeks with the pads of his thumbs. "And crying," he adds.

I use my shoulders to wipe the rest of my tears away. "I'm just a little shaken up."

I let him take my hands in his, and he just holds them quietly for a while. Somehow his palms are warm even though he isn't wearing gloves. He watches me as I take deep breaths, but he doesn't say anything. Just gently rubs his thumbs over my knuckles.

"Better?" he asks, after we've been holding hands for more minutes than I've ever held hands with anyone. And I do feel calmer. My lips aren't trembling anymore, and when I touch my cheeks, they're dry.

"Yeah," I say. "Better now."

On the ground a few feet away, I see one of the lenses from his sunglasses sticking out of the snow. I point it out and he smiles. "Guess Tom Fords ain't meant for rescue missions," he says.

"They were pretty douchey looking anyway," I tell him. He laughs again, and this time it's a real one. His eyes get all crinkled in the corners, and he even lets out a little snort. Then he goes as quiet as the snow.

My head is still hot with all the feelings I had before I was almost taken out by that truck—indignity, embarrassment, and I still low-key want to fight him for the white girl music comment—but in the back of my mind, I know he's right . . . about everything. So, over the course of the next few minutes, as I change the strings on my guitar and pray to the rock goddesses that it can still be played, I tend to my bruised ego too. I decide Téo's apology, heroics, and unexpected tenderness are enough for me to let it go.

"Thanks, by the way," I eventually say. "That was, like, an Edward Cullen–level rescue. Less graceful, but effective." I look up at him slow, but I keep my eyes steady. It was pretty hot, the way he picked me up like it was nothing, and I can't wait to tell Sola about it. To him I say, "You kinda saved my life."

He smirks. "Couldn't let you go out like that," he replies in a low voice.

I stand up and throw Delilah's strap over my shoulder. I tune her up, strum her once, and I almost squeal because she doesn't sound too terrible. I let out a sigh of relief, grateful she's still playable. Still my lucky baby girl.

Téo looks behind him at the door of the theater, then he turns back to me. "I, uh, saw that you called a Ryde. That wait is probably gonna be a brick, right? Why don't you come wait inside with me? I know you're cold. Guessing you hungry too, and I got a ton of grub in the green room."

I do a double take. Like a full-on look-at-him, look-away, look-back-at-him double take.

"You have access to the green room. At the Fox Theatre." I say it like it's not a question, but I clearly have many questions.

"Oh, yeah. Guess you wouldn't know that. I was supposed to be the opener at tonight's show, but . . ." He gestures to the snow all around us. "Everyone else—the headliner, my band and crew—got stuck on 285 on the way here. Only reason I was already in Midtown is cuz I was swinging by Vovó's for some QT before I went back on the road. Once we heard the forecast, she dropped me here early so I wouldn't have to worry about traffic. I just been in the green room, chillin' since before the storm started. Only came out to stretch my legs."

I imagine myself in the green room of the Fox, sitting on a couch where a real rock star might have sat, and I'm nearly vibrating with excitement.

Téo smirks. He can tell I'm starting to fold. "It's big," he says. "And warm."

"Oh hell yeah, I'll wait inside."

I grab my things so fast I beat him to the front doors. As I pull one open, I hear him laughing his goofy, snorty (kinda cute) laugh from somewhere behind me.

The theater is empty and quiet as a church when we step through the doors and into its huge atrium. Which is fitting. If there's anywhere I'd want to worship, it would be in a place that has seen as many musical gods as the Fox has.

Téo walks toward a carpeted staircase and beckons me to follow him, and we head upstairs and through a series of mazelike hallways. We pass a few maintenance people, who nod in our direction. Then he opens an unmarked door, and inside is a wannabe rock star's dream.

The room is sunshine bright and warm, and it's big enough for a dozen people to be here, moving around all at once. There are lit-up vanities along two of the walls, a few sofas and plush-looking chairs, a mini fridge, and a long and low glass coffee table with a wide spread of food, from charcuterie and fruit platters to chips, cookies, and granola bars. Téo walks over to the mini fridge, grabs a bottle of sweet tea, and tosses me one too. I almost don't catch it. He flops down on one of the sofas and kicks his feet up as I envision the bustle of an imaginary band and sound crew getting ready for a show. "There's Wi-Fi too," Téo tells me.

I yank off my beanie and shake out my yarn twists before tucking them behind my ears and unzipping my coat. "This is even cushier than I thought it would be."

Téo doesn't say anything, so I glance at him, grinning. He has a strange pained look on his face. It's then that I realize I never asked him if *he* was okay after our semi-near-death experience. I toss my stuff on a chair, then walk over and sit beside him on the couch, my excitement about being here diluted by sudden worry.

"So . . . I definitely should have asked this a while ago. But are *you* okay?" I lean forward until I catch his eye. "That was some scary shit."

He nods slowly, his locs flopping back and forth. He runs his fingers through them so they all point toward his left ear, then clears his throat.

"So, I'm good. But what you said earlier kinda got me in my feelings."

I frown. "What did I say?"

"All that stuff about me being discovered and how I don't know what it was like to have to work for anything. None of that's true."

I turn around to face him fully. "Wait. Are you saying you weren't discovered?"

"Nah, that happened. Even though I hate when people say that. It's like, I been existing. You the only one just finding out. Shit reminds me of colonialism. But we don't gotta get into that tonight."

I bite my lip because this is a level of depth that the TV interviews and magazine articles skim right over. When we were kids, he'd regularly get into it with teachers who wanted to gloss over the parts of history that they didn't like, so he was always in detention. I can't believe I forgot that about him—that he was only quiet until he had to speak up.

"But, like, after that exec signed me, I was kinda on my own. You know my vovó adopted me, right? That my moms and pops are still in Rio? She just wanted me to focus on school, and she *definitely* didn't support me getting into the rap game. But I saw what it might mean, you know? I could repay her for everything she's done for me, send money back home to my fam. So, I basically ran away. Forged the consent paperwork and left when she wasn't home. One thing about me, if given the opportunity, I'm gonna hustle. As a kid of would-be immigrants, I don't know no other way to live. So yeah, I guess I made it. But it wasn't like it was easy. And it could all go away in a second."

I swallow hard and look down at my hands, away from his dark, serious eyes. "You're right," I say. I know I say mean things when my guard is up, but that's no excuse for bad behavior. Téo didn't deserve that reaction. (Kennedy and Rakeem didn't either.) Granny Vee always says, "Excuses sound good to you and no one else," so I don't offer any of mine. "You're so right. My bad," I say weakly.

Téo takes a swig from his tea and puts it down on the floor beside the couch. He nods. "You good," he says. "And not gonna lie, some parts of my life are a lot easier now than they ever have been. But it's still work. Every day is work, whether I'm on the road or in the studio, doing interviews or just writing, flowing, trying to come up with something new. You should remember that if you wanna do this music thing for real."

I nod, and I expect things to feel awkward, but for some reason they don't. "Since we're being honest here, that white girl music comment had me ready to fight. I hear that enough from everyone else. I don't need it from you too."

He puts his hands together and nods again like he did outside. "Respect," he says. "I meant it as a kind of acknowledgment. To show that I saw you. I see you. It's what I remember you listening to since . . . forever. When we were like thirteen and everyone was all about Cardi B and Lil Nas X, you were on some indie tip, into artists I never heard of, or bands playing pop or punk or pop punk? Stuff white kids listen to."

I just look at him. "Most of the white kids I know love Cardi B as much as the Black kids do. Remember Whitt?"

"Oh shit! Whittaker James Prescott the Third!"

"The whitest white boy name ever," I say. "He pretty much exclusively listens to V-103. In fact, whenever I see *your* ass on TV, most of the crowd is white kids. So what are you even talking about?"

We look at each other. When he starts laughing, I can't help but follow. Pretty soon we're both cracking up.

"Yooo, it's funny because it's true, though!" he says through snorts and chuckles.

"I know, right?" I say when I can speak. "My granny always says, 'Everybody wants the culture, but nobody wants the color.'"

Téo lets out a low whistle. "That part," he says.

Something warmer than understanding, better than belonging, passes between us. And out of nowhere, Téo reaches forward and touches my hair.

"This is fire, by the way," he says. "The color, the length. It's everything." While touching a Black woman's hair is usually a no-no, the way he does it—gently palming a twist and then letting it fall, and paired with that compliment—is too kind and unexpected for me to be mad. In fact I flush, remembering his poem from middle school. I wonder if he's thinking about it too.

I turn to prop my feet up on the coffee table and clap the toes of my shoes together so I don't have to look at him. "Those boots lit too," he adds, and I'm grateful for the subject change. The vanity lights make the pink patent leather shine like just-licked candy.

"Oh, you like? That's a big deal coming from you, Mr. Fashion Week."

"You saw that?" Téo chuckles. "Man, I don't even wanna be rockin' half the stuff they have me rockin'. But I can tell this is all you." He pauses for a second. Licks his lips in a way that feels purposeful. "You look good, Jimi Jam," he says, using a nickname from middle school I'd nearly forgotten about. "And for what it's worth, I only heard the end of your song, but you sounded real good out there too."

I nod and say, "Oh, I know," and he laughs again. I choke down a bit of pride and tell him his stuff's not too bad either. "I really like 'Fake Fire.'" It was an early song, from his first EP, not one from the debut album that made him famous. Something about the song is dark and desperate and reminds me of his poetry; of who he used to be.

He does the thing where his eyes go wide. He blinks and shakes his head a little, like he's surprised. "Damn, J, that's a deep cut. I didn't even know anybody knew about that song. You stalkin' me or something? Gonna show up somewhere and reveal all my secrets?"

I roll my eyes. "Boy, bye. But is that why you're scared of me? Do I know too much about *Téo* while you out here trying to be Kinsey?"

Téo shakes his head and shoves my shoulder. He must be getting comfortable because he's suddenly very . . . touchy. Not that I mind.

"I didn't say I was *still* scared of you."

On the corner of the table, I notice a homey-looking plastic container that seems out of place compared to the fancier snacks. I point to it and Téo nods, so I lean forward and pry it open. Inside, half a dozen round golden-brown pies sit in two tight rows of three. "Are these . . . ?"

"Vovó's famous empadas? Yeah. Half are chicken, half are beef." I pull one out, take a big bite. It's flaky and salty and I taste both butter and bacon in addition to the beef. For a second I forget what I was about to say.

"Jesus, that's good. But . . . you actually *did* say you're still scared of me. Or at least that it was scary to see me," I say, covering my full mouth with the back of my hand. "What's so scary about me? Then or now?"

"Hmm," he says. "It's kinda complicated." He scratches his chin and adjusts himself on the couch so that he's sitting all the way back. He yawns and stretches, and the smoky-sweet scent of him wafts across the length of the sofa. "Sorry, I'm wiped. Gimme a minute." His face looks like he's concentrating, thinking hard about how best to answer my question, and I admire his willingness to be so open. I eat more of my empada while I wait.

"I guess it's like this," he begins. "Even then you knew what you wanted. You knew poetry, and you wrote and performed it with no filter. You knew you wanted to sing, so you were always singing. You knew you liked me," he says, and I freeze, empada in midair, only halfway to my mouth. He looks away a little when he says that part, like he's feeling shy about saying it out loud. "Or at least *I think* you did. And then you kissed me. I was shook. It was a lot to take in. Not just the kiss and the . . . feelings, but that you knew all that stuff about yourself. We were *thirteen*. But you knew who you were and what you wanted. I didn't. Still don't. And that was scary to realize. Still is. How much you know about you. How little I know about me."

I don't know what I was expecting, but it wasn't that. "Oh," I say. I make a mental note that he didn't mention the song I wrote. And it occurs to me for the first time that maybe he never got it. Or that if he did, maybe he was too intimidated by it—by me—to respond. I pop the last of the empada into my mouth and I chew it slowly, a million different thoughts colliding in my head at once.

"I guess I feel like everything in my life just happens *to* me, you know what I'm sayin'?"

"Mmmm . . . not really," I admit. I rub my hands on my jeans and scoot closer to him, fascinated, because he keeps saying things I don't expect him to and it just makes me want to listen to his rumbling voice, to be surprised by his ideas and feelings, indefinitely. "What do you mean?"

"Like being sent here to live with Vovó, and the whole music thing. With the stuff I wear. My parents said, 'You're moving to the States,' and I said okay, even though I was terrified. I just liked writing poetry and recording stuff for fun with my friends, but when the same friends entered me into that freestyle competition, I went with it. My manager or some designer picks out my clothes, I put them on. It all just kinda happens, but I don't feel like I choose any of it. Then, if things go well, I feel like I owe everyone, and I work my ass off to make sure they know I appreciate it all."

I pause mid-nod, because I can see what he's saying. But I also disagree.

"I'm sorry, Téo, but I gotta call bullshit. Because isn't going with the flow also a choice?" I ask. "You didn't fight your parents on their decision to send you away. You decided to go to the freestyle competition *and* to sign a contract. You choose to put on the clothes. Maybe you go with it, with all of it, so you don't have to think about what you really want. Especially if you're afraid that what you want won't matter in the end anyway."

He blinks slowly, like he's thinking about what I've said. "Wow, Jimi Jam. You ain't have to take me to church like that." He's quiet again, looking around the green room like he's lost. I feel a little bad.

"Sorry if that was harsh. As you know, I can come on strong sometimes. I guess, if I'm being honest, I don't like you thinking that you're powerless. That this stuff is happening and you can't do anything to stop it. So, tell me, Téo, do you know what you want?"

His bright, wide eyes circle back and land on me. He bites his bottom lip, and when his chest heaves with a deep breath, I smile to let him know it's okay if he's unsure.

"Some quiet, maybe. Some time and space to think, to create. To help my family in every way I can. I think . . . I think I want someone who sees me. Who sees past Kinsey to Téo. And I guess a nap would be nice too."

His nostrils flare, and he smiles a little crookedly. He looks down at his hands, then he asks, "What about you? What do you want?"

"Oh, me?" I say, thinking about my band and fame and my name in lights. I imagine Rescuing Midnight back together at the New Year's Eve party and then us playing a thousand other gigs. I wonder what it might feel like to perform here, *inside* the Fox Theatre, or to sing in the rain (now that I have in the snow), and what it would be like to finally kiss Téo again. I smirk. "I want it all."

Téo grins and shakes his head like he's trying to wake himself up from a dream, and his locs flop all over the place. "Today has been the longest. I need to get up. Move around before I pass out." He stands, and I'm surprised when he grabs my hand and pulls me up too.

He leans closer to me, like he's got a secret.

"Wanna see the stage?" he says.

It feels illegal to be inside the concert hall all on our own. But as I jog down one of the long aisles, Téo's right behind me. When we get to a side door that leads to a narrow hallway, he opens it, and we follow the dimly lit corridor past black-and-white photographs of Prince, Patti LaBelle, Mariah Carey, and countless others who have performed here over the years until it empties us at the entrance to the stage. I blow a kiss at a neon sign above the doorframe that reads PLAY IT PRETTY FOR ATLANTA. It's hot pink, like it was made for me.

When I step out onto the dark stage, I die a little. The theater is cavernous and shadowed, the walls stacked with elaborate brick architecture that resembles the facade of a castle, and each side of the stage is draped with heavy velvet curtains. The ceiling is an otherworldly shade of blue that makes it feel like the room has no roof and I'm staring up at an endless sky. Everything about it is ornate and gorgeous and I can't believe I'm here. The only thing that would make this moment better is if Rakeem and Kennedy were here too.

I open my gig bag, grab Delilah, and slip the shoulder strap over my head. I strum a few times, marveling at the room's amazing acoustics, and I close my eyes imagining a crowd chanting my name. I can hear the roar of imaginary applause, and I can almost taste what it would be like for this particular dream of mine to come true. It's sweeter than pouring Pixy Stix into my Granny Vee's already-sweet tea.

"Tell me about the first time you performed somewhere like this," I say.

"Hmm," Téo murmurs. He had been hanging back, letting me have the whole stage to myself, but now he steps out of the shadows, comes to stand beside me in the center of everything.

"It was probably when I opened for Lil Yatchy. I was scared shitless. I actually puked three times before curtain, so my whole dressing room smelled like ass. When my manager walked in, she thought I was dying."

I laugh and turn to look for him, but I can barely make him out since none of the stage lights are on. Just the leftover light from the hall spills out across us, like a pretty voice from far away—we can hardly hear its brightness.

"So she brings me a liter of ginger ale and I drink more than half the bottle. I'm burping so much by the time I need to go on that everyone's on their phones, looking for someone to replace me."

"No way," I say. I'm still playing Delilah, something soft and slow, providing a soundtrack to his story.

"Yeah. It was, I don't know, maybe a thirty-five-hundred-seat theater. A little smaller than here. But I pulled it together, went out there, did my thing. Hyped up the crowd for my boy, and it was all fine. I puked again as soon as I got offstage. But yeah. Probably one of the worst best nights of my life."

I nod, but I don't know if he can see me nodding. When I hear his voice next, he's closer.

"Tell me about the best worst night of your life," he says.

The night that comes to mind isn't one I like to think about. It's easier to pretend it didn't happen, like it's a chapter of my life I imagined instead of one that's real. But Téo has been so honest with me all night, and I feel like I can trust him. Everything about this moment feels a bit unreal, from the snow to the boy beside me to standing center stage in a place I dream of performing. He saved my life and shared his secrets, so I take a deep breath and share one of my own.

"It was the first show Rescuing Midnight was playing in front of an actual, real audience. One of my granny's friends had hooked us up, gotten us on a list at this big-deal Battle of the Bands competition at Benz stadium, even though we'd missed the deadline to sign up. I knew my dad and sisters would be there, but I'd texted my mom too—something I rarely do. She actually said she'd come. I don't know if I ever told you, but my mom hasn't really been in my life for a while. She left when me and my sisters were kids, got remarried, has this whole other family. Daddy moved us in with Granny Vee so she could help raise us. I think that was part of the reason I liked you so much when we were kids—because you lived with your grandma too. When I was with you, I felt less weird, less like I was missing out on something."

"I had no clue, J," Téo says.

"Yeah. Most people don't." I look out at the huge theater, and the gaping void of space above the seats, and I know I could fill it with all the rejection and disappointment I've felt in my life.

"Anyway. We're about to perform and we're so excited and I just keep checking my phone, because I'd told her to text me when she got there. But before I know it, it's our turn to hit the stage. We play a song I wrote called 'Left on Read,' and it's all about that feeling of knowing someone sees you right in front of them, but that they don't really *see* you, you know what I mean? They don't get who you really are. And then you meet that one person who does. The person who sees your messages and your soul and they *read* you, you know? You finally feel seen." I don't know if I'm making any sense, but Téo is standing right in front of me, looking into my eyes so seriously. I strum Delilah and sing a little bit of the chorus while Téo listens. I'd forgotten how good he is at listening.

"Did your moms ever show?" he asks when I stop singing, and I'm just standing there, looking at him.

"No, but my best friend, Sola, and her boo, Stevie, did. And they danced together in the audience. It was the first time Sola had let herself be seen that way in public—seen as she truly was, as she fully is. It was everything. Which is why I wanted my band to meet me. To record the song. To help Stevie win Sola back."

Téo steps closer to me, and I get all nervous, worried he's going to try to pull some kind of *move* on me, but he just reaches into my pocket and pulls out my phone.

"I'll record you right now," he says. "We should probably just do audio since it's so dark in here, though. We both know that voice of yours can shine anywhere, even in a voice note."

I can hear the grin in his tone, though it's too dim to see him smirking. Knowing the innocent reason behind his sudden closeness doesn't stop my heart from pounding, but I reach over to unlock my phone for him. He opens the voice memos app and tells me to start whenever I'm ready. I close my eyes and take a deep breath.

"But one thing first," he says.

"Bruh, I was already in the zone."

"My bad. It's just . . . I been thinking. You said you hate love songs, but this song sounds like one, and you're recording it to help a literal couple get back together."

"So?" I say. "And 'Left on Read'? A love song? Nah."

"Yeah, it is, Jimi. Love songs don't have to be about hookin' up or sex or flowers to be love songs. Wanting to be seen? That's romance. Doing this to reunite a couple. Romance. And even if you don't think 'Left on Read' is a love song, you've definitely written at least one." He pauses and licks his lips again.

I freeze.

"The one you wrote for me." His face is lit up by my phone and his eyes are as quiet as his voice—softly shining in the dark. My neck heats up. My muscles tense. My affection-rejection is fully activated.

"Shut up," I say, but my voice comes out softer than I mean for it to.

"Nah, J. You did. I remember."

"Ancient history," I whisper. I look down at the stage. The wood is shiny and worn. I strum my guitar again, just to do something with my hands.

"Is it?" he whispers. He reaches out, places his fingers on my chin, and tilts my head up until our eyes meet.

I take a step away from him. "Well, why didn't you say anything back? Why didn't you call? Where the hell did you even go?"

"LA," he says simply, looking at me in a way that feels like his warm hands are still on my face.

I think back. Do the math. Realize I must have sent the song to him the week of the freestyle competition. The week he got signed. The week his whole life changed.

Of course he wouldn't have had time to respond to a lovesick thirteen-year-old nobody, when he was in the early stages of blowing the hell up.

"Oh," I say. "Right." And I'm embarrassed about the song all over again, but this time for a different reason. He was doing things that were so much bigger, so much more important than me. I wasn't even on his radar.

"I didn't respond," he says, like he can *see* what I'm thinking, "because I was scared, Jimi. You were so sure about me, and I wasn't sure about anything. Except that . . ."

My hands go still on my guitar again. My phone goes to sleep in his hand, and I squint into the sudden darkness, trying in vain to see him. "Except that . . . what?"

His voice is gruff and lower than it's been all night as he says, "Except that . . . I knew I wanted to kiss you again, and I was worried I'd never get the chance."

I feel his hands on my waist before I realize he's closed the space between us. Delilah is the only reason our bodies haven't collided.

"Can I?" he whispers.

I swallow hard, and tuck some of my twists behind my ears. I nod, then realize he probably can't see me nodding. And I feel like we're thirteen all over again.

"Yes," I say, rising to my toes. I lean forward until my lips land on his, and I wonder if he missed the taste of my cherry cola lip gloss.

* * *

Several minutes (and several kisses) later, Téo pulls back a little. He turns on the little flashlight on my phone, and I'm relieved at the sight of his face. Even though he's lit from the bottom and looks like he's about to drop a ghost story on me.

"I could be wrong," he whispers, "but maybe we're afraid of the same thing."

I'm feeling right and warm, but I frown, confused. "What do you mean?"

"We're both afraid we won't get what we want, so you never let go of control the same way I rarely take it."

I try to wade through my buzzing hormones to read between the lines of what he's saying. Maybe I don't hate love songs, or love. Maybe I've just been too afraid to unlock my heart, to let anyone or anything in.

While I'm still trying to process all the ways that he might be right, he speaks again.

"Yo, why is your phone in airplane mode?"

"What do you mean it's in airplane mode?"

I yank the phone out of his hands, scream when I see the tiny airplane floating at the top of my home screen (beneath a crack in the screen that partially obscured it), and immediately tap into my settings to switch it off. Within seconds, dozens of messages and missed calls spill in, notifications piling up on the screen like a Jenga tower. Most notably, my dad and Granny Vee have each called over a dozen times. They're both going to kill me.

"They wanted to come," is the next thing I can decipher from the mess of notifications. "Kennedy and Rakeem," I say, glancing up at Téo. "My sister too. They all wanted to come!"

B **BAND CHAT**

Kennedy

I'm still mad as hell at your stubborn ass and I can't get nowhere in this mess, but I don't want this to be the end of RM.

Rakeem

The bus I'm on just straight up stalled out, so I'm not gonna make it. But yeah. I'm still in if you ease up about love songs.

Kennedy

And also, like, why the hell ain't you happy for us?

Rakeem

Not the time or place, K.

Kennedy

Shut up, Keem.

There's more, but that's all I need to see. Happy tears fill my eyes and spill over my lashes before I can stop them. I tap out a response as quickly as I can.

> I'm so sorry. I love you dum-dums.
> Thanks for always rockin' with me,
> even when I'm doing the most.

I text Jordyn and let her know that I appreciate her efforts to get here and understand that she couldn't make it—and I tell her I'll see her at home (eventually). Then I check the group chat. Someone has posted a video of some sorta light show. Different words and symbols—"dance" . . . "when" . . . "must" . . . a giant heart . . . a couple of music notes—shine in a dark night sky, and I have no idea what that might mean, but I don't try to figure it out because I want to spend every moment I have left with Téo actually *being* with him.

As I look at his floppy hair and tattoos, thinking of his soft voice and tender hands, I see that maybe he's right. I do know myself. I know what I want. And in addition to a stage and an audience and a band that I love, I'm pretty sure I never stopped wanting him.

"Ready?" he asks. He lifts my phone again and I strum Delilah, smiling as his eyes go wide.

I nod. He smiles back.

Then he hits record.

A Grand Gesture Over the ATL?

Staff Writer, 10:01 p.m.

If you've been anywhere near the ATL today, you aren't just
dealing with snow . . . there's something in the sky, and it ain't
just snowflakes. Theories abound. The UFO enthusiasts have
spammed the internet about it. Here's what we've got so far:

6:04 p.m. Random floating lights are spotted in the sky
around Mercedes-Benz Stadium.

6:28 p.m. More lights appear and move around, seemingly at
random.

7:01 p.m. A shape vaguely reminiscent of a music quarter
note forms in the lights.

7:11 p.m. The lights vanish.

8:01 p.m. The lights return and appear to form the word
"when."

8:19 p.m. More lights appear, and music notes are confirmed.

8:23 p.m. The lights vanish again.

9:10 p.m. The word "changes" appears fully formed.

9:22 p.m. "Changes" has morphed and is now a heart shape.

9:54 p.m. Conflicting reports. Some say they're seeing the words "dance," "the," "when," and/or "must."

Bookmark this page for the latest. We'll keep our eye on whatever's in the sky—be it snow clouds, floating words, or alien spaceships. Comment with your theories about who's doing it and why. Our bet is on a rapper who's cheated on his girl? Lil Kinsey's in town . . . maybe he's in trouble already.

NINE

STEVIE

Stadium field, 10:03 p.m.
One hour and fifty-seven minutes until midnight

MY LEGS SHAKE as I keep looking at the time. A little less than two hours to midnight.

I sit, practically freezing in the bleachers beneath the night sky, looking down at the field covered in small light drones. Sola cleverly described them as mega beetles set in a synchronized rhythm, ready to swarm when we first learned what Ern could do with them. What type of show he could put on up in the air.

Even though he *wasn't* able to get the stadium roof to close. Works in my favor, obviously—it takes the thing eight minutes to shut *or* open, which has the potential to throw a wrench into the timeline—but I hope his failure with that isn't a bad omen.

"Calm down, Stevie. Calm down. It's almost time," I whisper to myself. "Ern is just doing the final check. It's all going to work." A small voice inside me adds: *It* has *to work . . . you have no contingency plan.*

I watch Ern and his assistant wipe off each light drone and

scrape off any patches of frost that formed the last time he sent some of them up. I wish I could do more. I hate sitting around here waiting. I obsessively check the weather app. It's supposed to start snowing again right at midnight, threatening to ruin everything.

My phone pings, and it's more angry texts from Mama and Dad, but also a link from Ava.

A AVA

THIS YOU?

I click it and scan the news article about what have been identified as unauthorized light drones in the sky above Atlanta, and how the cops have been unable to get to the stadium to investigate due to the car accidents all over the city. I squeeze my eyes shut and try to will away another terrible scenario—what if the cops *do* come? Will Ern's permit hold up? Why *didn't that* get reported to the news stations?

Thankfully, the sky is the clearest it's been since this morning. Looking at it, you wouldn't even know that it had been snowing all day and that Atlanta was still under a severe weather watch. A full moon glows so bright and sharp, it makes the darkness around it almost seem purple. Like it's twilight instead of almost midnight. A jellyfish of a moon, Sola would say. Maybe it's a trick of the light, but somehow it makes my nerves settle.

Whenever there was a full moon, Sola would text me, or if we were together, lean over and whisper in my ear, "Do you remember the moon jellyfish?" and a ripple of heat would rush down my back and the backs of my legs.

I smile. I can almost recite every fact about them. And not even because I love science. I just know that if Sola were to be reincarnated as an animal, it would be one of those. I laugh for the first time today, thinking about how her childhood notebooks had moved from stories of the worm burglar to stories of a moon jelly kingdom.

Sola has always loved moon jellies, but it became a thing for *us* during the spring of our sophomore year. I'd been wanting to surprise Sola with a little excursion—we'd been cooped up at home for weeks juggling online school during the pandemic. I pulled into my mom's special parking space at the Georgia Aquarium. "Keep the blindfold on," I told Sola in the passenger seat.

"Why?" Sola whined, though I knew she was secretly very excited. The end of our sophomore year had been turned upside down by another variant surge.

"Where's your sense of adventure?" I'd said, turning the car off.

"I snuck out, didn't I? Upon penalty of death." She stuck her tongue out at me, pretending to be annoyed. "And I thought we were just running errands for your mom."

"We are. You'll see." I leaped out of the car and went around to open her door. She always complained that I wasn't romantic or spontaneous, and she wasn't wrong, but this time, I knew just what to do to make her smile. Mom needed files from her office at the aquarium, and I needed to show Sola something she'd never ever forget.

I walked her through the back door, using Mom's ID card. The empty aquarium felt desolate, like a reminder that the world was still paused. I remembered coming to work with my mom when she was first named senior director of zoological operations, and marveling at how she got to see all these majestic aquatic animals every day. Though she'd always say that it was mostly paperwork and meetings and approving this order and that budget sheet, it felt like my dream to be a scientist got firmly embedded in me then. I knew that one day, I'd walk into my very own lab with my very own staff of other scientists as we made discoveries that would change the world.

I looked for the security guards, James and Wayne, knowing they'd pop up at some point. Mom had alerted them that I was coming in to pick up some things for her while she was on bedrest recovering from COVID.

"What's that smell?" Sola perked her nose up, desperate for any clue.

"Antiseptic and chlorine and salt. Stop trying to cheat. Be patient." I marched her quickly through the different galleries, loving how the fish and sharks and other animals swam past the glass, eager to see who had come to visit after hours. I wondered if they were a little sad to not have all those faces staring at them every day since the pandemic had shut things down . . . or maybe they were secretly glad to have a break from humans. I led her to the jellyfish gallery.

"Now, count to sixty, then you can remove the blindfold," I ordered.

"Sixty!" she complained.

"Yes, you brat."

"Your favorite one."

"My only one." I turned her shoulders away from me. "Start counting, and out loud."

Sola stomped her foot, pretending to be upset but hiding a big grin.

I quickly spread out the blanket, set up the picnic basket, and pulled out the lilies I'd gotten her. I reviewed the snacks I'd packed—cookies, cheese, grapes, and candy. Not as pretty as a basket she would curate, but the thought counts, right? I chuckled to myself, knowing that as soon as she saw it, she would ask me what the theme of this basket was, and I would shrug.

"Forty-five!" she called out. Snapping me back into action.

I stood and wiped my hands on my pants; they suddenly turned clammy, and nerves shot through me. We hadn't gotten to see each other much due to quarantining, and part of me felt nervous, like the distance might've changed things between us in small ways. What happened when you went from spending almost every day with someone to just seeing them through the phone or a computer screen? Was the connection gone? Warped? A little bit of it lost?

I took a deep breath. "Okay, open them."

Sola snatched off her blindfold like it was suffocating her. She looked left and right, taking everything in. A smile stretched across her face as she spotted the beautiful jellyfish floating all around her. "Stevie . . ." Her eyes found the picnic, the deep blue light from the tanks casting rippling shadows over everything, making it fancier than it was.

"This is the first time we've seen each other since, you know . . . the lockdown and everything. I just wanted it to be special and for you to know how much I missed you." Heat warmed my cheeks.

Sola grabbed me and dragged me to the floor. We stretched out on the blanket and stared at the moon jellyfish flickering and floating past in the tank directly in front of us. The glow of their light made Sola's deep brown skin even more beautiful.

Sola launched into all her favorite things about moon jellyfish: "Did you know that a group of jellyfish are called smacks? And that they're very social? I love that they go with the flow of the current and don't actually swim. How awesome would it be to just float all day out to sea with your friends?"

I smiled. That didn't actually sound awesome to me, but it made me happy to know her imagination was running.

"They're just the most beautiful things under the sea," she continued. "I should dig out my old notebooks and reread all the things I wrote about them."

She turned to me then. "This was the best surprise. I've missed you."

I kissed her forehead. "You always say I'm not romantic . . . or I don't know how to be."

She laced her fingers between mine, and the warmth of her

palm made me tingle all over. "You did good. Your basket theme needs a little work, but we all can't have *my* skills."

I laughed and turned to tickle her. She nuzzled her head against my arm, and I pulled her closer to me. Our legs tangled with each other.

"Won't we get caught?" she asked. "And, like . . . get in trouble?"

"I have the security schedule." I flashed my phone. "Plus no one comes to this side of the aquarium on Tuesday nights, according to my mom. We have the whole place to ourselves."

She looked away from me then and back at the tank. "Moon jellies don't have hearts, did you know that?"

"You told me I didn't have a heart yesterday."

"Uh, that's because you didn't cry during that movie."

"You sobbed enough for the both of us," I teased. "I thought your phone might've needed to be turned in for water damage."

She elbowed my side.

I laughed. "You always cry. About everything."

"It's good for you."

"My drama queen." I pulled her even closer, and she put her mouth next to my ear. "You have my heart," she whispered.

My heart backflipped. "And you know you have mine."

"I know now."

I stared into her eyes, finding insecurity and tiny bits of confusion. "What do you mean?"

She traced her fingertips along the edges of my face and down my neck, leaving a warm trail. "You hold things close. I don't always know how you feel. I think you *think* you show me or tell me, but I'm not always sure"—she put her index finger on my temple—"what's going on in that brilliant head of yours."

"Oh," I said, not really knowing what else to say.

Then she put a hand at the top of my chest. "And don't even get me started on your heart," she said. "You can be a puzzle."

I gulped, feeling like there were a thousand things I wanted to tell her about the way I felt, but the words just piled up one after the other, stuck and swirled all together. Her eyes combed over my face as if she was searching for my thoughts in my expression. "Sometimes . . . I don't know how . . ."

"I get it," she said, and then she gave me a kiss. "If you can't tell me, I need you to show me. I want to feel it."

She took my hand and placed it on the bare skin beneath her collarbone and the feel of her skin made my mind spin as she shifted my hand lower and lower. Leaving it on her chest—and I didn't dare pull away—she reached for my shirt and began to undo my buttons one by one. I was wearing her favorite short-sleeved pink button-down.

I caught her wrists then. Not that I wanted any of it to stop . . . it's just that we'd talked about not going too far before we were both absolutely ready. "Are you sure?" I asked, my eyes drifting down to her bare thighs.

Sola nodded. "Yes, I am." And kissed me long and deep. "Are you sure?" she said once she pulled away.

I nodded too. "I am."

Her hands moved to my face, and as she held me there, I took in the way she looked under the blue glow.

"If we were like them"—she motioned at the moon jellyfish floating above us—"I'd float alongside you forever, Stevie. Follow whatever current we find." I pulled her to me and kissed her, slowly leaning back until she was lying on top of me. I really wanted her dress out of the way so I could feel the skin of her torso against mine, but I also didn't want to rush anything. "You okay?" I asked her.

"Always with you."

I rolled her over and put my lips to her throat. She let out a sound that was like nothing I'd ever heard before, and my body responded in kind. After a few seconds of brushing my mouth against the beautiful blue-cast brown of her neck—and feeling her rapid pulse against my lips—she said, "Hold on." So I respectfully pulled away.

Which is when she sat up, shifted to her knees, and removed her sundress . . .

And I gasped so hard, I almost choked.

She just laughed. It was the most musical sound I'd heard in a long time. "You can come back now," she said.

I didn't hesitate. After sweeping one of her braids away from her face so I could see all of it, I kissed her, then gently licked her full bottom lip before slipping my tongue into her mouth.

She shoved my shirt from my shoulders and reached to unbuckle my belt before working at the button and zipper on my pants.

And I neither flinched nor held back. Her skin felt as electric as the jellies when I ran my hand from her chest down into the curve of her waist and over her hip. As we allowed our bodies to have their way with each other, I hoped she could feel what was in my heart, all the things I couldn't say. The love, the admiration, the respect, the desire. Our mouths and fingers explored every inch of each other, and in that moment, I resolved to make sure she'd never question how I felt again, no matter how quiet I might get.

"It's going to look beautiful against that big full moon." Ern's voice cuts into my thoughts.

"Huh?" I look down at him, almost out of breath from the memory of my first time with Sola.

He waves me down to the field and hands me a granola bar. "Eat. Despite how cold it is, your forehead is covered in sweat and your pupils are dilated. It's been a long day and will be an even longer night."

"Can I help?" I have to do something. My head is a mess.

He hands me a clipboard with a checklist. "Technically no, but you can shadow me. Put these gloves on and let's do a formal check so I can start the next sequence. The weather is perfect and we're like an hour or so out from midnight."

I feel like we're in a lab together. My heart squeezes in a good way for the first time in days.

He lifts up one of the small light drones, demonstrating how to check its battery. "Be sure to place it back correctly. We've already set the storyboard and timeline in the computer. Everything needs to be precise and in order."

"I can do that. Order and precision are my favorite things." I wish my whole life could be like a light drone show—everything perfectly arranged and in place, a well-designed and thoroughly thought-through plan, a highly intelligent computer program, and an adept radio signal, all ready to synchronize my desired outcomes. I'd be able to see what was ahead and anticipate it before it happened.

There would never be any surprise variables.

There would never be a need to want another version of an event.

There would never be a desire for a different version of me.

Nothing would ever go wrong again. The odds of me messing up would be minimal. No one would get hurt. Least of all Sola.

I'd be the perfect girlfriend to her.

Ern clears his throat, popping my bubble of concentration. "If you're so into order and precision . . . why are we here again? You still haven't told me the full story." He doesn't look up at me, still checking each light drone.

A cold chill drops into my stomach. I haven't *actually* said what happened aloud to anyone. Mom and Dad did so much yelling that night, I didn't even get a word in or a chance to explain.

"I messed up."

"I already know that part. And that you're trying to win your girl back. But what happened? Evan-Rose said you ran over your parents' mailbox with your car while under the influence one night.

But you're totally not a drinker. I remember that time when I let you and E.R. taste an old-fashioned, and while E.R. seemed to like it, you spat it out and said you never wanted to taste alcohol again. So I know there's more to the story. Out with it."

I clutch the clipboard to my chest. "I was meeting Sola's family for the first time."

"But haven't you known her forever? You mean to tell me you'd never met her family?" His forehead crinkles with confusion.

"Ugh, I'm a mess. Sorry. That's not what I meant. I'd definitely met them before, but this would've been *re*meeting them . . . not as Sola's best friend, but as her *girlfriend*."

"Ahhh, I see," Ern says. "And that ended with you running over your parents' mailbox?"

I shrug. "Well, it started off bad this past Saturday night. For my senior project, I sort of did an experiment on the biochemistry of love and how it's just a chemical reaction in our brain, and I shared it with Sola. I got an A and wanted to brag and show off."

"Guessing that didn't go well?" he replies.

"Not at all. Sola is *super* romantic and she got really offended."

"Makes sense," he says.

"Well, then on Sunday, the day of the dinner, I was running behind. If I'm honest, it's because I was nervous, so I tried to distract myself with work. Our chemistry teacher lets me come into the lab at school on weekends when he's there. I'd been experimenting all day, then was supposed to run home and get cleaned up for dinner . . . but I lost track of time. I didn't even have time to change my clothes, let alone shower when I got back from the lab. I got so nervous I took two of my mom's muscle relaxers—the ones for her back spasms—thinking it'd help me chill out."

"Guessing that also didn't go well." He rearranges two light drones.

"Correct. I wound up being a loopy asshole at the dinner with her entire family. Aunties and uncles and Grandma from out of town included."

"Ooof, kid." He shakes his head at me.

"Finally Sola said I had until midnight tonight to apologize to her and her family."

"Well, this is a hell of an apology—and if Sola knew how much these things cost, she'd have to forgive you." He turns to look at me. "So what were you afraid of?"

I take a long pause, even though the answer is right there on the tip of my tongue. "Them not liking me."

"What else?" He tiptoes closer to me, past the rows and rows of light drones and wires.

"That's it."

"You sure? Not many people—even scientists I know—go out of their way to test and prove a hypothesis about love not being real. Or share that with the person they're in a relationship with." His eyes find mine and they feel like Evan-Rose's, which makes his stare worse. It's incredibly kind, but also sharp and knowing. "You've grown up with so much good love around you."

My pulse races, and I open and close my mouth, the rest of the words stuck.

He puts a hand on my shoulder. Which is when everything spills out: "I . . . I don't want to lose control, Ern. I don't like the chaos of it all. I don't want to lose my grip on all the things I *know* and can prove. While I don't like the fact that I haven't seen or spoken to Sola in over three days, I *hate* that it makes me feel so terrible. And *off.* My head is all clouded and I can't stand it."

"You're in love," he replies, his eyes softening. "Loving a person affects every facet of your life. It changes everything, Stevie."

I cry for the first time since it all happened. Maybe for the first time in years. The tears are hot and heavy, soaking my scarf, and no matter how many times I wipe at my cheeks, they wind up wet again. He pulls me into a tight hug. "What if I'm too hard to love?" I ask. "What if I'm too afraid? Too all over the place for a good love story?"

"Impossible." His voice holds so much confidence. "I'll tell you this . . . love isn't easy. That's the truth. And it may be partly a bunch of chemical stuff in our heads"—he taps his temple—"but it's worth it every time. When I met my husband—you know Maurice—it was a different time. Even in Atlanta. I was terrified to love him out loud because what if, eventually, it got too hard, and he got tired of all the dirty looks and slurs and senseless hate? So I was reckless in the beginning of our relationship. Pushing him away before he could leave me. I messed up a lot. And so did he. My love story is full of second, third, fourth, and even fifth chances.

Maurice was very patient with me, and that created room for what we could grow into."

I look up at him, and he smiles.

"What if it doesn't work?" I say. "What if Sola won't forgive me?"

"Then at least you tried. You told someone you loved them. You really told the entire city of Atlanta. And, like . . . the entire internet."

I nervously laugh.

His watch pings. "It's time."

Now I can barely breathe. "Really?"

"Mm-hmm. I just pressed go—we need to take advantage of the clear skies before round three of the snow starts. You'll meet your deadline ahead of schedule."

We watch as the tiny drones lift into the air, headed to the sky to tell the girl I love that I'm sorry.

Headed to fix the worst thing I've ever done.

○ OPERATION SOLA AND STEVIE SURPRISE

10:28 p.m.

E.R.

> My dad got trapped in the cell phone lot, so we got on MARTA from the airport. They're back up and running. Bring everything to the stadium. That's what my brother said. Gate four will be open.

Porsha

> We're on the way. Had to grab a Ryde because of flat tires. It has Christmas lights and a disco ball! But sadly, even with the holiday music and chatty driver, traffic is still terrible.

Kaz

> At least dude is taking some back roads. The plows are out.

Jimi

> Have y'all looked up? The sky is already lit. She really did that.

E.R.

> We're underground at the moment, but only have two stops to go. Can't wait to see.

Jimi

> Cool. I'm on the way too. With . . . a guest.

10:31 p.m.

Jordyn

Wait, with who, Jimi? Traffic on the highway is finally moving a little. On the way.

Jimi

 Where's Ava? Why she so quiet?

E.R.

And anyone heard from Sola? Can someone make sure she's even looking out her window? Y'all know how she is. Jimi?

Jimi

On it.

10:36 p.m.

S STEVIE

Sola, look outside your window.

Please!

I promise you it'll be worth it. I really am sorry.

CHANNEL 3 ACTION NEWS REPORT

10:37 p.m.

Though traffic is now beginning to move on three
of the four major highways, Highway Patrol has
reported numerous stalled vehicles and minor traffic
accidents. If you must travel, take alternate routes.

The mayor's shelter-in-place order has been
lifted, but the city is still in a declared state of
emergency. Efforts to clear the roads will continue
through the night. The National Guard has been
deployed to assist with road rescue missions.

TEN

A V A & M A S O N

Georgia Aquarium, 10:39 p.m.
One hour and twenty-one minutes until midnight

Ava

LATELY I'VE BEEN looking up quotations about time. Most of them are pretty interesting. Miles Davis said, "Time isn't the main thing. It's the only thing." In *The Color Purple*, Alice Walker says, "Time moves slowly, but passes quickly." Tennessee Williams said, "Time is the longest distance between two places." Some of the quotes are just plain wrong, though, like the one about time healing all wounds. That's for sure not true. I mean, depending on the size of the wound, you might need some antibiotics and gauze and maybe even a splint. At the very least you're going to need a Band-Aid and some ointment. So it's not time healing those big wounds. It's the medicine.

Anyway. I'm still on my volunteer shift at the aquarium. Ordinarily, I wouldn't still be here but, even with the storm, we stayed open late for a special holiday event with some bigwigs.

Then, the roads were such a mess it took a while for them all to leave. I'm wiping down the new Changing Seas exhibit in the atrium. Stevie's mom—Auntie Rochelle to me, Dr. Williams to everyone else—chose the atrium for the exhibit so everyone who came into the building would have to see it. "Changing seas" is a gentle and noncontroversial way of saying global warming. The exhibit is one of those multimedia display tables that shows a top-down view of the world's oceans and how much they're warming, because my parents' generation has a real problem when it comes to planning for the future. The exhibit lets you control the future by increasing the global temperature by a little—or a lot—and seeing what happens. It's morbid, but effective. Anyway, basically the whole point of the exhibit is that unless we do something Right Now, human beings will run out of time.

"We're supposed to be cleaning the exhibits, not playing with them," says a voice from the doorway.

Two things:

1. The voice belongs to my ex-boyfriend, Mason St. Clair.
2. He broke up with me because I refuse to wear rose-colored glasses about our future.
3. He's wearing a Santa Claus diving suit because . . . actually I don't know why he's wearing it.

Mason

FIRST OF ALL, that was three things.

And, second of all, she broke up with me.

Ava

NO, I DID not.

Mason

WHO YOU GONNA believe, the girl so fatalistic about the future she's standing in the dark for sure turning up the temperature dial on the Changing Seas exhibit? Or me, the kid so nice and so responsible he took on an extra dive shift because the regular volunteer tank diver couldn't make it in due to the snowstorm? I'd believe me, the nice kid in the Santa scuba suit. Just saying.

It's been three weeks since Ava and I broke up. Three weeks since I've seen her. We don't go to the same school, so avoiding each other is easy. On top of that, she changed her volunteer shift here at the aquarium, so I don't run into her here either.

Looking at her now, I'm noticing how many things can change about a person in just three weeks. She finally put in those faux goddess locs she's been wanting. And she got herself a new volunteer staff shirt. I don't see the little ink stain that used to be on the hem of the old one. Also I see two dolphin pins I don't recognize on her collar. I guess the gift shop got new ones in.

We're in the atrium, and it's all decorated for the holidays; blinking Christmas lights and huge silver-and-white snowflakes are strung up everywhere. There's a ten-foot-tall Christmas tree, an enormous menorah, and Kwanzaa decorations. Plus the PA system plays holiday music in all the nongallery rooms. Dr. Williams loves the holiday season more than almost anybody I've ever met. If she could somehow put lights into the tanks, she would.

I walk closer to where Ava is. My wet suit squeaks with every step.

She looks at me with those big doe eyes of hers. Her eyes were the thing that got me the most when we met, big and bright and so curious about everything. Okay, the eyes plus the way she bites down on her bottom lip plus the way she looks in her jeans plus the cowrie shells she had in her braids plus these little freckles that look like chocolate sprinkles that she has only on the left side of her nose. When I kiss her face, I always start with that little sweetness right there.

When I used to kiss her face, I mean.

"Why are you wearing that?" she asks.

I know she means why am I wearing the Santa wet suit instead of the regular wet suit, but I pretend I don't. "What you mean? I was just in the tank—"

"No, I mean—" she starts, but then she stops herself.

I walk closer. *Squeak. Squeak.*

"You got any ideas about what we should get for Sola?" I ask.

Her face lights up like I hoped it would. There's no one in the world who likes giving out presents as much as Ava, except maybe her mom and her sister. In my family, we barely remember each other's birthdays. She'll spend weeks—weeks, I'm saying—making lists of ideas for whoever has a birthday or some other occasion coming up. And when it comes to wrapping those presents? I've spent over half my life in a stationery store with her. Double-sided tape is her best friend. I've seen her wrap a present for thirty minutes. Three. Zero. Minutes.

"Yeah, I was thinking we—" she starts, but like before, she stops herself from finishing what she was going to say. Her smile fades away. "I have an idea what I'm going to get her. You should think of something too."

I get what she's saying. There's no we anymore. We don't have to get her a present.

I should probably take that hint and leave, but I don't want to stop talking to her. I squeak closer.

"So you see the rest of Stevie's message yet?"

She shakes her head no, and I hand her my phone.

For a quick second our hands touch, and I get the little zing I always get. The zing that makes me want to touch her more. I can't believe I don't get to do that anymore.

The sky message has SOLA with a heart next to it now. "Probably every Sola in the ATL thinks the message is for her," I joke.

Ava hands me my phone back but doesn't say anything.

"You think it'll work?" I ask. "Stevie's really going all out with the apology."

"Stevie better be going all out. That's my cousin and there's nothing but love there, but this was a major screwup."

I turn my phone over in my hands. "You sound like you're not rooting for her."

She narrows her eyes at me. "I didn't say that. I'm just saying Sola has a lot to forgive Stevie for."

I know I should leave this conversation alone. I know we're not just talking about Stevie and Sola anymore. But I don't leave it alone. "People forgive each other in relationships," I press.

"But what if the thing is not forgivable?" she says, voice soft. She doesn't sound angry, just sad and resigned.

She stares back down at the exhibit. The table lights her up from below, making her look a little unfamiliar. I get a sudden vision of running into her in a bar or, more likely, a lecture hall, say, ten years from now. Maybe her hair will be different again. Maybe she'll be with some other guy. We'll catch each other's eyes from across the room and do the half-smile-and-glance-away thing you do when you see someone you think maybe you used to know.

I look away from her and down at the Changing Seas exhibit. I was right before. She did turn the temperature all the way up. Most of the electronic map is flashing danger red, past the point you can recover from.

Mason

ME AGAIN. THE reason I'm wearing the Santa wet suit is because I ran into Dr. Rochelle right after I got out of the tank. She told me Ava was still here, stuck because of the storm, just like her.

"Just in case that's information you'd like to have," she said, and winked at me.

Instead of going to change, I put on the Santa gear. Why? Because it reminds me of the first time Ava and I met. I'm hoping it reminds her too.

Ava

"YOU'RE IN LOVE" were the first words Mason ever said to me.

We were on a field trip right here in the aquarium. It was just after Thanksgiving break, and both our schools had chosen that day for a field trip. For some reason, Auntie Rochelle was doing the tour herself instead of one of the junior staff members. She'd just taken us all into the Ocean Voyager exhibit.

Exhibit is not really the right word for Ocean Voyager. Imagine the biggest fish tank you'll probably ever see, with over six million gallons of water and more than fifty species, including sea turtles and sharks and coral. To see all the animals, you walk through this hundred-foot tunnel made out of thick acrylic glass.

When I walked into the tunnel that day, a squadron of manta rays swam right over our heads. Their pectoral fins look like enormous wings, so it seemed like they were flying through the water. I could see their smooth, pale underbellies and their wide mouths. I stopped walking in the middle of the path just so I could watch them glide.

When I was little, my parents used to take my sister and me to the aquarium all the time, but the day of the field trip I hadn't been there in years. As soon as I walked into the tunnel, I couldn't understand why I didn't come every single day. I felt like I was in another world.

It was my first time seeing Auntie Rochelle do her job, and she was beyond good at it. She told us all sorts of facts about the species in the tank. Everything she said made me want to get closer and see them for myself. I whispered to Sola what I was doing and went over to the glass. I got there just in time for a school of tarpon to swim by in perfect sync right in front of me, their scales flashing silver.

I got even closer to the glass. I couldn't believe the oranges and the pinks of the coral. Or the sea anemone with their weird tentacles. How could a thing that looked like that not be from another planet? Not to mention the leafy sea dragons that look like a seahorse that fell into a pile of leaves. Probably my mouth was open, the way it always is when I'm amazed by something.

And that's when Mason came up to me. "You're in love," he said.

I didn't even realize he was talking to me at first, but then he stepped closer. "It's incredible, right?"

Even back then, he was at least a foot taller than me. I had to tilt my head all the way up to see who I was talking to. As soon as I got to his face, I looked away because he was too good-looking. The kind of good-looking that makes you want to stop and stare and figure out how a face could even look like that.

I turned back to the tank just in time to watch a huge octopus unfurl its arms. "Really incredible," I said. I was talking about the octopus. And also his face.

"That's the giant Pacific octopus, scientific name *Enteroctopus dofleini*," he said. Then, like he'd been dying to tell someone, he let out a long list of facts about it. How some of them had two hundred and fifty suckers on each arm and that the males live for about five years and that the biggest ones could weigh six hundred pounds.

Then it was facts about the goliath grouper, which makes a loud booming noise when it's trying to mate, and the tasselled wobbegong, which is an excellent ambush predator and also one of the ugliest sharks I've ever seen.

He pointed out all different kinds of animals and told me all he knew about them. By then I had to look at him, because it would be weird if I didn't. It was even worse than I thought. He had rich brown skin, a perfect fade, nerdy square black glasses, a small gap in his teeth, and dimples on both sides of his face. I looked away again.

What was the scientific name for hot and nerdy, I wondered. "It's so cool how much you know about this," I said.

"Thanks, but I don't even know that much," he said. "I'd be in here learning a lot more if I could."

There was some sadness in his voice, so I looked at him again. "Why can't you?"

He tugged on the basketball jersey he was wearing and shrugged. "Got practice every day after school. Most weekends too."

I wanted to know why he couldn't just quit, but then he ducked down and pressed his finger against the glass. "You see that sawfish in the sand bed?"

It was hard to spot, but finally I saw it. "The long ugly thing trying to swallow that comb?"

He laughed. "I never thought about it like that," he said. "It's called a longcomb sawfish. Scientific name *Pristis zijsron*. The comb part can grow up to five point four feet."

"That's taller than me," I said.

He straightened up and looked me over. "By how much?"

"Two inches," I said.

"You'll have him beat by next year," he said.

"You have him beat already," I said.

He smiled wide at me, and I smiled wide back at him. I was definitely blushing, and it took all my willpower not to touch my face and give it away.

"I'm Mason," he finally said.

"Ava," I said.

And then I heard one of the kids in my class, Kaz, yell, "Look at that." When I turned my head, my whole class was looking in our direction. I was ready to die from embarrassment because I thought they were making fun of us standing there grinning at each other like fools, but then I turned my head and saw Santa Claus scuba diving in the tank.

"Ho ho ho!" said a voice over the PA system.

Scuba-diving Santa Claus waved to all of us. It turned out he was part of our tour. He had his own underwater mic, and he and Auntie Rochelle went back and forth telling us how they cared for all the species inside Ocean Voyager. When they started talking about the tank diver's job—feeding and checking on any animals that might be sick, as well as cleaning the acrylic—Mason's face lit up. I could tell he wanted to be in that tank one day.

We stuck together for the rest of the tour. Whenever Auntie Rochelle explained something, Mason would go even more in-depth. But no matter how in-depth he got, it wasn't enough for me. I asked so many questions even he couldn't answer them all.

Finally the tour ended with us back in the atrium. My teacher told us to meet over by the gift shop. Mason's teacher had them meet by the café.

"I'll find you before you have to leave," he said, and took off.

I went into the gift shop. "Who was that guy you were talking to?" Sola asked me. "He was *fine*."

She bumped my shoulder with hers and we both laughed.

I shopped for a while, got myself a dolphin pin and a little crab plushie for my sister. When I got out of the store, I didn't see him anywhere. I waited by the door until my teacher called my name, saying it was time to go.

I was halfway back to the bus when Mason finally caught up to me.

"Sorry I took so long," he said. He was out of breath and holding a sheet of paper. "I got you something." It was an application form to volunteer at the aquarium. The deadline to apply was a week away.

"I didn't even know you could volunteer here," I said.

"Yeah, I figured."

I clutched the application to my chest. "Are you going to apply too?"

"Yeah, probably. We'll see. Have to talk to my pops." He tugged on his basketball jersey again.

"Ava Munroe, this bus is leaving with or without you," my teacher yelled.

"I gotta go," I said. "Thanks for this."

I ran for the bus, thinking how nice it was for him to get me an application and wishing we had more time to talk. It wasn't until I got on the bus and looked at the application that I saw he'd written his full name—Mason St. Clair—and his phone number. And his email address. And his actual home address.

We were going to get more time after all.

Mason

"ALL RIGHT, I guess I'll just grab something from Mabel at the gift shop. She's probably still here doing inventory," I say.

Ava does the thing where she scrunches up her nose real tight. That look can mean one of two things: she doesn't like the way something smells, or she doesn't like the thing someone said.

"What's wrong with that idea?" I ask.

"What are you going to get?" she asks.

"Something cute," I say, and shrug. "Maybe like a goldfish plushie or something."

"Stevie screwed up bad. If she has any chance of getting Sola back, she needs to get her something special to their relationship, not just some random thing. You actually have to be thoughtful."

She emphasizes "thoughtful." Again, we're not really talking about Stevie and Sola. We're talking about us and our breakup. And she's calling me thoughtless.

I raise my eyebrows at her, and we have a mini staring contest. "How many times do I have to say I'm—"

She holds up her hand before I can finish my sentence. "I wasn't talking about that," she says.

"Fine," I say.

"Fine," she says back.

I look down at the small but expanding puddle at my feet. I need to go change out of this wet suit. I feel stupid for putting on the Santa gear in the first place. I thought I could get a laugh out of her, and if I could get a laugh, then maybe we could talk, and if we could talk, then maybe she'd realize how much she misses me, and then maybe . . . but obviously that's not going to happen. Obviously she doesn't miss me at all.

I turn around and walk out the door.

Ava

OF ALL THE things I miss about Mason, I miss being friends the most.

(Okay, that's not completely true. I miss the kissing too. The problem is, he's a good kisser. No. Let's be honest. A phenomenal kisser. A greatest-of-his-generation kind of kisser. A once-in-a-lifetime kind of kisser. The boy has technique.

A good kiss is not just about the lips. It's about the hands, and where you put them. It's about how hard or soft you squeeze the part you put them on. It's about the angle of the head and the warmth of the lips and the pressure you apply with those lips. It's paying attention to the little sounds the other person makes, and when they make that little sound—the one that says they're losing their minds—then doing that thing again.)

Anyway. I miss being friends. I miss telling him about my day and hearing about his day and helping him with math and him helping me with my essays. I miss nerding out together over some new documentary. I miss knowing about his day-to-day life. Like, I wonder if he got a chance to do the Ocean Voyager dive with an audience yet. Auntie Rochelle said she was thinking of letting him do it since he got his dive certificate.

And I wonder if he thinks Sola is going to forgive Stevie. Though Mason goes to Midtown High, he and Sola live in the same neighborhood and have known each other since they were kids. The four of us used to go on double dates all the time. Stevie and Sola are the only couple I know who've been together longer than Mason and me. The only couple I could see staying together forever. Despite what I said before, I hope Sola finds it in her heart to forgive Stevie. I hope that they get to be happy.

I watch Mason walk out the door, leaving wet footprints behind. Why am I being such a jerk to him? I'm not even really mad at him anymore for our breakup. I know it's for the best. But just because we're not going out doesn't mean we can't try to be friends, right?

"Mason, wait," I call out. "Meet me at the gift shop. I have an idea what we can get."

He stops walking but doesn't turn around. Maybe, after everything, he doesn't want to try to be friends. But then he says, "Okay, I'll change and see you there in ten."

I turn the temperature back down on Changing Seas, finish cleaning the other displays, and flick the lights off.

Mason

A YEAR AFTER we started dating, Ava couldn't decide what day to call our anniversary. She went back and forth between the day we met and the first time we kissed, which was on our third date. The kiss, by the way, was so good it made me stupid for a minute. Like I-couldn't-remember-my-name stupid.

We ended up celebrating both, the day-we-met anniversary and the first-kiss anniversary.

Funny enough, though, I don't think either of those days were the most important one for us. That happened a couple of months later.

One of the presents Ava got me for the first-kiss anniversary was the ultra-high-definition 4K version of the best documentary ever made about the oceans and sea life, *Blue Planet II*. It's narrated by this old English dude, David Attenborough, who sounds like your slightly drunk and way too sentimental favorite uncle. We'd both seen the doc before, but never in 4K, where you could see every last pixel, even in those deep ocean trenches where sunlight barely penetrates.

A few days after she got it, we decided to watch it in the basement of my house on my pops's giant-screen TV. It was after school and nobody else was home yet. We both had our bowls of kettle corn. The lights were off. English dude was talking about surfing dolphins. Ava and I were right next to each other on the couch. I had my arm around her shoulders. Everything was perfect. For about an hour.

Upstairs, I heard someone come home. I assumed it was my older brother, Omari—he hadn't gone off and left me for college yet—but it wasn't.

For some reason, Pops got home early that day. He turned on the stairwell light switch and came jogging down the stairs. I tried to turn off the TV, but Ava had the remote. She hit the pause button instead of the off button.

"Hi, Mr. St. Clair," Ava said.

"Hey, Ava girl," Pops said. I could hear the smile in his voice. He liked her from the very first time he met her. Said it was good for a jock like me to find myself a nice nerdy girlfriend to keep me grounded.

I put my bowl of kettle corn on the coffee table and turned around. "Hey, Pops."

He frowned at me and checked his watch. "Don't you have practice?" he asked.

"Took a pass today," I said. Our coach lets us take three absences a season, no questions asked.

Pops looked back and forth between me and the TV screen. "You took off from practice so you could watch some trifling fish?" He came down the last two steps and stood behind me on the couch. "I don't know where your head is at these days. If I had even half your talent coming up, you think I'd be working for the man now?"

How many times was I going to have to hear him say that? "I'll be there tomorrow," I said.

"You got a good life waiting on you," he said. He turned around and started to leave, shaking his head the whole time.

I could feel Ava staring at me, urging me to say something. "It's just one day off," I blurted out.

Pops stopped where he was on the stairs. "The days add up, son," he said. "Believe me when I tell you they add up." Then he left.

Ava knew how I felt about basketball, how I wasn't sure if I wanted to play in college, how I wasn't sure if I even wanted to play the rest of this year.

And what Pops said was true. I had a lot of talent. I'd been varsity since I was a freshman. What I didn't have was the love. He was the one with the love. He was so excited for my future. My mom too. They both knew I liked volunteering at the aquarium, but they didn't know what it truly meant to me. They didn't know that I was thinking of colleges with good marine biology programs instead of good Division 1 basketball teams.

"You need to tell them," Ava had said. "Once they know how much you love it, they'll understand."

I got a little pissed at her, to be honest. Ava had the kind of family that had dinner together every night and talked about their feelings and loved each other more than they loved anybody else. They're like superheroes.

"Yeah, and what am I going to say? 'Hey, Pops, you know

that basketball dream you have for the both of us? I don't want it anymore. I want to study some trifling fish.'" I dropped my head into my hands. "Just leave it alone, Ava," I said.

But she didn't leave it alone.

A week later, I was doing my first shift as a habitat guide at the Cold Water Quest touch pool. My first group was a second-grade class with a bunch of seven-year-olds. Dr. Rochelle called it trial by fire. If I could keep the kids entertained and keep the anemone and starfish alive, then she'd think about letting me do the ray and shark tank next.

Just as I was getting ready to start, Ava walked in. With my parents. I knew she was trying to help. She wanted my parents to see me in my element, but I was still mad. Getting the chance to be a habitat guide was important to me, and I didn't want to screw it up. Having my parents there made me even more nervous than I already was.

But it was too late to do anything about it. Dr. Rochelle walked in and stood right next to them. Then the kids and their teacher came in and lined up around the pool. I didn't even say hello or welcome them or anything like that. I just started reciting facts, and not the interesting ones either.

"Who can tell me the scientific name of the sea anemone?" I asked.

None of them knew the answer. Because they were seven.

"The answer is *Urticina piscivore*," I said. "Let's try an easier one. Who can tell me their range or their habitat?"

Still nothing from them.

A little girl right in front of me stuck her whole hand into the water and tried to touch a starfish. "Please don't touch the animals," I said.

The teacher looked at me and frowned. It was a touch pool exhibit, after all.

I glanced over to where Ava and Dr. Rochelle and my folks were. Ava was biting her lip, nervous for me. Dr. Rochelle was grimacing. My mom looked sympathetic, but Pops just seemed confused, like he couldn't figure out what he was doing there. Like he couldn't figure out what *I* was doing there either. I glanced back at Ava, and she pressed both hands over her heart.

I looked down at the little girl. "What's your name?" I asked her.

"Priya," she said.

"Well, Priya, I'm sorry I said you couldn't touch. Today is my first time giving this talk and my parents are here and I'm a little nervous."

She shook the water off her hands and shook her head at the same time. "But you don't have to be nervous 'cause my mama says parents love us even when we mess up so can I touch the starfish and the sea any money now, please?"

The teacher laughed. When I looked up, Ava, Dr. Rochelle, and my mom were laughing too. Pops was still frowning, but I was all right with that. Because this little girl in front of me was curious. Maybe today would be the day she fell in love with the ocean, and it could be because of me. I answered every single question the kids had for me, even the ones from the little boys trying to trip me up. I showed them all how to use the gentle two-finger touch with the animals and told them how the sea "any moneys" used their tentacles to sting and stun fish so they could eat them. By the time I was done, the teacher said I had probably created some future marine biologists.

But that wasn't even the best part. The best part was the look on Pops's face. I could see he understood something about me that he hadn't before. He wasn't happy about it, but I could see he understood it.

We got into it hard back at home. It took him a while to come around, but he did eventually. It was after midnight before I could call Ava and tell her about it. I never told her this, but that day—the day she showed my parents what I really loved—that day was our real anniversary in my mind. It was the first time I started to really think about how much I loved this girl and how I didn't think it was just a high school thing. I was starting to think maybe I loved her for keeps.

Ava

WHEN WE GET to the gift shop, Mabel, the store manager, is still there, but her purse is strapped over her shoulder like she's getting ready to leave.

"Hey, you two," she says, looking back and forth between us. There's a smile in her voice, and I know right away she's going to say something she shouldn't.

I glare at her preemptively, but she ignores me. "You two get back together yet or you still being stupid and wasting time?" she asks, and then laughs.

"Ha, very funny," I say.

But Mason actually answers. "Still being stupid, I guess."

I glance at him, but I can't see his face properly. He's looking down and playing with the penguin keychain display. Is he being sarcastic?

I walk up to the counter and explain the Stevie and Sola situation to Mabel and ask her if we can have a few minutes to shop.

"Take as much time as you need, honey," she says. "My husband isn't here yet anyhow. The snow made a mess of the roads."

I watch Mason wander around the shop. He picks up a penguin plushie and a mermaid one and then puts them both back down. By the time I get over to him, he's next to the octopus stuffed animals. He puts one on his head, and the arms hang down in front of his face. "Like my hat?"

I shake my head. "It literally sucks," I say.

He gets my joke right away and laughs. "Good one." He puts the octopus away and looks around. "If I ran the gift shop, I'd only have the ugly, nonsexy animals," he says. "Like you ever see the water bear? Looks like a microscopic anus with feet."

"Oh my god," I say, snort laughing. "No one would ever buy that."

He grins and does that thing where he looks at me like I'm the coolest person he's ever met. My heart squeezes, and I just have to look away.

"My turn," I say. "I'd choose the blobfish. It's like someone made a wax sculpture of a regular fish and then melted it down."

Now it's his turn to snort laugh. "All right, how about the giant siphonophore?" he asks.

"Eww, gross," I say. "It just looks like hundred-foot-long intestines with weird shit hanging off it."

"I know, but it's amazing," he says, eyes shining. "I was reading about it last night. The way it clones itself is out of control."

I already know all about it, but I love watching how excited and nerdy he gets. It's one of my favorite things about him.

I walk over to where the jellyfish plushies are. "How about one of these?" I say, and hold it up for him to see.

Mason comes closer, takes it from my hand, and puts it on his head as well. He's grinning, and the iridescent tentacles hang down his face and he looks silly and so handsome at the same time. If this had happened a month ago, I'd go up to him and brush the tentacles apart and give him a kiss.

"Why a jelly?" he asks.

I tell him about Sola's love for jellies and how Stevie has bought her a new one every year on their anniversary.

He takes the jelly from his head and frowns down at it. "Doesn't do real jellies justice," he says.

He's right. In real life, moon jellies are translucent and have a faint blue or pink glow. This plushie is nice, but it doesn't compare.

He looks down at the jelly, thinking.

"Got it," he says. "How about a Name a Jelly certificate?"

"Oh, that's a great idea," I say. "Better than that thing."

"We can give it to her together," he says. "Don't want to damage your gift guru reputation or nothing."

"Good looking out," I say, laughing.

Our eyes meet. It feels nice to laugh with him. Maybe we really can be friends. Maybe it won't always hurt to remember what we had.

"Ava," he says. His voice is nervous but firm, the way it is when he wants to say something hard. He wasn't always good saying what was on his mind, but after he and his dad hashed out the basketball stuff, he got better at it.

I shake my head. "Please don't say anything," I say. I must look sad or desperate or something, because all he says is "Okay."

It would be easy—so easy—to slip back into being with him. But I know we shouldn't.

Ava

THE PROBLEM BEGAN on our second anniversary. Mason was a senior now, so he'd started touring colleges. On our day-we-met anniversary, he was out in California with his parents at University of California San Diego, so it wasn't like I was expecting a present or anything. (I did get him the perfect gift, a custom snorkeling set with his initials carved on the inside of the goggles. I wrapped it in this really pretty vintage-style teal-and-gold paper.)

We'd been texting each other all day. He sent me pictures of the campus and lecture halls. I sent him back pictures of the practice PSAT tests I was taking.

I kept expecting him to say "Happy Anniversary" at some point, but he never did.

The next day, when I told my mom about it, she asked me why I hadn't just said the words first.

"I don't know." I sat down next to her on the couch. She gave me a look that said she didn't believe me.

The truth was, Mason had been busy a lot lately. He was studying for the SATs and getting his college applications ready. Things were still great between the two of us, but he was preparing for a future away from here. Away from me.

"You know, honey," she said. "These relationships don't last forever."

"What does that mean?" I asked.

"Don't tell me you haven't thought about it," she said.

"Somewhere in the back of your mind you know the end is coming."

I started to protest. "Mom, I—"

"Wait, just hear me out," she said. "I know how much you love Mason, honey, but you're a junior in high school. There'll be other boys for you when you go off to college."

I shook my head. "No, there won't."

"There'll be other girls for him, too."

I jumped up off the couch. "I come to you because I'm sad, because my boyfriend forgot our anniversary, and you tell me he's going to break up with me eventually anyway?"

Finally it dawned on her what a messed-up thing it was for her to say. "Honey, I'm sorry."

"Whatever," I said, and walked out of the living room. I knew she was doing the mom thing, trying to protect me from a broken heart, but I was still mad. Just because Mason was going off to college didn't mean our relationship had to end, did it?

Later that night, she came to find me in my bedroom to say she was sorry again.

"It's all right, Mom," I said. She kissed my forehead and tucked me in like she used to when I was little.

After she left, though, I got to thinking.

Maybe she was right. Maybe the reason I didn't remind Mason about our anniversary was because I was worried about what was going to happen to us when he left. And maybe the fact that he forgot our anniversary told me all I needed to know. He was already in the future. A future without me in it.

Mason

I MESSED UP. I know I messed up. I forgot not only the when-we-first-met anniversary, but the first-kiss one too. Worse than that? I didn't even realize I forgot until she called me at 12:01 a.m.

"You forgot our anniversary," was the first thing she said when I picked up.

I was in bed half asleep, so I didn't realize how mad she was at first. "That was today?"

"You forgot the other one too."

"My bad," I said. "I'll make it up to you."

"Don't bother," she said.

That's when I started to wake. I stacked my pillows and pushed myself against the headboard. "What you mean, don't bother? I want to—"

She cut me off. "I mean, it's not like we're doing this thing for much longer, right?"

Now I was all the way awake. "What are you talking about? What thing are we not doing?"

"Well, college is starting for you and you're going away and—"

"Wait a minute. Let me get this straight. You're saying I don't have to make it up to you because we're going to break up when I go to college anyhow?" I couldn't believe what I was hearing.

"No, don't you try to turn this around on me," she said. "You forgot both our anniversaries. Both of them, Mason. You might as well be gone already."

I went from feeling bad to feeling mad. "Well, why didn't you say something then? It's both of us in this thing together. Why didn't you remind me?"

"I remembered all day. Both times. I was waiting to see if you'd remember, but you didn't."

It seemed like she was accusing me of more than just forgetting. "Hold on. You didn't answer me before. You're saying I don't have to make it up to you because we're going to break up anyhow. That's what you're saying?"

"Aren't we?" she said. But she didn't say it like it was a question. She said it like she had already decided. Like it was a done deal. And that just made me madder. I didn't know we had an expiration date.

"Might as well do it now then," I said. I don't even know why I said it. I was mad and it just came out.

"Fine," she said.

I could hear her breathing into the phone. I kept waiting for one of us to take it back. But neither of us did. And that was that.

Ava

WE MAKE OUR way over to the Tropical Diver exhibit, where the jellies are. One of the janitors, Thomas, waves hello and wishes us merry everything.

Without the people and with most of the overhead lights off, Tropical Diver is even more beautiful than usual. It's a re-creation of a tropical Pacific coral reef, and you can find fish in every single color in here. That, plus all the coral and the wave maker, makes it my favorite exhibit.

"I'll go get the certificate," Mason says, and heads over to the information desk.

I walk over to the jelly tanks. During the day, these tanks are always crowded. It's easy to see why. The jellies are beautiful, like dense, brightly colored smoke curling through water.

"You're in love," Mason says, reminding me of the first time we met. Déjà vu.

I turn to look up at him, but he's staring into the tank. "Did you know a large group of jellies is called a smack?" he asks.

"And their scientific name is *Aurelia aurita*."

"Their bell can grow up to one foot," he says.

"They enjoy snacking on smaller jellies," I say.

I wait for him to come back with another fact, but he doesn't. "Looks like a nice life," he says. "They don't have to make plans, just drift through life eating zooplankton and fish eggs."

"Yeah, but they don't have brains or hearts," I say.

"And no worries either," he says.

"Is that what you want?" I ask. "To drift?"

"No," he says. He puts his forehead against the glass. "I'm sorry I forgot our anniversary."

"Both of them," I say.

He laughs. "Both of them."

I touch my forehead to the glass, too. Then I say the thing I should've said when we fought. "I'm the one that should be sorry."

He doesn't say anything, just waits for me to go on.

"My mom says these things don't last."

"What things?" he asks.

"High school relationships. She says we have so much growing and changing to do. She says we might outgrow each other."

"But that's true even for people who've been together for twenty, thirty, or forty years," he says.

"She also says long-distance relationships don't work. We're going to be apart and—"

"But it's only a year, Ava. Then we can go to UCSD—"

"What if I don't get in?"

"You'll get in," he says.

"But what if I don't, Mason? What if we're separated for four years? And then there's grad school after that. It would be so hard."

"You're right," he says.

This, what's happening to us right now, is what I've been afraid of. I was afraid of him admitting that there was no future for us. I just ended things before they could fall apart.

My heart hurts. Mason is right. Being a drifting, heartless jelly would be easier.

I look at our reflection in the glass, knowing it's one of the last times I'll be looking at us. Mason is looking at our reflection too. Our eyes meet.

"You're right, it's going to be hard. But I want to try, Ava. I'm sorry I forgot our anniversaries, but I promise you I wasn't forgetting about you."

I can't stop the smile spreading across my face. "Promise?" I ask.

"Always," he says.

I slip my hand into his.

"Did you know eighty-eight percent of all high school sweethearts end up together?" he says.

"That's not true," I say.

"True fact," he says. "Scientific name *Homus nerdus improbalus*. Their main habitats are libraries and aquariums."

I laugh and play along. "They meet young and sometimes they get separated, but they always find their way back to each other."

I move closer to him and rest my head against his forearm. We stay like that, watching the jellies drift up and down, like we have all the time in the world.

"We need to get this jelly certificate to Stevie," I say. "She and Sola have to get back together. They just have to."

"They will," he says. He leans in and kisses my freckles, the way he always used to. Then he kisses me like a promise of more kisses to come.

⬤ OPERATION SOLA AND STEVIE SURPRISE

11:22 p.m.

Mr. Olayinka "Baba" has been added to the group.

Jimi

Hey, Mr. Olayinka. We need your help.

Mr. Olayinka "Baba"

Yes, dearest Jimi. How can I help? And what is this you've added me to?

E.R.

Hey hey, Mr. O.

Ava

Is the snow terrible over there?

Mr. Olayinka "Baba"

It's terrible everywhere, but the plows have come through here. I hope you're being safe.

Jimi

We need your help getting Sola to the stadium. Promise she won't be out late.

Mr. Olayinka "Baba"

Give me a call, Jimi.

Kaz

Come thru, Papa O.

ELEVEN

STEVIE

Mercedes-Benz Stadium, 11:49 p.m.
Eleven minutes until midnight

I CAN'T TAKE my eyes off the sky. The light drones have started their second version of the message. As each word and image form, my heart lifts a little, and for a moment, I forget that I'm alone in the stands watching it and Sola isn't at my side. But watching it light up the dark, for the first time in my life, it all feels like magic. Something I've never believed in. Ern added an "I'm sorry" to this storyline, and I'm hoping that might help me get her to respond.

WHEN THE MUSIC CHANGES,
SO MUST THE DANCE.
I'M SORRY, SOLA. FORGIVE ME?

"It's perfect." Ern pokes his head out of the tech room. "Better than perfect. The whole city is talking about it now. Did you hear from her?"

I'm too afraid to look down at my phone, to see if she's texted back. I grip the edges of it so tight, just to keep my fingers from shaking.

"Stevie."

I whip around at the sound of my name. Evan-Rose stands at the top of the stairs beside her brother-in-law, holding the hand of a gorgeous brown-skinned girl with shoulder-length locs. The sight of E.R. almost breaks me. I dart up to her, almost tackling her to the ground. "What are you doing here? How did you get here?"

"MARTA," she says. "They cleared the tracks. Mo, Van, and I came straight from the airport."

I hold her so tight, she can't even answer. "Good to see you, Maurice," I say over E.R.'s shoulder. "And nice to finally meet you, Savanna. I told y'all not to . . ."

"You're shaking." E.R. tightens her grip on me, and it feels like an earthquake trembling beneath my rib cage. "I've got you," she says. "Everything is going to be okay."

Once she lets me go, E.R. lowers her backpack from her shoulder and pulls out a long tube. "We would've been here earlier, but once we decided to take the train, I had to go and find Maurice. I made sure to keep it safe."

I uncap it, remove the poster, and unroll it. Definitely the one from the bulletin board where Sola and I had our first kiss at Barthingham Girls' Academy. One of our biggest milestones. I hug her again, but then doubt crashes through me. "I'm too late. It's all too late—" In my head, Sola would've seen the message and rushed over here, and I would've given her the poster to represent the real start of our love story. To remind her that it's all been worth it even though I messed up.

"It's not even twelve yet, Stevie." E.R. hugs me again.

"Well, I haven't heard a word from Sola. It didn't work." A single tear falls from my left eye, and before I can brush it away, Evan-Rose does.

"She knows how much you love her, Stevie. She knows what the two of you have. I can almost guarantee she won't just throw it all away." E.R. peeks over her shoulder at Savanna and smiles. "Especially not after you lit up the skies above Atlanta. That's maybe the most romantic thing ever. Have a little faith."

"You know I don't like that word." I ease into a nearby seat and think of all the sermons Dad has given me about being faithful, trusting in a higher power. I trust the numbers, the science, the things I can see, like my friend E.R., who trekked through this storm to get to me . . . but tonight part of me wants to believe that something else, someone else, someone *bigger*, will intervene on my behalf and make it all right again. My experiment isn't working. I drum my fingers across my observation log, and I want to rip out the pages, erasing all my potential outcomes, all my hypotheses.

"What's meant to be will be. Isn't that what people say?" Evan-Rose tucks one of my locs behind my ear and gazes at me, fishing for eye contact.

Another round of light drones lift and head for their positions in the sky, and I wait for their buzzing to subside. "I envy the believers sometimes, and I wish I could have faith that what's meant to be will be, and that all will work out in the end." I rest my head in my hands, defeat filling my insides.

"Yo!" a voice booms from behind.

I look up to find Kaz and Porsha barreling down the staircase. Kaz is holding up a kit of LEGO roses like it's a championship trophy. "Had to fight a kid for this!" he says.

"That's a lie." Porsha shoves him playfully, then looks up at him, and I can't help but smile. Something's changed between them. I think about how happy Sola would be to see this. She'd been so proud to tell me all about her coaching him, helping him get the courage to tell Porsha how he feels.

"We barely made it. We were in traffic for six and a half hours." Porsha rattles off the obstacles they faced getting here—the flat tires, the wild, Christmas-themed Ryde, the back roads, the tailing a plow and almost getting pulled over, the accidents everywhere.

"You didn't have to . . . ," I start to say.

"We wanted to. You're our homie," Kaz replies.

"Hey, y'all!" Jimi, Jordyn, a guy I'm pretty sure is my cousin Ava's ex-boyfriend's older brother, and . . . I blink twice.

"Wait, is that . . . ," Kaz begins.

"Lil Kinsey," E.R. whispers.

"There's no way," Porsha says. "That can't be him."

"Definitely looks like him . . . ," adds Savanna. "Those neck tattoos are pretty telling."

I'm too much in shock to even speak as they barrel down the stairs of the next seat section over.

"Y'all play it cool," Kaz says under his breath.

As they approach, Jimi looks around. "Where is she? Where's Sola?"

Ern shoots out of the tech room, and Maurice heads back up the stairs to join him. "Glad you all made it, but watch for the drones!" He waves his hands all around. "They're landing."

And as the drones come down, my cousin Ava and her ex, Mason, arrive, holding hands and stealing kisses. That is, until Mason sees the guy with Jordyn. "MARI!" he shouts, and runs over and hug tackles him. Definitely brothers.

As soon as I feel Ava's eyes on me, I crash back in my seat. Jimi and company walk through the layers of bleachers and join everyone. I don't have the energy (or the heart) to explain how my entire mission, my entire plan, has failed, and that their plan to secretly help me even when I told them not to failed. They ignored my instructions and traveled here in the snow for nothing.

Sola didn't see the message.

Sola didn't reach out or acknowledge it.

Sola didn't accept my apology.

It's over.

I bury my face in my hands and hope I can keep it all together and not be upset in front of all my friends (and these strangers).

E.R. tells Ava and Mason that no one has heard from Sola. I hear Porsha try to crack a joke to lighten the mood. Kaz says he's "starvin' like Marvin" (whoever that is), and Lil Kinsey pulls out his phone and starts scrolling, trying to figure out if there's any late-night food still delivering . . . in the snow.

What am I supposed to do now? I gulp down the rhetorical question, mostly to keep from vomiting or crying or falling apart.

Jimi puts a hand on my shoulder. "It's okay, Stevie. Maybe she just needs to cool off. We could drive you home."

"My tour bus is down in the garage," Lil Kinsey offers. "Hella chains on the tires. Or I could call the helicopter." The outlandishness of it all doesn't even register. The whole night feels so ridiculous, I might as well go home in a helicopter, landing down at the dead end near the park. I can already see all the neighbors with their faces pressed against their windows. Dad would be too curious to be super mad, and Mom would be too shocked to yell. It might delay the inevitable lecture and grounding routine.

I shrug and struggle to my feet. In this version of my life, this night turned out differently than I hoped.

This version of me failed. The mistake I've made is *too* big to correct. My universe is shattering. This reality, this me, couldn't fix it.

"You tried." Ava rubs my back as I climb the stairs and we head for the exit.

I take a deep breath and hold it in my chest, only to push down the disappointment, the vomit, the anxiety, the heartbreak. With each step I take, I imagine the infinite ways this might've turned out better:

Imagine if she'd actually *seen* my apology in all its glory.

Imagine if I would've just gone over to the Olayinkas' house and formally apologized to her mother, aunties, uncles, cousins, grandmother, and father in person, impressing upon them how much I regret that dinner and my actions.

Imagine if I wouldn't have let so many days go past without attempting to fix things, instead of hiding in my room and being afraid of her rejection, my own embarrassment, or facing an even worse punishment.

Imagine if I hadn't let this wound between us fester and rot and become something that can't be repaired.

We reach the atrium level, and my friends follow behind me. The noise of their voices and footsteps makes the tears fall.

It's all over. All of it. I roped them all in, Ern included, and they came through with the things I asked them for, but it was all for naught—

"Stevie?"

I barely hear the voice through the noise of grief in my head.

In fact, I would've sworn I was hearing things if not for the fact that everyone behind me goes quiet.

"Hey," the voice says then. I look to my left.

Sola.

My heart freezes. The sight of her feels unreal: a figment of my imagination that I'd willed to arrive.

"Sola!" Kaz shouts.

She takes several tentative steps forward. Behind her, near the escalator, Mr. Olayinka stands holding a newspaper. He tips his hat to me and smiles slyly.

I rush forward, closing the gap between us. "I'm so so so so sorry," I stammer out.

Her beautiful eyes are filled with tears.

"You . . ." I still can't believe it. "You came."

"Baba drove so slow I thought we wouldn't make it," she says. "But of course I came. You wrote me a message in the sky. I could see it the whole time we were driving here." Her voice is gravelly and full of the memory of tears, and it kills me that I know how much she's been crying. Her nose is red, probably from blowing it.

"A grand gesture . . . is that what it's called in romance novels?"

"More like the grovel," she says, and I think I spot a small smile tucking its way into the corner of her mouth.

I take a deep breath. "I'm sorry for what happened at the dinner. I'm sorry for showing up a mess. I'm sorry for the bad impression I left behind. I'm sorry for ruining our moment." I reach out a hand, hoping she will place hers in mine. It lingers out there, my fingers twitching with anxiety.

She sighs and meets my touch. "I'm sorry I put so much pressure on us. I wanted it to be the best memory we had. The one where we could orchestrate the outcome. If the dinner was perfect, everyone's responses would be too." A tear drifts down her cheek, and I sweep it away. The feel of her skin is electrifying.

"Do you think you can forgive me?" I ask.

A silence stretches between us, and I feel the weight of all of our friends' eyes. My heart knocks around inside my chest, threatening to burst. I bite my bottom lip and search her face for some indication of what her answer might be.

She suddenly throws her arms around my neck, startling me. "Yes, I'll always forgive you, Stevie. But can you ever forgive me?"

I look up, and Mr. Olayinka winks at me. "Of course," I whisper.

Everyone claps and whistles and shouts. They swarm us in the best and biggest group hug ever.

"So all right . . . ," Lil Kinsey says with a clap. "Now that everybody got their girl back—me included—can we party?" He motions to Ern and Maurice, who are standing just outside the tech room. Ern disappears and within a few seconds, the giant screens that circle the field fill with color and light, and the stadium speakers start blasting music.

Sola and I stand there, my arms locked around her. I don't want to let her go just yet. It hasn't quite settled in that this version of me *did* manage to fix the biggest screwup of my life.

Everyone is laughing and moving around us, and since I know I'm about to be grounded forever and this might be the last time I see her for a while, I sway left and right, pulling Sola into a slow dance despite the Lil Kinsey song pouring through the speakers. I'm curious to know whether or not this is awkward for him, but I can't take my eyes off Sola long enough to check and see.

"Oh, so you like to dance now?" she says, her grin mischievous.

I spin her around, then pull her so close she can probably feel the pounding of my heart.

"With you?" I ask, kissing her. "Forever."

WEATHER.COM REPORT

ATLANTA

29°

Snow Showers

H: 36° L: 18°

Snow Showers in the Forecast for the Next Two Hours

(and Love!)

AUTHORS' NOTE

EXPERIMENT TITLE: THE KEY TO LOVE

SCIENTIFIC QUESTION: Which author wrote which part of this love story?

WHEN WE DECIDED to write *Whiteout*, we wanted to challenge ourselves to tell a love story that felt like a big, glorious puzzle, because so often the process of falling in love can feel like that: two people trying to figure out who they are, where they belong, and how they fit together. If you're curious about which author wrote which pieces of this big snowy love story . . . look no further than the following key:

Stevie and Sola were written by the self-professed love grump of the group.

Kaz was written by a Christmas queen.

E.R. was written by the only Atlanta native among us (who is also an airport lover).

Jordyn was written by the only author who is a rapper.

Jimi was written by the author who has always been a wannabe rock star and whose books always include music.

Ava and Mason were written by the author who once wrote a kiss scene that lasted for four pages. (Her editor made her shorten it.)

ACKNOWLEDGMENTS

This book was a fun, complicated challenge, and every member of our fabulous team deserves a shout-out for helping us with this snowy love story.

Thank you to our families and friends, for all their love and support, for being our constant cheerleaders as we wrestled yet another big project as a team.

Thank you to our HarperCollins/Quill Tree Books family: Rosemary Brosnan, our fearless editor who is always up for a challenge and made sure everything fit. Suzanne Murphy, Erin Fitzsimmons, Courtney Stevenson, Patty Rosati and team, Jenn Corcoran, Mark Rifkin, Shona McCarthy, Laaren Brown, Audrey Diestelkamp, Shannon Cox, and Lisa Calcasola. Thank you for continuing to rock with us.

Thank you to Molly Ker Hawn for steering us to the finish line.

Thank you to the librarians, teachers, and booksellers who make sure our books find young people.

Most important, thanks to the readers who follow us into story after story. Thank you for diving into another love story with us.